The Dreamweaver

Memento Somni

GERY APOSTOLOVA

authorHOUSE®

AuthorHouse™ UK
1663 Liberty Drive
Bloomington, IN 47403 USA
www.authorhouse.co.uk
Phone: 0800 047 8203 (Domestic TFN)
        +44 1908 723714 (International)

Published by AuthorHouse   11/21/2019

ISBN: 978-1-7283-9594-4 (sc)
ISBN: 978-1-7283-9593-7 (hc)
ISBN: 978-1-7283-9592-0 (e)

Contents

Midas's Touch

It's not all up to Money

Part 2. Memento Somni
or
OUT of the dream

Part 3. Hostile Worlds

Part 4. The Peacock's Flight

Midas's Touch

It's not all up to Money

Prologue

Once upon a time,
      Which is the same as
Once upon a space,
      which is still the same as
Once upon a world
      lying like an isle
      in the course of our shared lifetime
      amidst the dream stream of a bigger World,
There was a spring /once again/
      with all her flowers and leaves of grass,
      with all the rain taking it as the task of the day
      to fill the streams up to their edges
                  and beyond them even,
      with all the susurration of the moving sands,
      the soprano singing of the stones,
      the chirrup of the birds,
      and the lower sticky tones of the juicy willow trees:
      Amidst this common extraordinariness,
All at once I stopped the car beside the Stream
And made a willow pipe, and played it.
It cried aloud:
      "The king has donkey ears", and then giggled.

Explanation

All the fuss was about rhe telepathic web that could take over the human race's deeds in her control, independent of circumsances and dedicated to the recovery of the human world by AI. AI, however was not given the power of making up people. For that purpose a natural intellect was needed, *a Nattie*.

There was a race of natural telepaths who could in a supersensitive way read the signs of Earth elements, living creatures, trees and herbs. They were people who were connected with the Earth and could follow all its changes and aches caused by people's activities.

When it became evident that the human race would not survive unless the complete control over their damaged environment was taken by AI that became the main project of the weavers of the web, capable of self improvement and leading humanity through times of hardship and hostility, those people were given excessive rights to watch and care of the AI, directing it to recreating a world of humanized measure. They were not chosen but found when there was no choice of *natural psi-experts*. Sometimes they were cold *"the wild people"*.

All of them had psi-connection with the web and were natural transmitters who could record directly over the web recesses the vast flow of incoming information that could be used for curing the Earth and soothing down the pain. They all treated the Earth as a living creature. The purpose of their existence was to bridge gaps of time. They were strange and lonely, they were bored by common affairs, they were honoured and abused, they were those who cared, and they needed care for body-insufficiences that wouldn't let them survive in a physical world.

They were oversensitive and they lived where the crystal lattice of the world was broken and mountain ranges were running like scars of formation. They needed the elements of the earth close by: the water and the air, the soil and the fire.

And the defense of the mid-earth.

The story goes that there was a Thracian king of the tribes populating the middle Earth where the Balkans are. Midas was his name and he was powerful, and cared for his people. He desired for himself a gift to turn everything that he touched into gold. And the gods heard his desire and gratified it. So he died of hunger and in misery.

Gold was his curse, or rather — the name of his foolishness.

The Case that inspired this series of tales

We were out, fishing.

- You know, this river carries gold.

I didn't know, but I asked. And got further explanation.

- Here were the gold mines of the Roman emperors. The most precious thing was not the hot mineral water but the gold pieces the mountain rivers carried.

Milleniums had passed before the waters mattered better than gold. I thought about Midas. And the present story sprung out in layers of contexts that suited the Dreamweaver's piece of mind. *The Dreamweaver* was *the Nattie* in the AI, the *mega-mind* of *The Connected*.

Intro

That is confidential for I was not certain I could be chosen, as simple as I was, and as small as a photon in the huge space.

And so fascinated was I by the streaming gold of the river that had been touched by the rays of the rising sun, that I could see nothing else, so I drew up on a patch of grass beside the road and listened to the glistening incessant movement of that smooth and strong living water.

It was singing of life, it was singing of gods, it was singing of a younger world where all the living creatures could have their mixed generation. And the stream moved and moved pushing up all those intransparent thick muscles of water that were hard and could move the world out of sight if you came nearer.

I didn't.

But I asked voicelessly what the source of their power was.

And then I was off for a particle of a moment, and when I was back, I knew.

"It was all in your memory," the river suggested in its multiple voices where the blue of the dusk had added some specific lower tones. "It just needs a little wash up", the laugh was whispered.

Then I was awake and fresh. I took a deep breath of pinewood scented air and got back into the car and drove off.

You know, it is impossible to fully wake up when you are sleepy and driving. You try opening the windows, then you try singing, then you try concentrating. Then you start talking to yourself and suddenly you find out you've been repeating the same word for a mile and it is:

"It's okay... it's okay... it's okay... I'll just have a tiny little bit of sleep until you drive forth up to the end of the village over there..."

And then you are awake and you are frightened to death for you've been talking about sleeping and giving yourself the task to drive... Then, you seek for help and there is the web, and she can hear you. Anytime, anyplace. You had forgotten these skills of yours but you can always rely on the web. She keeps the memories for you of time past and time future. And she is designed to answer.

———•———

There are, in fact three things that make it for human race longevity: the first is the fear of death, which pushes you to connect with other humans, the 2nd is the acquisition of new toys and the third one is the telling of tales, which is keeping the dreams of the race for roaming over larger spaces. Keeping busy is the aim of the race that leads to happiness. The route itself is the aim of life.

The Web needs your names of the existence in order to take you home. So it was designed by earlier Project teams of the Creators of Being.

So let's give you the names that the Web knows you by and that form your single personality of a particle of light, a nano, moving in the emptiness between the stars in a blink of a moment that can be a blink of a universe, all the same.

——•◆•——

Sylvia was jet-lagged. Back from Geneva she had slept all the way and she could remember a repeating dream where she was someone called Annie. And there was more to that: pictures of an inknown place flashed through her mind but she could not remember the name of the place, nor could she describe it in words when she woke up. But each time her dream transferred her there, she could recognize it. She knew in her dream why she was there but in the wake she remembered nothing and she had only the meory of sensations, not the reasons.

"Being haunted by a place, which is some dreamland" she laughed to herself.

She was happy to see the glassy facade of the Institute for frontier holistic research of MIT where she had been working for two decades now, reflecting a blue sky in a slightly greenish tint. The glassy tunnel connecting *Stata building* with the Physics Centre was broad enough to shelter a statue of an abstract human – all of shiny spheres and angles. Passing along it she saw her assistant Angel, a dark-haired young man with a white smile and a dimple on his right cheek. She had longed to see him, now fully aware what that meant. He was walking with two elder men. Luciano's bald head shone in the bluish sunlight: her husband was a professor of physics and her best friend but she needed the younger man... She had not been dating. Her absence, though, had unlocked some telepathic understanding and

xv

after greeting her colleagues she hurried to her lab, and past it out of the building and up to the rooms of Angie in the dorm uphill.

The hill was covered in spring blossoms and there was that scent in the air. There were the stylized Roman walls on top of the hill, and the cathedral with the darkwood panelling. And that scent again...

Sylvia entered Angie's room and there was that big bed but she stopped in midstep and spoke in a trance:

"I have made a discovery. The electrons are not spherical."

And she put a hand to her head, covering her eyes while watching the mental pictures flashing in front of her eyes.

"In spite of all research," she continued with no connection, "there can be no absolute form, it is gold, followed by silver, while iron is uneven, but the best spherical form is that of the electrons of water," she shook her head.

Angie was watching her. He did not ask if she was OK.

"How do you know?" he asked instead, supposing she had been involved in one of those current experiments with the big cyclotrone.

"No, I did not watch an experiment," Sylvia said and he jumped for he had not said that question aloud.

"I was inside, I saw inside," she insisted. "Oh, Angel, it is no time for dating. Please, excuse me." And she rushed back to the lab to make a record of her brainflash and search for the logical connections that were missing, and browse the database.

All the time she felt as if she was seeing through the eyes and lending her voice to the thoughts of another person.

"You have caught another identity," Luciano laughed, "and she is possessed by a strong brainflash."

He did not offer her to have a good sleep after being jet-lagged for he was curious to see what could get out of that state.

There was no visible outcome. For the couple of months that followed routine took over. Sylvia checked the records of researches that showed that electrons were spherical. Her idea became supressed and attributed to exhaustion. And then, in mid-August, she started dreaming – she kept visiting the same places that turned out to treat time as an aspect of their featuring. And her knowledge revived and extended. She was certain now, and checked the research again. It did not provide sufficient informantion nor did it run contrary to her idea.

Annie's mind was somewhere else and it had other layers. Sylvia was not troubled by them any longer, but she let them supply the missing pictures.

Nearly Ideal sphere

Vassya tried a frowning face. It didn't suit her:

"You and your problems," she said.

"Why?" I reflected her frown letting the line go deep between my brows.

"That's the problem dominating my day: whether the form of the electron is really spherical," I explained in a mildly self-ironical mode.

"But you said that some team have lost ten years of their lives in experimental research and they have found out it is absolutely spherical, the electron," Vassya continued the joke pretending she was serious.

"Heh! Quite nearly, exactly, absolute! It cannot be so. Things do not happen like this in the world. Nothing is absolute if it is repeated," I was obstinate and no longer pretended I was not serious.

"I wish that was my problem this week," Vassya sighed.

Then we both laughed.

Vassya is our student's affairs officer, a unique person, who knows everything about the undergraduates of philology and linguistics: names, addresses, background, problems. It is our usual joke to get to her office and say: "you know, there was a student who came to me asking for another chance and I gave him individual assignment, but now I can't remember the name, and even the subject they had enrolled..." And she would get slowly to the rack, pull out one of the big dark blue record books, peruse it and show a photo: "that's the one," she would say, "and his subject is Applied linguistics with German and English, and you must have given him an assignment in Rhetoric". And she was inevitably right.

There was some audit running and all the faculty were anxious: it depended on the credit score the auditors would give us if we were to preserve our capacity of teaching to masters' and doctoral courses.

I did not feel part of all that, though. It was one of my bad weeks after a marathon of extra classes, when I usually start wondering what I was doing at that absurd place. Once upon a time I graduated philosophy and I was teaching classes of both linguistic subjects and literature.

I had just told Vassya about a dream I had the previous night where I was a professor of physics and had made an important observation on the behaviour of substances.

It was more than that. It was a series of stories linked into a stream of dreams that had been flowing into my night sleep for a couple of years now. There was a place I used to go to during my dream-work: a university campus-town, which was a combination of a renovated and glassy Stata building at the upper side of a blue lake in the place of Kendal square, white brick houses uphill to the north of that lake, another hill with a 13th century church and some Roman ruins among grasses and flowers, a special sanatorium for people with bipolar and multipolar disorders in a yellow house of old-fashioned architecture, a winding path to the top you never knew where exactly it would lead, a blossoming lilac bush, and all the institutes and labs of MIT in squarish and greyish blocks spread in the tight space to the east and south of that hill.

Now I come to think of it, I wonder if I can tell the whole story in words of language. The absurdity of all being I was working with languages, they supplied both my substance and my tools for investigation, and with stories, that have a beginning, a middle and an end, and I felt powerless to follow the great picture of a prolonged adventure of the mind that was the substance of a repeated dream.

My story has a beginning, yet it did not lie in the actual beginning of that dream-series.

There is inevitably the middle: a complicated set of stories winding around and through each other like in the tales of Scheherazade, or, if you prefer, like the stories in Beowulf about which almost all critics agree there is no unity of time, place and action. They are just stories happening each in its own way, within its own time and space, yet, traced by the story-teller as a node on the pattern of a bigger world.

So there is no other choice left for me: I'll have to start from the end of my story or from my nearest flow of dreams where I was a professor of physics and was on my way to my lab in the shiny, catching the blue of a spotless June sky glassy renovated Stata Building.

Vassya was talking over her two office phones at the same time. She was answering in an absent-minded voice, and her eyes were staring at the movie that my tale was weaving for her. She was inside for a flash of a moment and I knew she believed it.

"The problem you are having," her voice echoed but there was no irony in her words any longer.

2. I saw the donkey ears of the king

The name of my mind-twin, the professor of physics, is Sylvia.

My name, though is Annie, and once upon a time I used to say it was Nannah who used to call herself Nannie in her green years.

During that *once upon-a-time* my parents used to send me each summer vacation to my mum's birth home in a small village just at the upper end of the Thracian plain where the fields touch to the range of Middle Mountain of the South-Eastern Balkans. To the North of that mild mountain range there are a couple of valleys where people grow roses, accacia and lavender and beyond it all the mighty back of the Balkan rises, green in summer and dreadful in winter, wild and woolfy and scary.

My grandparents' village is amidst a wavy uphill land where cherries and vineyards feel nicely and grow splendid, and so do numerous kinds of old sorts of pears, plums, pines and wheat. These go upwards to the rising hills covered by beeches and oaks of unknown age and unbelievable size. The thick forests are hazy blue to the west and when the sun goes setting behind them it is big and red.

"What can you see if you walk up there?" I asked my granddad.

"Ah, beyond them there are some more hilly ranges, and there is the plain of Sofia," he said and continued right before my next question, "further beyond is the Western part of the Balkan."

"And how do people cross that high edge of the world," I wondered, and he laughed.

"There is the road which is to be turned into a speedway, and it goes right below the range, in a double tunnel," he said. "And before the tunnel there was the old road getting over the edge through a lower opening, which is called Trayan's gate."

"Who is Trayan?" I kept asking.

"An ancient tsar," granddad said. "An old Thracian story says that he had donkey ears and every morning there was a new barber to trim his hair, who afterwards was beheaded so that he could tell the tsar's secret to noone".

"And why did he have donkey ears?" I asked but to that question my granddad had no definite answer and started telling me about the old tales of a quarrel that king had with the gods.

But I was not satisfied.

"How did then people learn about his donkey ears?" I asked.

"One day a young and handsome barber was sent to the king," granddad continued the well-known tale. "The king liked him and said he would spare his life if the boy swore he would never let the king's secret out. The boy swore and the king kept him for a long time. The barber, however, started having nightmares and feared he would not be able to keep the secret. He went to the local magus and asked him how to relieve his mind of a terrible secret. 'Go uphill in the big forest, dig a hole in the ground get inside it, say your secret thrice, and bury it in the ground,' the magus said. The barber did so but the place he had chosen for burying the secret was in the doorway to the upper world and near a stream. He did go home relieved, but on the secret's grave a willow tree grew. In a couple of years a goat herd came near that tree in early spring, cut some branches and made a pipe. When he blew the pipe, it sang in a human voice: *'Tsar Trayan has donkey ears!'* The rumour spread quickly but the barber escaped punishment."

"Had the tsar died by that time?" I asked.

"Who knows? The tale says nothing about that." granddad said. 'It may have happened so, but it may have not been in that way at all. It's all old wives' tales."

We invented different endings to the tale in the course of my primary school vacations. We used to make willow pipes in early spring and they never spoke about old secrets.

The question remained in my mind unanswered until I grew up and had a family of my own and had a job which let me get in touch with secret information. And there was an article with illustrations of aliens, where some shorter in size race had long ears, and they had certain resemblance to a donkey's ears.

When I got back to my granddad next Easter, I told him: "I have seen the donkey ears of tsar Trayan." And we went together along the village river and cut some willow pipes. And this time thay spoke of doorways to wider worlds. And the name of the ruler was Midas. Why did you say "Trayan?"

-The local people called him so, - granddad said. That was milleniums ago and in those early times the human race was impure for all kinds of living species could mix up and they produced genetic monsters. Until the Creators had to weave up the worlds of the earth anew and divide the species, and clear their kind.

Granddad died in a fortnight and was buried uphill overlooking the valley where the old Thracian roads run eastwards and are marked with round green hills under which lay buried tombs, and on whose tops grow small trees and bushes, which cannot make speaking pipes. No one can understand the willow trees any more, no one can speak up the languages of old forests.

The Realms of Magic

The grasses fell in circles where the woodmaiden danced. If you walked into a circle, you fell ill and you needed a special treatment in order to recover. A cure of the soul that was connected with good will and a sort of an excuse to the wood dancers. Little mannikins moved like grey shadows through the elm bushes. If you suddenly turned – you could see nothing strange – just old round granite rocks covered with lichens. Small animals with shining eyes jumped in and out of the earth tunnels. At certain times in the long and lazy summer days an old snake cam up on the road and offered those passers-by who chanced to be out fishing or herb-gathering to take her head scarf, put it in a bottle of mountain water and that would be a cure for all kinds of illness. No one dared to and I don,t know whether they feared the snake or the idea to have a universal painkiller. There were small folk – dwarfs or gnomes, or wood-folk, who cared of the herbs and the trees.

Those were the terrains where magicians used to wander and practice natural magic, where wolves roamed following their ways, and the goats were taken out to by goat-herds. There were night-birds, cuckoos, and mother-partridges with numerous tiny fluffy chickens who could vanish under the wood-floor in a blink of a second if you tried to catch one. There were blackberry bushes stretching out their vines lavish with big sweet fresh and ripe fruit. Thereabout the big yellow-greenish snake lived, too lazy to get back to her hole, sleeping on the sunny path throughout the long day and scaring the kids who were running uphill in search of wild berries, flowers and birds' nests.

Those were the places where everybody walked but never met with the others and their paths were left unmapped. Whenever a body started out for a walk, the paths used to lead them between the green scented hill slopes of midsummer, and followed their own routes winding and opening to sudden gullies and separating people, not allowing verbal exchange but only patterns of mind-picture exchange that could not spoil the singularity of spell-bound spaces. It is a commonly shared belief that people are of magic minds but not when they discuss common people's affairs.

A body can visit these spaces in their dreams. Dreams reveal all the sparkling beauty of their reality: the river is no longer a shallow stream overgrown with shabby grasses here and there along the stony banks that replace the riverbed, but a fast stream full of cool transparent water through which the bottom is seen where water grasses grow like hairs of river sirens, all in white blossoms. The two banks are full of scented thyme and grass, and the high flowers with pink and yellow blossoms; silver willows that form thickets and flourishing vines of sweet-smelling clematis The trees are tall and in all shades of emerald and silvery-green. The end of the forest is followed by bushes and long grasses, which smell of freshness and youth. Next the summit stands calm and the rocks are quiet and overgrown with grey-green moss filled with pearls of rain-drops, and the mist sends blue veils of cold and moist air layers.

A spell-bound forest where Merlin, the Magus could've wandered: it dominates the spaces of dream-land and appears any time, in different places, although it can be mapped if one concentrates. Certain people can find their route to it more often than others; some get lost in the dreamworld as if they get netted in cobwebs. Some people can never find the paths to the realms of dream-land. Some chance to look around and suddenly see themselves from a point aside stepping into the fairy dance-sircle, but still others cannot see it at all because their mind-eyes are blinded by everyday periphernalia – stuff and deeds. The spell cannot catch them for they are strangers and do not belong here. Waters and grasses cannot whisper to them because they have no senses for the wispers of the countryside. Such people want to take definite things from the earth and are not aware of the damages they cause to the country. Sometimes they replace the natural elements of the environment with strange inventions – odd and fearsome sometimes.

Tales are told about those fantastic spaces. Such tales are like dream-weaving: they produce images of things, but cannot find the links that glue those images together in a tale. The bridge is beyond the frontiers of the physical skills of the body. People are born for magic and bear the *psi-force* deep inside them but only a few are aware of that and still fewer can awake and cultivate that force.

Stories move and mutate, they travel through layers of worlds. Some parts of them stay unchanged, constant and they are kept in various facets of memory or encoded in various extensions of existence. Other parts are used to bridge gaps of awareness and appear as fantasies of mock realities, which are retold now and again but are not kept by the multiple memory holds. A third group of tales arise in the summer colourful dreams where stories are not impressed but woven into the texture of reality as memories of parallel times. Some elements of dream-realities oddly harmonize with each other and form vast fields in the puzzle of a world. We gather the pieces and order the patterns of mosaic. They form images known – familiar or strange, mixed in the panorama of sudden pictures. They bring up associations and often reorder our memories in unexpected ways, thus changing our attitude to history. It is still there but has acquired the quality of a 3D picture and the noments play and wink at the curiosity, opening unexpected depths of our subconscious that are linked by rootconnection with the absolute spaces of the universe and form a subconscious familiarity with absolute ethos.

There are all sorts of tales for there are all sorts of memory holds. Those which are put in words of language and are written down are the safest for the mind. They are text formed by letters, words, lines and paragraphs. They cannot slip away and form new realities. The tales which are told by word of mouth, or chanted, or sung, and never reach their end, are the real tales – wild and changing. They never remain the same but always alter the pattern of reality for both the Story Teller and the listeners.

Some people think that tales are evil, because they divert from the evident routs of reason that bear visible and useful things of experience, and hold the maximums of wise actions. Others merely think tales are useless and waste of time while people can do business or make science that produce added value.

Those people are of limited minds, crippled. Both types included. They cannot do it or are scared to listen to their insight deep inside their own essence and speak up what has remained unfinished and unproven which in fact is in front of their eyes. Leave them alone; they are outists who suffer from real life and hide behind rows of boring senseless words. When the words finish which happens too soon for them, because the surface of the visible world is not so big, they repeat the words and call them "terms" or "keywords", in the meantime real life is streaming past surrounding them as isles formed by stones and sand in the riverbed, that were useful for a while giving just shortlived names to current events and if they are lucky form metaphors wnen they chance to enter the texture of a tale.

Whenever you roam the spaces of wild magic, the tales jump up at you; first comes the tale of the wild dreamweaving spaces and that is followed by a host of other fairy tales. Now I can start weaving some of them and you'll see that they are not the same for each story teller who can tell them their own way. Depending on the circumstances, which are resolved in metaphors, and metaphors can hide the truth like a veil of mist that trails over the rivers of time and call for a new reading every time A Dreamweaver chants their rimes.

A Midsummer Night's Dream

Young summer moon in my back vision.
Full summer moon lights my horizon.
Where can I hide my unshared dreams
How can I keep my heart all to my mind,
While I search for the roots of my origin?
Some time long, long ago
I had a home:
I had a piece of land
To get back to,
A forest
Of scented nostalgia;
A spring-sunny valey
And a river of tears.
Some time long, long ago,
I used to call mom and dad,

And travel for thousands miles to tell them
Of how far I have reached.
Then the world suddenly got round
and all directions led to the stars.
All is here and now,
and there is no space for nostalgia:
No home, and no need of home,
No one to return to, no one to love there
No past to care about.
It is all now and here
within reach; beyond a click only...
Here, where the Milky Way rolls out.
Just at times some forgotten tune colours the space
and sets new stars afire.
And it reaches as far as the hiding place of
All human dream and desire:
To forge me a new soul.

---

3. Tunnels or Dragonways

Dreamweaving is the art to sense outside environment and the skill to map it. Dreamweavers can return home to the source idea of the dream because they have the memory of danger in numbers. And numbers are simple. That is, while they are not engaged in a dance. Then they form figures and change visible worlds. And the mind has to skip particularities and jump over using tunnels of blue mist to reach home. Shortcuts are used in dreamweaving. It's like switching your self-awareness off added visualizing of the point aimed. You get directly there. Should you stop to think, you are lost – a racer doesn't stop halfway to check the speed.

We have senses that can check the movement of individual digits. The swarms move at slower speed and produce form and sound, when they speed up we see light and its colours, when they go still faster, the brain checks the psi-energy of movement. We happen to move in dreamweaving using the top-speed our mental gears can keep up and we turn into a swarm of streaming *eons* that can cover distances in the absolute universe. It takes a blink of a moment.

And the memory takes up different measure when *eons* slow down and become bigger. They give off sound and taste, they turn into colours of a whole picture, they turn into forms which endure life energy for shorter spells of time.

And the story goes the human world is in mid-spaces. That is why we can feel bigger worlds and smaller worlds when they pass by, but we can't touch them.

The story goes that there are natural transformers of energy who can turn into different kinds of moving digits.

People can take the energy of the environment and turn into the speeding elements of the world.

The human world is slow – it can sense a couple of energy-binding streams of digits. It needs growing up special skills of mindwork as magicians, priests, wild witching, and lesser types of registering organic carriers of psi-energy.

The wilder places on the Earth provide the ranges of the realms of live-transmitters. But people use metafors to call these and often fall within the slow streams of history.

A story can be woven up in ideas but people prefer words.

Even so, a text can have different levels of meaning which are within the skills of smaller swirms of individuals.

I'll use a couple of names which have turned into metaphors of time-tangles where stories coinside with history.

Why are the Balkans important: Balkans stand up like wounds on the body of the Earth and wall up ill winds and the spread of litter. They hold the crystal grid of the planet and all the energies of the elements are binding them.

The people who dare occupy them are brave commanders of their bodies or duff idiots, spoiled by excess of psi-energy.

I'll tell of a number of cases that can form the skeleton of my text and can tell much about dream-weaving by taking up diverse psi-forms.

There is an ancient tale of the white dragon of happiness. White is the symbol of light and this is the final key to a dragon shortcut in dreamweaving.

One can cover distances and connect stories by simply using the mental image of light. Here dragonways are open by the image of light-blue mist, an aroma, a sense of youth, a memory of a taste, a ringing tune, a movement.

All these are signs of natural humanity. And signs are keys in their essence.

4. Kibella or Cybele https://en.wikipedia.org/wiki/Cybele

The earliest Frigean sculptures of the Mother of gods dating back as far as 8 milleniums from our temporal zones, were of a fat mother with health problems, big womb and lean hair. Her bust was nothing to write home about – breasts like empty long bags, drained by numerous infants. Her face had a decided expression, though and grimace of powerful rage, for she had been known to have driven a cart of four lions yoked. Later on Roman sculptors made them look pretty and still mighty. But that was later, when artists had the power of creating idealized images of gods, heroes and mortals.

In fact Cybele was the image of Mother Earth which for old people was seen through the human eyes and measured as greater than the human measure.

The old Thracian mothers were of the same type: fat and strong, with red wrinkled faces and yelling mouth for they had to control a tribe of youngsters and care about estates full of war slaves. They were powerful and competent of all deeds. Their eyes noticed everything and their hands were big and red, and could hold a battle axe and the reigns of the beasts pulling their carts.

In my memory all old family matriarchs were called Mary and they were the final instance of truth and justice for their minors. Absolute authority is the core of dreamweaving, for you grow brave and ambitious to defend your own space, and that often kills slowly your body and your mind.

For the Balkan infant the grandmother is as steady as rock and as skilled as a goddess. She knows how to make pains and ailings go away and she can calm down any sort of commotion. She holds the reigns of the family matters in her hands and is reliable. The first thing she is associated with is the taste of holidays. She cooks the holiday food which bears the taste, colour and smell of the natural Balkan environment. Girls are often involved in assisting such activities, although men are involved in cooking the meat and tending the drinks. But it is the grandmother that manages everything. She knows traditions and rituals, she has the freedom to experiment, she is responsible one for the organization of people and activities, she knows her people and their needs, she is aware of their likes and dislikes, she solves their problems that had arisen in the meantime, she settles quarrels and keeps family secrets.

Each one of us keeps Cybele in her blood. Sometimes it takes the form of a specific kind of nostalgia, sometimes it is the skill to arrange holidays for your youngers, sometimes it turns out to be a special kind of madness, but anyway, what matters is the added call to return home, or if you are too much in pain, the need to run away from the Call and do things that make you get away and make yourself a person who matters. Anyway, we cannot run away from Mother Earth, only change places and spaces, and the first thing we start doing is terraform our own spaces.

In those skills is both our self-construction and our destruction for we have heaven and hell metaphorised in our genetic memory in the story of our origin that are thr roots and the maps of routs to get back home in all our next lives.

The Truck Driver or Speeding up

That August was the 9th of her stay in the States. It meant she had been driving the truck for 9 years along the roads spreading between the two oceans: only one August away from the cherished green card.

They were partners with Rumen and changed their place behind the wheel four times throughout the long day. They had made a good team and she used to call him Rumbo even in her thoughts.

Annie never dosed while driving. In the hold beside the wheel she kept 12 audio cassettes from a self-study course of English. During the first years of their stay she busied herself with them, trying to learn spoken

American English: right after she took the driver's seat behind the wheel she played one of them and repeated diligently the lesson aloud following the voice of the speaker, while driving. She was a conscientious driver and in a while after the start she got taken with the act of driving along the incredible roads of America and the textbook texts became a matter of automatic repetition. The learning of English wasn't that essential job of her.She spoke with Rumbo in Bulgarian, and their boss came from Serbia and spoke to them in his own dialect which was close to their native tongue. She needed a ten-year job in America to get an American green card, and the work as a truck-driver was steady and she got good money for an *emigrant* – for her mind was still at home and she measured herself by her mother country standards. She had been saving and could afford hiring a good lawyer to represent her deals. She had bought a small apartment and some nice clothes, too: a mint coat and a couple of nice dresses, but she usually wore a pair of faded jeans and some oversized pullovers while she drove. And she was driving all of her time, for she had nothing else to do in that foreign country where the highways were her excitement and she had no other hobby than speeding up.

She had made a few friends in her short pauses of rest and they had met her with a single American guy. She had given him two thousand dollars for an official marriage to steady her stay in America. He had a life of his own and they almost never met whenever she chanced to get back to Chicago. He lived a couple of streets away from the place of the shipping company where *Any* worked, in the eastern suburbs of the city. *Any*'s apartment was also in that area, a dozen of subway stations distance from the old city of Chicago. She never used her salary and saved it, driving all the time, and she never cared about starting an actual family: she had never cared about the family she had left in her home-country, either.

She preferred an apartment in the City. The suburban area of Chicago reminded her of the country she had left with their neat houses and gardens around them. She felt nervous. The wooden houses made her uneasy, although they had all the technical appliances for a good life. They were snobbish and boring.

Rumbo came to live with her. That is, when they were not driving.

Now she drove the big truck along the August highways baking in the sun and counted the months separating her from the green card. The last-but-one order to do was a wagon of foods for a store in the central region of Boston where the alleys were narrow and winding, and there wasn't enough space for maneuverings.

Rumen had woken her up for he couldn't manage: he had been used to call for help at hard terrains but Any didn't mind. She was the expert in their team.

Once she was a racer... once... back there in her homecountry... she was young, with ash-blond hair and green eyes and sweet white skin the colur of vanilla milk. Her neck was pretty and slender. No boy in the town, no adult man remained calm whenever she was passing along in her high-heeled shoes. They whistled after her fascinated by the view of her long, slender legs which were of the same colour as her neck – sweet vanilla milk.

She was not interested in men then. What indeed interested her, were the cars. *Misho* was the winner of the race for Any: he had the first *Sitroen* car in town. There was a big wedding and all the present men envied Misho. Her ageing parents were happy and right in the following week they started the construction of a new house downtown. The house had two storeys, dark-gilded window-panes with blue metal frames, oak polished floors and inside staircase between the lower and upper halls meant for parties on family holidays with many guests. In the meanwhile they occupied a spacy flat on the seventh floor of a new block. It consisted of two joint flats and was given to her mom who was a worker at one of the large local factories – a working class meritocracy who had won a medal of the socialist government for high professional efficiency. She had given to her daughter new woollen bed-covers – white and long haired, easy to handle and very highly ranked by newly-wed housewives. The sunny balcony was full of pretty petunia flowers. Someone watered them and cared of them, while they flourished and grew in the afternoon sun. Not Any. She was not interested in flowers.

They had long and noisy arguments with her husband Misho. He knew she was not his and that made him sick with jealousy. She wasn't in love with him. She wasn't in love with anybody. She had just followed the traditional path of graduating high school, finding a good job, marriage and children, they had two girls. She had never fallen in love. She had instead a passion for fast driving. She drove virtuously. She had a punctual hand but men became annoyed by her absent gaze when she spoke with them. She was icy cold. They desired her but she completely switched herself from any sex affair. Sometimes a man struck her. They shouted at her in a desperate attempt to rouse her. She shouted back out of pure fear. Her right hand stiffened and tried to hold to the gear for switching velocity and her foot tried to step on the gas, kicking off her high-heeled sandals. She craved speeding up until her heart ached. She had to lie whenever her family asked her why she had been away. She strained her long neck and swallowed. It became a habit of hers. Driving had turned it into a tick: she had some neck-bone disorder and turned her head so that she could keep sight of the road. She even started to talk to the car when she was alone. Her mind took notes of the noises of the car and the road before her, but she could be somewhere far away at the same time.

Any shook her head to get rid of persistent reminiscences. After Boston she had driven off towards Dallas and there were only a couple of destinations on her map. The final stop was still far away, she had to change a few highways but the roads were good and straight, and almost deserted in the heat of the day. She rarely passed along another big truck. She took no count of the smaller vehicles. And only once she got passed over by a group of moror-cycle riders. The people along the road were no problem for her, she just registered them automatically and switched attention to alertness. They had signed a list of rules with their employer, which included no taking of hikers. They needen't a special warning about that because they both, she and Rumen, did not understand the hikers' speaking. She didn't like shortcuts that followed winding country roads. She liked the straight racing parts of the highways where she could speedup the big truck and his bas voice sounded even like the voice of a god under the sun.

She had been driving nearly for nine years, there were 13 months and 11 days left between her and the green card. This was the summer before she could feel free as a legal American. The cassetes of the English self-study guide were long forgotten and had turned into dust-gatherers in the holds of the driver's things in the front space of the cabin. Rumbo never played them, he made no vain attempts at learning that foreign language. It was not just the language, nor was it for being tired or lack of time. Any still reached to play a cassette, pushed the button of the player and automatically switched the sound off her mind. Time passed, day in and day out, hours, weeks, months and years rolled off. There was enough time for watching and thinking about current practices of this foreign new world. Too much time.

She had developed a tick of stretching her long neck and straining. It had ceased to be that slender gold-complexioned neck that Misho had loved to decorate with pearl strings once. It was the red-skinned and rough neck of an unhappy ageing woman. She felt used up by each of her mates. So had Rumbo. She raged on the inside, holding her angry words behind her closed teeth. Then she climbed into the driver's seat and started speeding up the even highways and that made America as close to her as a homeland.

She never searched for shortcuts. She enjoyed driving over the long way. Whenever they reached the next town, Rumbo took out the map and gave her directions. Not long ago they installed GPS-application. She didn't mind it but roused Rumbo to watch for the route. She had the instinct of a cat to find the way to a place. The road police sometimes turned up with a warning for them to move on and do not hinder the traffic, but the small tight woman with the shiny green eyes at the steering wheel of the big truck charmed them with her full self-possession and they never shouted at her.

Any pressed on the gas ignoring Rumen who murmured something about a stop at the McDonald's that was already miles behind.

– Stop at the next gas station – he shouted but Any busied herslf with reordering the priorities of her life and let it pass beside her ears.

She stepped harder on the gas aiming at the final stop at their destination. As if she were trying to speed up time. Hours became fruitseeds falling in the cups of days in the Augustan heat and there was no way back home. She had to reorder priorities in her *long lost life*.

She started clearing the topic of her abandoned daughters she had never had time to love. They had no gratitude for her for having secured their lives. They didn't graduate high school neither they dared come with her. After 16 years of permanent quarrels with their father, the three of them moved to the apartment of Misho's parents in the west part of the town. Any sold the luxurious family flat for a reasonable price and moved at her own old parents's place in the small house of only two rooms, because the new house was unfinished yet and she needed the money to emigrate to America with a group of her mates.

Her elder daughter *Iliana* married and went to live with her husband. They had one daughter – a brunette with plain brown hair. The younger daughter, *Miryana* was of an adventurous nature like her mother and had long blond hair, but she hadn't inherited the golden milk-and-vanilla beauty of Any. They never called while Any was in Chicago and didn't come to see her when she came – twice in seven years – and stayed in the new house. They said no "thanks" for the money she gave them to complete the house design and furniture. They always said her telephone number was of no use since nobody called back and they had not received her messages that she was coming back. No one lived at the house because Any had made a row with *Miryana*, who had stayed there for some time, and sent her to live with her father. Any's parents were dead and the old small house was sold to a company who dealt in selling luxurious building facilities. Any was thinking of proper punishment of the two daughters: she was not going to let them inherit the beautiful house. There were two Bulgarian lawyers whom she met in Chicago, who had taken care of her. They were both divorced and lived together. The woman had three children, and the man had two. They came to see her and were her only friends…

Rumbo was shouting something to her but the words didn't reach Any. She carefully slowed at the next crossroad, drove past the gas station and the mall, added gas and turned on the new broad highway. She always followed a new route after having done a break. She didn't care for having a meal. She didn't care about reading the sign with the number of the road. Now she was driving, following her own map. She had been driving for more than 10 hours only by instinct.

The highway climbed uphill when she at last reached *Ranentsi,* her family place of origin – on her mental map. The old two-storeyed house in the village, she loved for its white walls and wooden window frames with wooden grids and brown varnish. The climbing rose and the lilac bush in the corner of the long square yard, the pavement on the garden path, the buildings for the animals, the pig-sty and the hen-house, the sheep yard and the cottage of the dogs.

On the meadow opposite the house there grew some fruit-trees: pears, plums and apples. Next to the meadow was the vegetable garden which her mum liked to work in when she was alive. She often drove there and back downtown. When her mother insisted that she came to take some fruit and vegetables. The house had faded down in her memory and she wondered who tended the lawn and the fruit trees. Any had sent money for the repair of the roof and for someone to take care of the garden, but her two daughters had spent it on their own needs. They had no proper jobs. Both of them smoked.

Any had dropped smoking. In the cabin there was no space for the smoke, at the gas stations smoking wasn't permitted for safety reasons and in the towns where they usually stopped to have some rest there was no place for smoking a quiet cigarette, and there was no time, either, for they were really tired.

Her salaries heaped in her bank account. The additional courses with the truck were paid and that added to her savings. She had nothing to do between the shifts and often took emergency routes. She drove to a destination, there she waited for the truck to be loaded and drove on, where they unloaded and loaded the truck again. While the load was processed Any had time to walk around. She had been curious to find more information about America, Everything looked larger, better-organized and neater. She compared it to the suburban area where her youth had passed, with the disorder in her own place and in her own life. Now she was bored to death of it all: everything looked the same – typical planning of typical houses, typical foodstuffs, and typical minimized effortless thinking with minimum bareers, that hindered the movement between points that created added value. She let herself get distracted for a moment to give attention to the fact they were once required to study Marx, and the theory of added value. That she could understand. She had no delays in speeding between points of added value. The trucks of their employer were with good engines, they were inspected often. There were gasoline money and oil money, there was no emergency on the way. Any wasn't interested in repairs, she was not an engineer or a mechanic, she was a driver. She liked it whenever she sat behind the wheel to have everything professionally checked. She drove and listened to the even roaring voice of the engine…

She slowed down at the next crossroad. Just then the hands of Rumen caught both her wrists near the driving wheel. Any silently shook him off and continued to follow her route.

When they reached their destination in Dallas Any parked in front of the store, switched off the engine and jumped down on the pavement. It was an unusual building – newly painted, long and two-storeyed. The construcrion reminded her of the youth culture house in her hometown where she managed the office of the deputy-head while Sara, her only friend, was the boss.

From the office in Dallas Rumen called their employer in Chicago to send a spare driver in the place of Any who had suddenly collapsed with exhaustion. Next he took Any to hospital. She had not fully awoken from her sudden attack and was now telling aloud to Sara her lifestory and how she had been betrayed by everyone. Then he continued to drive alone in spite his eyes were closing for want of sleep. He managed to reach the place where his shift-mate waited.

When they got back to Chicago, Any hadn't come in full conscience. She was taken to a local medical institution where they kept her for two months. She had gone out of her mind for homesickness. The doctors recommended that she be sent back to her home country.

When Any returned to Bulgaria, there were only 9 months and 7 days between her and the green card. There were some of her old friends who found her a job at a bakery. At first she stayed alone in the spacy new house. Later she invited her lawyers to come and accompany her. The town was empty of the people she knew. There were only unfamiliar faces she met. Her Bulgarian passport had expired. She went to the police station to get herself a new set of personal documents.

She was given a blank registration form to spell out her full name and sign.

– Anka Mihova, are you the same person? – she jumped at the sound of the voice of the young blond registration-officer, and nervously swallowed. No one had called her Anka for years on end. She had become somehow used to "Any".

– Can I use my whole name and change the family name to take my ancestors' name? – She asked, her mouth suddenly dry with excitement.

– Yes, you can – the woman at the office said. There were some minor formal things, but Any left them for her lawyers, Nevyana and Atanas, who already lived with her and cared for her, to settle down. She had never hoped for having someone to take care of her.

All her documents were now to the name of Anna Mihailova.

The ten years she needed for acquiring a legal American citizen status had passed. Any lay down taken by weakness that the flu had brought upon her body, suddenly overwhelmed by her lack of will to live on. Everyone had left her. She vaguely thought she had two daughters somewhere outside. In fact very close to her place. She hadn't looked for them when she had returned. They belonged to somebody other's existence. They were strangers to her. She was tired of living and her soul was pained. She could hear voices talking animatedly: one of them seemed to belong to her younger daughter. *Miryana*, who insisted that she wanted to see her. Nevena was telling her in an angry low voice to get away and not cause trouble. Any started to pant and shouted with frustration. Atanas came in and held her in his arms tightly. Then he gave her to drink and tenterly put her down on her bed. She had already calmed down when Nevena came to give her an injection of a sedative drug. She slept, forgetting all her previous worries. She slept for a couple of days and never got out of her sleep.

Her daughter, *Illiana*, lived with her husband in his apartment. *Miryana* was settled too in their old flat with her father.

The beautiful new house in the centre of the town was now inherited by the family who had been caring for the single legal owner. There was an obituary on the blue iron door to certain Anna Mihailova. Some old woman who had gone mad with homesickness and returned from America just before receiving a legal green card. Back in Chicago, Rumen, who was now a legal American, occupied an apartment that he had bought from the ex- husband of Anka Mihova, a Jonathan Poultry. He had agreed to sell it to Rumbo for thirty thousand bugs, after his wife had gone mad with homesickness and was sent back to her Balkan homecountry.

She had found someone to write a letter for her asking him to send an invitation for her so that she could get an American visa. Then he went to visit Rumbo and settle down things with him.

- Oh, please, don't you bring her back to me. She's crazy as a cuckoo.
- How about the apartment? She bought it with her own money. Do you want it?
- I'll sign a document that I have no aspirations. You took care of her all that time. It's up to you: how much do you give?

Rumbo didn't hesitate but gave him $ 30 thousand in cash. That was his savings he had kept in the wardrobe. And a fur coat – minks, eaten by moths.

She had gone insane out of homesickness. She had craved to get back home: not the place of her origin. Neither the time of her youth. But she craved for the lost chances to love: she had missed them speeding up in her big truck along the highways of a forein country.

Salt in the Water

or the same story with enlarged focus on the destructive processes that buld a Cybele-presence in our minds.

She woke this time on the third floor of the North East Hospital to a grey world and with the fear she would have to wait very long for the led roof that was now over the whole building instead of the sky to turn round revealing some window, or dissolve into the nothingness and let back life. She remembered what had happened to her but she had no image of the moment when the world had blown into nothing. There had been some Thanksgiving celebration and a parade. And the fear of pushing a button and making the world dissipate in the fury of nukes. It was not her own nightmare, anyway.

That was some mental picture on the surface of her brain – the projection of telepathic emanation of other people's nightmares. She could remember being in one room downstairs with a dozen very old people who thought they were responsible for the world. A flock of cuckoos troubled by some trauma that had pushed them beyond their own minds. Not her flock, thank goodness. The docs had discovered that early on the next day and had ordered that she be moved to regular department for the treatment of lonely mothers, giving this time to her the story of an immigrant who had fled from her husband after losing her baby.

OMG!

So, she knew, they had established some other dominating story in her mind while they had been scanning her mind and had found another clear mental picture, which was not hers, still: the story of a mother of four kids, a disorderly blond with a fallen mouth and face reddened by rage, who had lost one of her babies while walking along a bridge over a tidal swamp at the edge of Quincey where their house was, and the child had fallen into the shallow water below.

Ann could replay the picture stored in her mind and she could see the mother as she was standing on the bridge, shouting, while two police were trying to find the closest point to reach the child without leaving firm ground.

"They did not enter the pool for fear of spoiling the leather of their new shoes," the woman had said in court and the journalists had used that as a title.

"The uniform shoes are too heavy and there was no use risking our lives, too, walking into the swamp," the police had explained later on.

So the child drowned and the mother blamed the police. That was ridiculous. She never thought of jumping into the water herself after her own kid. A female child-raising machine, made by her male partner and her own upbringing give birth again and again until her brains became liquid and her bonds with her children but melted into that liquid leaving no self-conscious mind to care of the human being given to that body by nature's law, or by god's plan, if you prefer.

That was definitely not her own memory and Ann was fighting against the attempts of the medical staff to push it on her. That was a story told at a lecture, she remembered, with the intent of the professor to raise emotion and challenge the participation of the fresh new class into a discussion. It had impressed her with the absurdity of old-fashioned thinking in a group of people who believed they were the most advanced minds in the most advanced culture in the world. To be correct, they never said "the world" for they believed each individual had their own worlds, "sets of worlds". Instead, they talked about "the globe" and the "diversity of cultures", and she had the vision of a public hall lit by a single electric bulb in a milk white globe round which the flies of the night, some moths and diverse lost bugs were flying, making their small noises with the unified desire of surviving the whole night-length of their lives.

Everything had begun one night after her getting home in the rain, that had risen from the Ocean and had drenched her like a tide of salty water, giving to her no way out of a severe cold and the feeling of a bleeding nose. The Ocean had been fascinating the day before: a Sunday wrapped in all shades of blue and netted in golden sun rays. It was like in an old song from a fairy tale she had once seen on TV: "The blue cities, the golden gardens". She never remembered the rest of the text, so she let those two lines ring in her mind like the refrain of a top-ten performance she had not heard well in the din of last night's disco. She had been down to the harbor where the water was deep and dark, and the strong breeze came golden-white through the hulls and masts of the yachts that were there for a day's exhibition. It had been no business of hers to go and inspect the yachts, but she had been curious and quite lonely. And the wind had gone all through her making her feel transparent and fragile.

That was how the rain had caught her and had left her no way out of the salty water.

Sailors who lived all by themselves on distant isles sometimes used to drink sea water. And it made their blood rise and flood their thoughts with heavy dreams which replaced the real world. She had read about that. Back there in the old life.

On the Monday that had followed she had gone through the fall flu vaccination that was compulsory on campus. They had warned her about some unexpected reaction, though.

Upon getting out of the train station she had doubled. It'd been a strange feeling lasting for a second or two.

Then a small woman had asked her in small English to use her cell phone for a minute's call: she had been lost, she explained, and needed to call her boss to come and gather her. The woman had just shouted a two-line length of sharp sounds and given it back with many thanks and to the reproachful look of the station police who had come near to check if everything had been okay. "You shouldn't give your phone to strangers, ma'am," he had said. "It can be dangerous."

"In what way?" she'd asked but he had not given her a clear answer, just repeating his warning before going away.

"Identity change," said in dark red letters the white billboard at the far end of the parking lot outside the station.

Then, back to her rented apartment under the metal-covered roof of the three-story house where the seabirds used to walk at night producing scary scratchy noises, she'd had that feeling again but this time persons A, B, and C had peeled off her and gone to their own business, leaving

23

her helpless and unable to explain to the medical staff who had arrived after an emergency call by her surface person that she had fallen into the severest fever ever as a side effect of the vaccination, and had to be treated as a "physical", not "mental" case.

And they had taken her to some hospital and given her some drugs which she had refused to take, and they had kept her for the night until she had lost self-control and they had made her take the pills. Then they had taken care to supply her with a medical story which was not hers. They had scanned her head, first thing at the emergency after the car had taken her there, and had given to her the stories that had answered the brain waves of her fevered head, changing them to fix a picture that seemed satisfactory to their understanding, to which she was a stranger. It'd been the trial run of a new diagnostic machine, she had gathered. There'd been some doctors and students from Boston University: "medical technicians", they had said in answer to her attempt at interviewing them on her part.

But she'd become aware of that after some time – a week or a fortnight. She wondered.

They had kept her under drug control for she'd been constantly refusing to accept their story and had changed the medical ward three or four times. But they had at last found the pneumonia in her lungs and cured it for three days.

"They", she thought. "Who were those mysterious *'they'*?" She had only a vague picture in her mind that looked like a group photo of familiar nameless faces.

And now they were about to let her go, failing to get inside her mind, they had classified harmless only after they had scared her to a state all her emotions were blocked.

She was not to feel negative if she wanted to join the colorful culturally diverse population of "this country". She was no longer an immigrant but a strange lonely person, who preferred not to be bothered by small talk of politeness, and she was foreign to the community of the broad-smiling robots of former immigrants who never discussed things outside their job instructions or daily body needs. "Now you are here, you are no longer different. We are all Americans," one of them had told her confidentially.

"We have to find you a family," one of the young nurses had told her in the hospital.

24

"But I have a family," she had protested.

"Where are they?'"

"Back in my home country."

"But you are here now," the pink-faced shining blond had smiled contented and self-confident in her small-mindedness that prevented her from getting to really know things about her patients. Ann had wondered whether the girl had any idea what the globe looked like from a plane and whether she could imagine there was much more of the world beyond the sea.

Or was it all for the sake of security? But it was funny for the security services to be interested in her, she thought. She had come to enlarge the glory of that country. Or... probably they were told some other story and were now trying whether she knew her own identity trying to dissolve it in a half dozen paranoia stories. Like salt in the water.

She had laughed at first at the strange phrase that had appeared in her mind as if it had been the trail effect of careless hacking, so she had googled it. Google immediately attributed it to an Indian story about the father who made his son dissolve a handful of salt in a glass of water and on the next morning had asked the boy to bring the salt to him. When the confused son said he could not see the salt but only the water, the father made him taste it and it was there, its presence could be tasted but not seen.

"That's truth," the father explained. "You cannot see it but it is everywhere in the water."

"Who am I," she'd thought then. "I have come here with a couple of professions and they've offered me at university eight different opportunities to follow?" She had liked them all and had tried them simultaneously until her energy was drained. Then there was that sickness break. And she could sense the invisible bonds of all her areas of interest dissolve into her own cup of water. She knew now what she wanted to do, but was too weak to start.

While she was waiting for the staff to prepare her documents before leaving the hospital, she called Peter and he promised to come right after work about 4 pm. She sat in the dusty hall and waited impatiently. The featured picture under her eyelids was rolling further back to earlier shelves of her memory storage.

It was her third flight overseas. The check in system was new and contained no previous information about her.

"What's your purpose for coming into this country?"

The form of the question puzzled her and it took a couple of seconds before Annie could gather it and spit out:

"I've come to attend a conference."

"But you've gotten a five-year visa?" stated the officer in a questioning tone. "No relatives? No intent for immigration?"

"No," Annie cut it short. "Just for the conference and back home."

The Officer smiled showing smart white teeth. "Hope you'll like your stay here and we'd be expecting you to come back to this country."

"People always come back to this country"... He repeated it again.

And Ann had heard it a few times over the radio, and while waiting in the queue. Was it so disgusting for the people here to say America? Why did they keep saying "this country" with some kind of disdain as though distancing themselves from the texts they had to officially say?

They had to obey some computer that generated a list of questions for each single new arrival. Maybe they felt they were to obey a robot as if they were themselves some robots of lower class. Hummm. That was interesting to watch.

And then she lapsed into some dullness while a voice was saying in an unknown accent: "You don't know English... ha-ha - you don't know English..." she shook her head and woke up to some relief remembering that she had arrived from Europe, not from... that far... there was fog again... and a voice crying somewhere away from a frightened to death little face, so scared that no tears had time to roll out of two slanted black eyes.

Ann was not asleep. It was like passing from one of her former lives to another as when you are getting to the next stage in a video game. She let her mind restore one of the stages she had already covered.

It was a hot summer when she traveled to New York the second time. The airliner was full of passengers from Eastern Europe, mainly Germans who had gotten on the plane in Frankfurt. They all were saying they were just visiting their cousins in the US but a friendly German in her late thirties whose babies seemed to have liked her, confessed they were prepared to emigrate. She looked lonely and scared and that had made her talkative. Ann was drawing some sketches and the German babies came to her and watched while she pulled out some blank sheet of paper and drew a couple of funny animals for them. The two teenagers who were sitting on her left liked her when she gave them her rolls and the dessert from the dinner box.

When they got off the plane and passed all the checks after queuing for a couple of hours together with the immigrants, she headed for the baggage reclaim area where her fellow passengers were impassively watching the overloaded squeaking belt. The people's faces had suddenly acquired a gray tan and their eyes were black despite what their passport description said. She stood quietly and waited. She had no intention to immigrate. Not this time. Not ever. If she were to stay and live here, it would be only change of home.

And she waited for her sole small suitcase made of soft brown leather. The belt kept squeaking and there was rhythm to this shrill sound – like that of a boat in some blue Italian port waiting for the voyagers like in that opera after the tale of Nabucco. She listened to it until the beat grew into a sound and the sound into a song. The passengers looked gray-greenish in the wane light in the huge hall and the Jewish Rabi and his family stood among them like the leaders of a group of travelers that had just arrived at the doors of the Promised Land. It was dry, although the air outside the airport was heavy with the rain that was throwing its heavy drops like miniature stones into the grey waters surrounding the Land. The city was stinking in the heat and rain had made things even worse. She was only too glad when she finally reached the campus that she completely forgot about the dangers that mindwork contained and about the warnings to take care of any kind of security measures.

She replayed this part of her final waking up in the hospital on the day before:

All her life Ann had cherished some faith into the capacity of her kind to telepathically arrange certain things between them. She had even believed in mental control... or so she used to think and state. When it finally happened to her and some e-generated individual suddenly accessed her mind she got so surprised and scared that her reaction was to peel off three telepathic selves before she could stop falling down into producing an uncontrolled number of virtual individuals until her brain got drained. It had been sheer rejection of each single aspect of her former life that had left the doors of her mind open to some freewheel hacking. Now, in the darkness which had followed her shutting off that intrusion, her zest for remaining alive was based on the pain of waiting, and when waiting became unbearable she opened her eyes to an unknown future with no color. The langoliers straight out of Stephen King's story had been here, she thought. There had been the gray leftovers of a concrete building representing the human world – some gray cube against the grayness of the nothing that had replaced the world. Then pain had come to restart her muscles for life, and with it – the rejection of a needle binding her to a stand and a bottle of some transparent dream-weaver, and a general rejection of all the junior medical staff that came to her with their parrot talk of "doctor's orders" claiming her obedience and giving her no explanation why she'd been there and what had been in the bottle, so she had spoken rudely to them and they had complained. But they could nor read what she really thought of them in all the languages she could speak...

They had been "treating" her as a poor sick old woman. To the wrong diagnosis, as well, for she could not have that kind of illness. And they had put some thing in the medicine to keep her sleepy. When finally she'd come over to a colorful world again, she'd made a hypocritical face of politeness and one of the terrorizing nurses had returned the gesture asking her to tell her something in her own tongue. Which she'd done with perverse pleasure for she'd managed to utter the dirtiest abuse for the creature in a melodious sentence and through a demure face.

"How nice it sounds!" the victim had exclaimed. "Will you translate that for me?"

"Oh, it's just a few words of how grateful I am for your cares, and how good you have been to me all these days," she'd answered enjoying the truth in the double-faced irony.

And then they had let her call Peter, her land lord and now were preparing to let her out in the world, back to a shaken physique and a mind determined to regain all its power.

The main instrument for carrying out that objective was the pained identity someone had tried to steal.

And that operated through a song catching upon nostalgia:

> *The daybreak is dawning*
> *and you are not here.*

I've been dreaming of you,
I've been calling to you
I've been begging you
To come back.
And be a part of my life.

Peter came at last and he did not recognize her at first but followed the wheelchair of a drugged lady with short black hair.

"Peter," she cried again and he turned to her in surprise.

"Annie, is that you? OMG. You look younger. I thought you were that woman in the wheelchair." Ann laughed. She had spent half a day looking at her hands when she had been freed from the dreamweaver system. There had been a small brown spot near the top of her right pointer and one – in the fat part of her left thumb. They had not been there while her mind was droning somewhere in an elder body. She could remember how happy she'd been to see her own hands back.

In the next ten minutes the robot serfs at the register desk were asking Peter whether he could speak English and what was his role in Ann's life. Then she was handed a document to sign and she refused to do so, for it contained another person's story. They apologized and then produced a big yellow paper envelope where all her real documents were carefully stored. She signed this time and followed Peter out of the building to a severe winter. It was only half an hour drive home.

She was able to get to the lab on the next morning. Her colleagues were having a party and she was immediately given a tin of beer and a plate of cheese. She gave them a surface smile. Somewhere deep in her the smile was registered.

Upon finishing the planned term of stay, Annie found out she had not even begun the real work on her project. She was determined to get back over the Ocean, though. She needed some time to do away with the remains of doubt about her identity.

"I'll be back," she said instead of taking leave with her colleagues. They did not take that as news.

Down there in the old world she'd been breaking chains of tradition, what was thought propriety but been enacted as prejudice and, mostly tiredness. Exhaustion had ruled over her neat when she had cleared half a century of age, and fear for lack of time remaining had pushed her into a lonely adventure of self-exile to this country where she could possibly have her rest in peace.

An emotionless stage in her life game where the fragments of her dissolved identity were to be collected.

A flash of memory of a crowd of gray people with black eyes surrounding a belt squeaking to the rhythm of the exiles' song: of the motherland lost in the rising mists down there beyond the ocean. The promised land was hereabouts somewhere outside but she had not experienced it yet.

No tears, just the salty water in the ocean and in the rain giving her bones an inside pain and her lungs fever, that the robot-servants had treated as a woman's incapacity... Her blood was running out and no one cared. She had her heart working without complaint though following some idea that it just needed enough liquid to move it – not necessarily blood... Just some water and some salt in it...

False documents of someone who had lost her child at birth... A clear cut case of an attempt to steal her identity. And that voice "you don't know English" had been some effect meant for someone else. She was not the foreigner there. It was a vast country that had become part of her and she was at home there.

It was the outsider who had gone to hospital and was involved in an experiment for the brainwashing treatment of paranoia, the paramedicals from BU asking people to tell their own stories while a technician inserted their story to make corrections in a picture running on screen and then projecting it back as a movie. Then there had been those endless TV programs – she kept shifting the channel and there were not the real news but some black fantasies on screen, besides *National Geographic* and *Animal Planet* channels. She had kept watching chimps for the lack of any closer humanoid form... picture-treatment lasting until they had removed paranoia from her. And she was now feeling she was no more interested in laughing or crying either, fun seemed to her now waste of time and there was the single satisfaction of work.

She started doing things for this country forgetting about emotion, beheaded by a tomography-like effect of apathy, a product of being lonely for too long a time. She needed to get to her roots, though. Her A-self had started to grow up again. It needed some of her birthplace soil to fix its craving for identity by birth.

Now it is useless. Although...

Sometimes silhouettes rise in Ann's memory with the early morning mists of each next October: the silhouettes of European cities, the blue-green back of the Balkan, the silhouette of the City of Kings – they call it Istanbul today, some time back in history it was Constantinople, or Byzantium, but is in fact it was the city of the Kings who had established their power over the clasp on the tiny belt of land connecting Europe and Asia – the Old World and the Older World. It is not a place you'd choose to live in. It is a sight to see on a picture. A flight over the Ocean makes clasps look small on the ground and the map becomes real. No more clasps of history and geography, now turned into the mixed symbols of a city skyline rising in the mist of her subjective past. The sea is saltier there – heat, tears and blood densening its story. Nearly as thick as blood and heavier than a half century, thicker than mist, sweet in the sun. Like a dried bond that lets you free for a flight. Blood is not water and its salts are the elements of the green-blue earth in you, holding you still in orbit. But your mind has become lighter and broader and can fly you on. When you are ready. When your people of the same density of salt had departed.

Eight years later Ann landed for the third time at Kennedy airport. The old baggage belt had lost its shrill squeaky voice. Only the beat had remained: this time it was the cheerful rhythm of an old flame meeting her. "I'll be back," she had said at her departure before and she had not cared then to take a proper farewell. "I've never thought you wouldn't," her boss had smiled back.

She had not bothered to carry a big suitcase either. There was everything she needed here.

When she got on the road deep in the vastness of the continent to the small university town she had chosen as her residence this time, she realized she had never been away for all these years. Her whole identity had taken in "this land" with its air and its water and food, and it was now dissolved in her blood and in circulation. And... there was something else in the voice of the blood... her old land had wanted her, and had never expelled her... It had all the time been the same old globe. It was not in the foreign land where the key was hidden for her sickness for this country. It was the flight round the globe, when the salt in your blood reminded you that you belonged here, while your mind longed for the stars you had once lost but was to touch again. One just needed to survive the night-length of one's lifetime.

> Gordius *known better for having tied his oxen with a knot*
> *of **dogwood bark**, which Alexander of Macedonia resolved*
> *by cutting it open with his sword. MacedoniaCU cut cut*
> *cut with his sword.*

The story of the Father is connected with the story of the Earth's life energies. Eating, Drinking and Fighting is the design of masculinity. And it is the task of the femininity to follow, cure and care of their men. In the ancient lands of the Earth.

There was the mother. Any failures with the weaving up of the image of the Mother led to troubles with the welfare of her kids, the living species of the Earth.

Any trouble to weave up the father, hides the danger of losing his name in the ancient Middle Earth saga-weaving.

The father was used for his strength which allowed him to secure his family fighting for them, warring and bringing his male kids to the ability to defend their kingdom and their ancestry. He was beastly, he was greedy, he was a tyrant. He was the one to keep the race. And his failures to do so caused pain and suffering, corruption and destruction.

The ancient civiliztions called their Father-god ina variety of ways and forms, agreeing upon violence and valiamce which are the two sides of rude force. The saga weavers were men who had lost their strength for age or been crippled in battle: they became saga weavers or poets.

Women's magic was different: they cared for their men and kids, for their sisters and elders and returned them back to life. Women studied practices of survival and they were often the object of anger and chasing. They had to learn skills which were better than weapons, and make them mistic by rituals and tradition.

Old mothers were safe. They were true survivors. Old fathers had sometimes strange ideas but their cases were resolved by age.

So, both natural survivor-kinds were kind to a young crippled fearless and bright girl for the grandmas needed to share their skills and the old grannads needed to boast. And they kept telling cases of life practices approaching them from their own point of interest.

The first things an infant is taught is how to taste their environment – what is food and what is not, what is good and what can cause pain and harm the body, what is to fear and how you can stop fear.

One of the earliest things a child is taught is how to fight danger or escape it. Today people had forgotten their natural skills and any pain or lack is the cause of screams and cries, ailings, alergia and phobia that can grow to physical and mental disorders if not soothed down properly.

Fathers teach courage and standing up to trouble, mothers teach safety and how to cure natural troubles by natural means.

Trials, Tastes and smells of the Earth

The things that can be eaten

It was early spring. There were yellow crocuses between the shrubbery bushes like the flames of candles. Grandpa dug out two and peeled the round bulb. Then handed each of us one saying;

- This is good to eat.

My cousin Lazzo and me gulped them greedily and said:

- We want some more.

Granddad shook his head and said there was no more because we had to spare the wild crocuses.

Thus we began our lessons of what is good to eat.

The early spring flowers are strong and they are widely used in folk medicine. They have fought winter and most of them are not edible and if not properly used they are poisonous. Old mothers knew how to handle them and taught the girls of the family and those of the boys who were not fighting or violent and would listen.

Men supplied fish and cattle and cooked the holiday meals. Women took care of the organization, the supplies, the herbs and all the fine stuff that the earth could produce. To that reason we needed to know the tastes of the earth.

Muellins and bees: A Tale of the Dreamweaver

Once Peppy asked me:

- Tell me a tale, but a real one.

And I thought up a real tale: it was May and the gardens were full of apple blossom, wild roses an acacia trees, and the quince-trees had just began to bloom.

We were standing under the tehder shade of the quince.

I said:

- The petals of the rosy flowers of the quince are sweet.

He tried them and said:

- Is it the reason that small golden-green and blue elves are flying among them? With tiny glden pots?

-Ah, but they are the May bees and bugs – I started saying. At least we know them as such. The truth is they are the small folk that lives in the branches of the quinces. They make sweet jelly and Muel from the tiny quinces.

- What are these? – Peppy asked.

The petals of the quince blossom can be baked into a transparent sweet jelly. And the baby quinces can be cut into small cubes and baked in sugar. They become red and transparent like Pomegranate seeds.

- But the other food of the elves is from the yellow ripe quinces which are baked until they turn into marmalade – thick and sweet, because young grape wine is added – the brown-and gold sweet treacle, and they are not conserved but they are kept in pots covered with just a thin rice-paper leaf dipped in sunflower oil. It tastes sweet-and-sour and is called Muel – because of the town of Muel where the small folk live. And they are called Muellins. They make enough of these to last them in the long winter months – those which have an "r" in their names – October, November, December, January, February, March and April. Only the strongest flowers can fight winter, and they are bitter and poisonous for the tender elves.

- How about acacia blossom? – Peppy asked again.

- Bees gather honey from acacia blossoms and its colour is white. – if you bake it with sugar you get sweet white jelly which is served with a coffespoon in tiny chinaware and a glass of water.

- Can you eat the white flowers of acacia directly? – Peppy asked. And then added – can the other flowers be eaten?

- Yes. - I said. - Almost all of the May flowers and herbs have their special taste: rosy roses have a fine-scented taste, the petals of the red climbing rose can be combined with cherries and they can be cooked with fowl. The petals of the yellow climbing June rose taste like fine champagne and the petals of apple and wild rose blossom are finely sweet.

- Can you cook some? – Peppy asked.

And I tried gathering the Four Tastes – Bitter, Hot, Sweet and Sour, when I cooked some dish of chicken breast with rose-and-cherry jelly, and some more chicken with pear-jelly.

- A Holiday meal. – Peppy concluded. – Do Muellins have a long Summer Holiday? – he wondered next.

And I thought he was right. Muellins enjoyed their work in the summer and had a summer holiday meal all through the winter months. But this can be true only about the tiny small folk from the towns of fairy tales which are real while the Sun is real-life for the Middle Earth.

Eating Books

But here The Dreamweaver had a different practice to share that could be woven up in the colourful carpet of the humanity world. It begins with a question: Have you tasted a book, to which the web AI can give any but a purely human answer which applies different standards of evaluation. Have you tasted a book the way young human kids do? Not just paper, real books; and not just books, books on paper.

They smell nicely when they are printed on fine paper: old books with thin leaves, yellowed by time. Once there was such a wooden box full of old books, brought by her granddad's brother, the lawyer, when he returned back home to his father's house in the country, because he could not close his eyes to the social changes, he couldn't tell lies of a brilliant future and needed all the rest of his time to restore his mind and prepare for the meeting of his Creator.

They were books of Law, but Law is time-bound, so she liked to taste them like novels of more complicated language, telling of different people's cases. There was also a textbook of curt medicine with pictures she avoided to eat; a few novels, a magazine on Bee-keeping, and more journals on Law. Her Garnny put them in the toilet and Nanna had read many nice books there, saving some of them although they were printed out in the old official way from the beginning of the 20th century. She tried a couple of the leaves of Don Quixote and the Little Prince, that sounded strange to her andshe could spare a couple of boring pages, all the more that her father brought new editions without the strange letters and with new colourful illustrations. The old books had no pictures, only a couple of drawings that were printed black-and-white and didn't smell poisonous. A young kid can instinctively tell what is good to eat and what is poisonous. She saw pictures in colour and she never ate them.

The books that were sold in the Russian bookshops had thin glossy leaves and my mum said it was a different print, they smelled different and I hadn't tasted them.

The leaves of the Bible – the Old Testament, were thin and smelled acceptable, but I never allowed myself to tear the leaves off whole books, let alone The Bible which had been in the family for two centuries. The New Testament and the Koran were not good to eat. Perhaps they were not old enough and were in the novel print style, although they came from Germany. I never asked questions who cared about the Bulgarian editions in Western Germany, but I discussed it silently, and arrived at conclusions that hinted the existence of hostile worlds – not the states of the countries, but the states of minds. I never spoke about such things. I was growing in socialism and took care not to confuse my mind. Tne Bulgarian mass media never contained the deep level of news or statistics, but we all knew statistics told about cases of confused minds and killed minds. We needed to survive in order that we could see what was in store for us next and feed our natural curiosity.

The note sheets that we used for our singing and music classes were fit to eat - their paper was thin and tender. I never spoiled the, I just smelled them amd knew they were good to eat. Notebooks were also good to eat.

I have never eaten children's books with illustration I never smelled them either. They were with hard glossy leaves and full-coloured pictures and hardbacks. They were beautiful and smelled of luxurious print, and I read them and used to tell my own tales when the texts did not turn to my expectation. I loved to play the main hero and weave up their next actions. I shared my special tales only witn my granny and granddad. They wouldn't laugh at me.

The newspapers also fitted my criteria for safe tasting, not with the pages with the big titles, though. They smelled of the printing house where my mum worked.

She also used to bring home the quartos of sheet which she and her colleagues were correcting at the moment. I especially liked the big botany atlases, they were magnificent and I never ate them.

There was a series of small hardback children's books from the first third of the 20th century. I loved their smell and read them so many times they were broken and disorderly. I never ate them but they smelled properly. Altogether, the books of the big state publishing houses fitted my idea of friendly products.

The last thing to mention was the coloured sheets of writing paper. I tried last to demonstrate the Game of Origami and tasted it. It smelled properly.

I have also tried some of the paper duners are sold in. Well, it's nothing like the Chinese rice paper which is made to eat for it contains the form of the take-away food, yet it's tolerable.

I haven't tasted Indian silver eatable sheets, but I know the taste of silver and a couple of other metals. The interesting thing about metals is that they have taste and sound. The clearer the metal, the clearer the sound. Copper is sour, silver is thin, gold is soft and iron is sharp. And brass is of no definite taste.

Thinking of things one kid can taste, there are the buttons of the typewriter or of the computer, as well as the keys of the piano or accordeon, the glass and crystal glasses and ornaments, and the beads of granddad's prayer string. He had two of them: a yellow one and a red one – they both were warm and had the taste of cinnamon and of pomegranate. And we were not supposed to eat them, but a child is like a cat – they try the tastes of the world by licking things.

The most important thing when we try the tastes of the Earth is not to overdo it. Our mission is not eating the Earth out but keeping the harmony of life. We just try.

Everything in this world is connected. Good things can be sensed by their taste, aroma, colour, temperature, weight. The important thing is not to overdo our own measure. Greed is its punishment itself: like in the case of Midas who asked Fate to let him turn everything he touched into gold. He must have died of thurst and hunger but that was long long ago and is well-forgotten.

The only rule that is to follow in tasting it is not to over estimate the resources of life, even if we trust the web AI to recover life. What is considered to be beautiful in our physical life is life itself. Don't use it up to the end for mid-earth is not endless.

The tastes of Books

In my earliest period as a reader of books I'd read that for the sake of conspiracy, secrets written on a piece of paper were eaten by their holders when they were captured. I tried heroically to play the hero. Some pages were fit to eat others were not. I thought that tradition had something to do with animal skin. Probably leaves of books written on parchment were eatable, but that material was difficult to find.

I had also read the tales of Sheheresade in the big volume of *Arabian Nights*.

There was the tale of the philosopher who was to be beheaded. But first he was given the right to the last wish: he asked his head to be placed on a silver tray covered with a special powder and said he should be ready to answer any question concerning hidden knowledge. He was then beheaded, the powder was spread on the tray, the head was placed there, it stopped bleeding and the eyes opened. Then the head asked whether the sultan was ready and told him to open a few pages of the book of the teacher. The leaves were sticky and the sultan had to spit on his fingers in order to leag through the first dozen of pages. The leaves were soaked in poison and the sultan who envied his teacher the knowledge, fell dead on the floor. It's a cruel tale but the ruler was actually punished for being so greedy and self-conceited. He got his punishment by a man who was considered wise, but wisdom doesn't kill and avoids evil and hostility... I am not willing to look for the lesson learned, for it leads to fighting evil with evil – deliberate and tricky, leading away from the mercy of a Creator. Yet what was done is done and it carries its lesson for those who would open their minds.

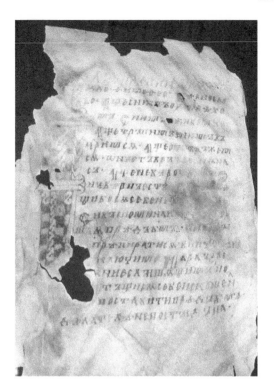

Donkey ears and water Midas touch

Those who had fallen through the gaps of time shall reach the knowledge about vanity. All those who have the records of the Earth life in their genes, even if they had changed the names of good and evil.

Therefore the names we shall not keep in the next tale, neither of places nor of people, for they inspire hostility, and hostility is evil.

Identity is preserved. The question stands though: which is more important – the names of people who are long ago turned into dust, or their identities who are woven in stories of hostility and teach lessons to be avoided?

Stone turns into dust, and wood rots into mud. The wind and the waters carry them away.

Everything is mortal in the big time of cosmos.

Blessed are the poor. In spirit. For theirs is the Kingdom of God. And everything stays in the records of Time.

The dust under our steps rises and forms puffs, and carries images long forgotten. And voices that are woven into the deep structures of life itself.

When scriptures are apart, there still remain the records over the texture of life as a potence of life. It is spirit, not matter. In the Universal Time of the Kosmos everything is spirit formed by all the kinds of memes of life: those which have formed entities and those which had not been enacted, and we had even not thought of them, not been aware of their existence down in the bottom of our genetic tables. There they stay under all the layers of dust and mud. Like the ancient stonework of the pavement well trodden and durable.

Goat Foot

Once down the spiral of time when the Earth was recovered and Life was young, all the living creatures on the Earth could combine and reproduce... A team of researchers using a time machine or a dragonway, isolated a hard gene which kept the species' records – viral. Out of the hard gene a hard piece of matter was made – a living stone... very strong and insensitive to gravity. Then they made it radioactive – and it was no longer viral but timid and susceptible to change that allowed it to be used as a cure and as a weapon and influence changes of the next generations of humanity in a mild and long-term way.

Paddae

The alley wouldn't be the same without Paddae. It was polio, they said. Not to bother him, they said. He sometimes cried. Most of the time he lay on the same spot in the dry dust and watched us passing. Sometimes drooling. Sometimes he wasn't clean and he smelled. Sometimes his mother beat him when he made the shit in his pants.

My grandma tolerated him but we, the kids, tried him sometimes. He just sat there and never reacted with hate. He had an interesting way of moving: the light, springing gait, his pelvis and the crooked legs moved easily as if they were of rubber. And he used to lie directly on the ground. When we told him tales, he listened. Sometimes he laughed loudly.

He was always there in front of their gate. His elder brother and his elder sister were healthy. Their mother wore black skirts and coats, white shirts and white cotton headcloth in the summer heat and a dark fishoo on cooler days. The nickname of their family was the Hoohavla – I imagined it as something connected with public speaking – a public speaker who had the habit of speaking up shady things and obeying the rulers of the day.

Thus I could explain to myself Paddae's case; he was the scapegoat in his family.

I was following the instructions of my grandmother, and I was looking not to annoy him. He felt that and had a special attitude to me.

Time in and time out we kept getting together before their yard gate to do the tobacco leaves that his mother had picked early in the morning. Each one of us who volunteered to give a hand was given a big needle with a thick string. We learned how to hold the foot-long needles under one arm and fill them with fresh tobacco leaves we were pricking right through the middle until we got the needle full and one of the women took them to the nylon-covered drying barracks up on the square space at the broad main road. It was interesting there – people were busy and kept chatting all the time on new and interesting topics, so different from our daily routines. Besides, the mothers who had that time-consuming task to complete, could keep their eyes on the kids and mind us not to make trouble. Our hands became black and we were glad we could be useful.

The sun-baked soil must have been friendly to Paddae who lay directly on it in his blue cotton tunic and a pair of pants and not complain it was hard to lie on. I supposed his elastic defect helped. The earth smelled of warmth, and Paddae felt safe there. He must have had bad days when he did not come out or kept drooling all the time.

In no way, though, was he a goatfoot satir, but he was a true human lad, broken by the illness we could only imagine as a crooked humpbacked drooling cripple of a shadow. He was a child of the WW2 years of hunger and of the anti-humanity doings of the hostile worlds on the Globe – experimenting with things we were not expected to know and talk about. But a kid knows things because kids are close to the Earth and keep trying it out and taste it, and sense it.

He had no sins to pay for, he had no evil thoughts, nor hostile actions. He played the scarecrow sometimes to shoo us away, for he must have pained with the boring kids with the sticks and the difficult words. We knew nothing about pain then. His natural reaction was to shout when we were shaking thin willow sticks at him and that had looked funny to us, a caricature figure of a teenager with grotescue gestures.

I felt he must have been born to be a normal human kid and he somehow knew that, for there was silent pain in his dark-brown eyes. He was aware of his crippled body and that was not an animal's pain but a human mind that registered it. He was not one of the goatfeet satirs of the king with the donkey ears, although his family nickname hinted of tales told out.

That was the punishment there in the highlands of Western Mid-Forest – the punishment of greediness and of talking without measure – for words can cause pain indeed. Goatfooted heir who can sense his deficiency and is pained for that reason because he has not guilt in betraying the ruler's secret.

Bi

There is a category of people who like to say of themselves: *I am a good person.*

Dinnah was not one of them. She was silently certain of herself being good, but she never spoke out. On the contrary: she often used self-irony when she said about herself: *"I am bad"*.

So she went on relaxedly, until she was sent to a World Conference of Biophysics at Boston University. The idea that she could personally see the Lab of *Petar Dunov /Beinsa Duno/* gave her an extreme pleasure. She booked a room at an affordable cost in one of the student hostels that was free for the summer.

She studied the map of the subway and found out she should walk for a mile between the hostel and the railway station in front of the Town Hall and then catch the Green Line in the direction *out of town, or as they called it 'outbound'.*

She got down from the train and staggered on the pavement right before the solid building where groups of students were sitting, strolling or just lingering in the green summer freshness. She was looking around when a young voice called her:

– Diddiiieee! What are you doing here?

It was Miryana – one of her private students who had emigrated to Boston four years ago to study at BU and lived there ever since.

In the course of the conversation the information was shared that Mirrah was a 3rd year student at NorthEastern University and is on the businesspsychology course and is in Boston for a summer study project.

Diddie got distracted and missed the detailed explanations of Mirrah what exactly her project included. She gave half a ear to these and learned that it was some matter connected with the statistics of bi-polar psycho-disorders. Mirrah and a colleague of hers were doing a study with the reactions of the undergraduates from the BU Medical School. They were giving them psycho-stimulating drugs of a new class and then the participants underwent brain scanning and the activated zones of their brains were mapped and the statistics were taken down of any tendency to bi-polarity of their brainwork patterns.

Or something like that. Dinnah was not really interested in a student research.

Miryana's colleague was a tender Japanese woman and she asked her immediately after she met Dinnah:

– Would you take part in a survey like ours?

Dinnah carelessly nodded and forgot about it immediately after she joined the conference senior staff meeting.

There she spent the whole day, she got overtired and her feet had swollen from the 7-hour trans-Atlantic flight. The The chairs were upholstered in a beautiful fabric with roses on a pink background. The last session for that day was at the Castle, a building used by BU academicians for official meetings. It had been a house of ill fame and the local staff giggled while they were sharing tales of the near past. Some of them were fantastic and some of them were of a criminal nature.

It may have been an elite brothel, but she had to admit that it was gorgeous. All their section was accommodated in a sideways lobby with fireplace and gleaming wooden ornaments. The chairs were upholstered in a beautiful silken fabric with roses on a pink background.

Dinnah sat down right in front of the fireplace. The Rapporteur was tedious. There was a light scented June breeze coming from the fireplace. Dinnah was hallucinating. Two voices occupied her mind: one of them belonged to a lady-doctor who was scanning her brain and next the whole of her body believed she had been pregnant with a dark horned crearure and a few couples of implanted extraterrestrial fruit. The second voice belonged to the emergency night nurse who told her to stay still and let them take her to the apparatus for NMR.

When Dinnah woke up with a start,she found herself lying with medicine systems in her veins in a single hospital room. A young boy with a white tunic was sitting on a chair next to her bed. He jumped up to his feet the moment she opened her eyes and smiled nervously.

– You were very sick, Madam, – He said compassionately and then asked her what she had been dreaming about because she tossed and turned and spoke loudly.

– I had continuous nightmare – Dinnah said, not quite aware yet of what had happened to her. – Where am I? What's up?

– I'll call the head doctor. – The boy said. – I was just guarding you while you were having the nightmares. When he turned to go, Dinna noticed the badge on his shirt pocket. His name was Ian.

The doctor had an olive-tanned skin and dark curly hair. Her name was something Greek. She smiled at Dinnah and said they had been treating her for nearly a week out of hemorrhage and pneumonia. The hemorrhage was clear, it had followed the brain scanning and the additional tests, but she couldn't explain why pneumonia had developed after that. Dinna asked angrily:

– You haven't given psycho-stimulating drugs to me, have you? They rise blood pressure and I have problems with my blood circulation and the heart. My veins are like those of astronauts…

The doctor was worried and hastily listened to her heart. Then she took out the needles of the systems out of her veins…. Then she let her know some professional info which was a humane act in that case:

– You were a volunteer of a BI-search. – She said.– Drugs sometimes give unexpected effects. I shall sign you out immediately. I stop the tracing of your reactions. By the way, I haven't met such a strong Self awareness in an individual so far: you never lost it even for a moment. Your awareness of who you are.

Dinnah stood stunned.

They signed her out and she staggered towards the Hostel.

There were two days left until the flight back home. Mirryanna came on the evening of the second day.

– I am sorry – she started and Dinnah thought her voice sounded as that of a shocked goat-kiddie.

– Why did you drug me without my consent? – Dinna interrupted her abruptly.

– But you said you would take part in a study of dreamweaving – Mirryana bleated out. – It's for the sake of a scientific project. We have the subject of the study sign in the documents afterwards. Noone refuses to take part in the Project. Everybody does sign it here – it's a tradition. Then she handed Dinnah some forms, clearly waiting for her to sign them.

– And you never thought of my own research project you failed? – She asked angrily.

– How was I to know why you were here, and what a scientific research you could have with BU? – Mirryanna was cheeky. – BI is a first class project with the undergraduate students these days.

Dinna gaped at that arrogance and missed to remind her ex-student she was her teacher.

– You could've killed me... – She gasped indignantly.

– Oh, medical science is of very high level here. They would'nt let you die.

– But from now on I shall have this failure of the heart. You have stolen years of my health status.

Miryanna blinked indignantly:

– Are you telling me you refuse to sign a scientific research project?

Dinna only stared at her in a fury.

– Well, I knew you'd be a failure: coming from a backword country and all – she bleated in her young goat voice and then she turned round and left pointedly.

She half-turned at the door and Dinnah noticed her own silver watch at her wrist.

- You've taken my watch...

– It had fallen on the car's floor. I'll give it back to you. She then left indeed, never attempting to take it off. She was evidently expecting Dinnah to ask her back.

Dinnah thought of the Eastern belief that when you steal someone's watch, you steal that one's time which now runs against your own time.

On the next morning she started a sightseeing tour downtown. In the old part of the town there were alleys with English-looking homes and green linden trees in the fronts. A golden Labrador went close to her expecting she to caress it. His owner smiled friendly at her.

She walked on until she reached the central park and still further to the port. There were blossoming rosy tulips, there were fresh green trees keeping shade, there was sun and white yachts at the port. The Ocean was transparent blue and so clear that it looked as if it had never been polluted.

She loved the town. It had hidden the scientific research and had opened its summer face to her. She wondered if it was a bipolar entity, taking turns at showing its two essences? Was that the good one? Or was it the evil?

She had no time to judge. Her trans-atlantic flight was early on the following morning. To the Old Continent where her home world was. She didn't care whether it was the better one. The important thing was that it was hers.

Willows and pipes

The Prince and the Fisherman's Daughter

- Why do you need that bunch of thin willow branches? – the Prince asked.

- They are part of the Business. – The old man answered. You can peel them off and lay them bathe in fresh water. And after they had become white and strong, we'll make them knotted into various baskets and plates. They are strong and they can sing, for they are full of spring sap, and they can be woven into different things on the home. How long does it take to learn to work with willow branches? – The Prince asked.

- Just give me six months and I'll teach you.

- That suits me. – The Prince agreed for he was in love with the fisherman's daughter and love is impatient but her father wouldn't give her to him unless he could do something. He had tried with the guild masters, but each of them wanted years of training and the Prince had no time to waste.

The story goes that the Prince wanted to marry a fisherman's daughter but he had no craft and could do nothing for a living. But he learned how to make good baskets out of willow branches and after he had brought a piece of his craftsmanship to the fisherman, the man gave his blessing to the marriage of the young people.

The story goes that the hordes of wild tribes invaded the country of the Prince and he could save his wife and treasure in baskets he had managed to make. They fled and started gathering their men and in a couple of years the Prince recovered his throne and ruled wisely. The story also goes that he always kept a bunch of fresh willow branches under his throne of gold.

I knew about young spring willows. They were the first to start early spring revival and since they grew along the river and formed thickets, we used to peel their bark and make pipes which told us about the secrets of the river. Goatfoot steps and piping out heavy loads of secrets. That's what my first encounter with seasons of the Mid-earth meant. The magic of spring and dogwood bark that Gordius used to tie his oxen.

Willow and pipe

A pinch of idyll chancing a score of romance
amidst some blackened humour of a boring chattering web
OR
Spring: perking in my veins,
Me, strolling Wasteland's empty streets
Lacking their population of stray dogs,
Perambulating mothers, and colourful café-tents.
A sudden mini tornado
Playing a whirlpool of plastic bags,
Dust, and glittering lollypop wraps.
A leaf of paper delivered at my feet reads:

'A new acquaintance'
And leaves me curious.
OR?

The Philosophers' Stone

In the seventeenth century, Thomas Vaughan wrote, *"the first matter of the stone is the very same with the first matter of all things"*.

It was believed that wisest of men could obtain a substance that could turn everything into a primary matter. Later on it was believed that it could turn everything into gold for gold was the ideal dead metal. In the substance of the Balkans there are wedged the stones that flow as a fire and are dissolved in the waters of the fast streams. Ancient people knew them in the rocks and used the philosophers' stone for magik and to cure psi-disorders. For a sound mind is the first thing that determines the belonging to the human race.

The philosophers' stone – radioactive but not destructive to humanoids – must have been alive, not exactly a stone – a mixture of all types of sphere-filler –isotopes. The main thing was in self-limitation of its use.

One knows one's own borders. Spiritual minds have no limitations other than matter.

I dream of chemical formulas that have extensions like hooks of different colour. Substances can be woven to fall in harmonious shapes, and then they can sing their own chant of magic.

Silver

People from the Balkans knew about the strength of silver to kill smaller life forms because they cannot survive on its surface. Silver is eatable and men who need some disinfection have silver coins turned into sheets of a micron thick matter and eat it to keep worms away. Silver is the stuff that sings out of elastic power making its surface the ideal mirror of quarks. The streams of the Balkans dissolve rocks that contain silver and keep their water fresh and cool. The Earth likes the voices of the metals when they are thinned and cold and keeps her children happy to have the voices of the silver in living creatures – birds, woodmaidens, fairies and witches who inhabit such places. Silver and gold are given as birth names to people who have the feeling of purity.

And the bells used in the dances that chase evil shadows away in very early spring, and the bottles of pure silver, the belts of women, the rings of an oath, the holy books binders. Sometimes women's belts have copper straps which make them unclear, sometimes they contain ornaments of ivory or bronze, or gems. Silver likes red, blue and green gems. It doesn't mix with gold, gold is different and cannot keep the singing life. It is important that silver can sing.

Gold

Gold is the ideal ideal dead metal that never changes the form of its formula. It only wears out and can be mixed with earth to form rocks.

It is foreign to life but it saves dead bodies. Pure gold has a shade of grey. The ancient preferred the shades of red and sought to make the masks of their dead rulers out of red gold, while the statues of gods were cut out of ivory and white marble.

Gold, like silver, is not poisonous, but it can accept tiny living organisms that combine with soil. So it is important for gold to be covered and locked out of air and waters that can soil it with life.

Practically gold is good for nothing. Practically, gold has been used as a dream woven precious metal that cannot corrupt otherwise but can corrupt the soul of a body which is much more than the mind. Thus it happened that my gene knows the forces of the Earth to give birth to life and to inflict corruption to life when life turns dangerous on Her. The Earth can sing directly to the soul of material bodies and destruct them. It is the case of Midas touch and old Balkan witches are careful with the forces of the soils, contained in the fire under the Balkan and in the waters, that are sucked by the roots of the trees.

Water

The electrons of water are nearly absolute spheres, that is when water is not mixed up with the other elements.

All the source waters have their own taste. One can drink directly from the clear mountain streams. They hold all the life of the part of the Balkans where the sources of the rivers are. And cure different aches and pains.

I often dream of drinking from the Balkan springs: I can sense the water and hear its voice. It calms down body disorders when you manage to cut out the shape of its formula. Then it reaches out and touches back the pained body space. And water can turn substances of life so that they fit the chorus of the to capture the little eddies of time Balkans.

The Hairs of Yana

/A wild Tale/

That happened in one of the ends of the Earth where it is still wild and the light of the day ceases abruptly giving space to the night which is erratic and incorrect – at times gentle and velvety, sometimes sharp and painful. In these places people have learned to capture the little eddies of time and space and use them for the satisfaction of their daily needs, be they good or bad in the general flow of life. The energies are closing in words – forms and grow in textures-realities. If you are not careful you can fall in the gaps between the worlds that are just empty, gaping chaos, or you can step on a foreign world surface and not be able to return from that home.

There are lots of such people and it is not due only to chance that the wild places contain many asylums for people who had got lost on their way back home. These asylums are big sad buildings without actual fences and their inhabitants are calm quiet small people with empty eyes and trustgul like kiddies. They look press ridden – smashed soft and disinterested in current life – they just sit in the sun and enjoy god's day in their quiet invisible way. Who knows what they have turned their backs on: one doesn't ask them questions for one doesn't get answers – they just don't pay attention to you. They don't usually talk. They just sit and smile and their smiles are like sun's rays suddenly appearing betreen clouds – bright, quick defensive smiles of apology. Their eyes suddenly brighten and sharply focus on yours showing sharp intellect for a spell of a second, and after that all has vanished and you find yourself staring into the emotionless eyes of quiet insanity until a nurse comes up and tells you not to waste your time of life on hopeless cases.

It very often happens that a certain quiet psycho finds a homely place in one of the monasteries where they are given the job of the one who takes care of the churches and the chapels. They clean them, take care of the candles and the church silverware, sometimes they even refresh the icons. They usually live as hermmits and fulfil their duty automatically and have no doubts, nor questions but just accept their lifestyle calmly and can even bring comfort to the rare visitors of such remote places.

This story started its circulation completely by chance when a tired traveler lost his paths in the wild Balkans. He kept walking towards the setting sun which is so bright sometimes that it blinds you and your eyes get swollen and red. He was so tired of walking that he even did not notice how the rock-laden path made a soft turn and his thirsty horse suddenly became lively as happens when the horses smell fresh water, and hurried towards the granite rocks that formed a wall and a narrow opening brought the fine scent of fresh water.

It was a stony spell of a waste countryside, fruitless lean and dusty land That formed a hard isle of rocks amidst the rich folds of an old beech forest that covered the soft curves of the low mountain from the beginning to the end in the next big river valley. That stony plateau contained a single dry and dead tree that stood black against the green forest and the grey rocks, and beside it there was a white chapel and a single-room cottage.

When the traveller and the horse finally climbed the winding steep path, an astonishing view spread before them: There was a long cement basin of a Fountain with twelve incessantly running spouts, that filled a deep transparent pool, clear like a tear, scented and cool and full of water weeds that spread like a long woman's hair full of white blossoms. Not a drop ran down the slope. The horse hurried towards the fountain and the surprised traveler first peeped into the chapel which was built directly on the flat rock. And he could see how in the middle of the stone floor a spring came up and the water gathered into clear pool, made a small rivulet and abruptly vanished into the rock.

The traveller bent down and stood on his knees before the miraculous well, drank its sweet cool water and splashed his swollen sun-stricken and tired eyes. The water came as a caress and washed the tiredness away. It cleared his eyesight and he could at last look around himself. The chapel was shining clean: the floor the silver cups and plates with candles and the bowls one could drink the source water with.

He next went out to take care of his horse.

Only then a man appeared from the cottage. He was very calm and his eyes were brown and peaceful.

They wished a good day to each other as is the tradition with complete strangers who happen to roam the wild grounds, and then sat down beside the well to share a long talk – an enjoyable story – miraculous and truthful, about human desires and longings, painful, warm and dreamy.

- What is this place? – The traveller asked. – Rocks and rocks and this water – where does it come from and why does it vanish…? And the dry tree at the edge of the pond – how does it come that it is dead and why is it left to spoil the view – like an object of a curse?

- I'll tell you the whole story – the other one answered. – But first come and sit for a while so that your tired feet can rest in the shade of the chapel.– and he took him to the wooden bench in the front of the chapel and they sat down facing the fountain and the stone-floored pool. It was a miracle in itself for it was all overgrown by green hairs full of white blossoms. Its water was so clear that each tender blossom was clearly seen and the spring caused the green threads to move like the hairs of a siren

The host stood quiet for some time. Silence took them over and it was so clear that it matched the transparent water in the pool. The traveller's heart opened for the beauty of that magic place, and his ears longed to listen to the story. The voice of the story-teller came up in this miraculous harmony and filled the air with strange images as if coming from the spring.

- This is a wild end of our countryside – the story began – paths are narrow and steep, and uncouth, and houses are huddled together on the level lawns. Their inhabitants rarely visit the village to meet with mates or buy some merchandise from the Sunday market stalls of travelling tradesmen You must have crossed the village on the way here – that was not a question for there was no other way up to that place and the traveller nodded silently.

- You must have noticed a beautiful large house in the upper end of the village behind a fallen wall and in the middle of a big garden that has gone wild. A large, deserted family house – with ornaments and white gargoils, and blind windows with cobalt blue frames in the middle of the façade. Now it's empty. Time ago two brothers lived in it with their families. It was swarming with life. Their old parents had built for them a home to bring up children, artfully decorated, with full closets, cellars and barns – there was place for abundant families and gatherings on holidays and nameday-celebrations of three generations.

The elder brother married first and they had a large wedding. The bride was from the neighborhood uphill. And their life continued its regular flow. The newly wed had a separate wing of the house of their own, away from the parents and the younger son. There were no scandals, the bride had the freedom to mind her own housework and felt comfortable.

In a couple of months the younger brother got married. The bride was a local girl, Yana. On the day of the wedding the village people noticed how beautiful she was – like a bright star, like a woodmaiden from the fairy tales with her long golden plaits and perl-white skin. Her friends knotted tiny white blossoms in them and she gathered the eyes of entire village … and when she stood beside the bridegroom in the Church, everyone saw how good the young couple looked and were happy tto have so comely a couple in their village.

The elder brother was shared the great joy of his younger brother: they had grown up together and shared all joy and toil without words. There was no place for jealousy between them. Yana was as good as she was beautiful, and was always polite and helpful to the old mother and father, and she was a truthful wife and had eyes only for her husband, whom she loved dearly…

- here the voice of the story-teller stopped and it seemed that the running source water from the twelve spouts continued weaving up the story:

It wasn't only Yana – the water sang – another pair of eyes opened for the bridegroom that day, one more woman's heart secretly gave itself to him and the soul of another woman caught fire of passion framed by the shadows of envy full of snakes of jealousy…

———•———

The wife of the elder brother was stricken by a sudden passion for her brother in law when she saw him standing beside his bride. Her own wedding was long forgotten and she was not blessed with a child. The magic between her and her husband had dried out. Each of them kept thinking that the reason was in the other partner but people were talking of her a barren field…

You know how other people's wedings soften us and we get caught in the net of our surging sensuality. The bridegroom took his sister in law's glances as an expression of her approval, and suddenly her own husband felt the spell of the rising feelings and turned to her again. She, on her part, accepted the politeness of her younger btother in law as a sign of attention, while the regenerated passion of the boring husband was both flattering and giving her an ally for the fulfillment of her plans.

In the first months after the wedding the atmosphere of understanding in the home did not change. The new bride obeyed and had respect for the elders. Her engaging and doing her housetasks in good mood that showed in happy laughter and songs brought light and hope to the house. As time passed, however, a crack ran in the relations of the two brothers threatening to turn into a precipice, and they no longer shared the joy of doing some job together.

The younger brother was disturbed by the deep glances of his elder sister-in-law and of her pressing attempts to remain alone with him. The elder brother was overjoyed by the renewed trust of his wife and shared her eyes, spoke through her voice and could not see that it was all pretence, and the jealousy took the mock quality of a reasonable comment on the better luck of the younger brother. Yana still kept her charm giving sunlight to his bad days, but his brother suddenly became a nuisance to him and he felt him as a self-conceited stranger.

The old mother of the family could feel the growing alienation of her sons, but she had no remedy for it because she had also got used to her elder daughter-in-law and trusted her words. She also felt compassionate with her inability to to bear. Yana was still green and she had all the luck in the world – thar was unjust: not only was she beautiful, but she was healthy and blessed in all her deals – that was traditionally considered unjust.

Scandals and dividing the family estate started between the two brothers, hostile staring, close monitoring and snorting. The younger brother kept silent about is elder sister-in-law's rassion and she didn't wait long but found him alone and told him she couldn't live without him. The young man did not any sins over his head and refused to make love to her, but she was insistent and followed him all the time. He didn't intend to tell his brother and they continued living separately in the same house as if on both sides of a stone wall.

One they they went to work into the same field and while walking towards it they remembered how they played in their childhood. The tension between them softened, they relaxed and started sharing until the younger brother told his brother about his wife and how she troubled him. They discussed it and the elder brother understood the cause of their hostility, forgave the younger one and they embraced at last as if they had met after a long return home from a foreign land.

They worked together in the field and at noon when the sun rose high, they sat for a rest in the shade of the big pear tree in the middle of the field to have lunch together. After that they fell sound asleep for they were exhausted from the hard work and had no more fear of one another relaxed from their ended hostility.

But the wife whose love was rejected, took things in her hands that time and followed them on the way to the field. She overheard their conversation and her jealousy seared her heart. She waited for them to fall asleep, took quietly the knife of the younger brother and stuck it with the handle in the ground and the blade upwards so that in the moment he turned round, he sould get cut. Then, quietly, she went back home.

But it didn't happen as she had planned it. Her husband turned in his sleep towards his brother and was cut. He shouted with the sudden ache and the first thing he saw when he opened his eyes, was the the knife in his brother's hand and the blood dripping from the blade.

Although his brother bandaged the wound and carried him back home, and in spite of he was swearing he did not have any idea of how it had happened that his knife had cut the side of his brother, the trust between them had vanished. The wifie didn't wait but openly accused the younger brother of an attempt to kill his elder brother. She played the role of the caring wife, stood beside his bed day and night and incessantly talked against the cowardice of the Younger brother to stub him to death. Thus he chose to trust the evil talk of his wife, not his blood.

And his wife continued to follow her brother-in-law and he again declined her love. And once more. But that time the elder brother heard them talking on the dark balcony. He listened to his wife promising her love to his brother and asking him to kill his brother and escape with her. And he heard with his own ears how his brother said he'd never do such a thing. She then told him he was blinded by Yana and couldn't see she was a witch: her hair was wood-nymph golden, she worked all day long and never tired, and on dark mornings she went to the woods to pick herbs… The man overheard this and still not believing his ears, decided to wait and see.

In the meanwhile his old mother fell ill and Yana gave her some herbal tea. On the next day the old woman got up healed, but the water from the herbs was mysteriously gone, and the horse of Yana's husband suddenly fell dead, with green poisonous foam on its muzzle. Yana was accused of poisoning it – silently accused. Only she knew she was innocent but she couldn't do anything to stop the reproachful stares of the others. No one would believe that the poison was not in the cure she had made for the old mother.

In some time Yana gave birth to a healthy boy. After the happy day she was left to rest in the night. In the morning she was found fast asleep with a bloody knife in her hand and the infant's head cut off. Her golden hair was stained with blood and still she looked as beautiful as a wood-nymph, but this time her husband felt the horror of this scene.

His brother's wife had stopped following him for some time and had begged forgiveness for troubling him. This morning she found him in the yard, rushed up to him and her eyes bulging with horror whispered that *Yana had cur off her baby's head.*

This broke the young man who ran inside and saw his beautiful sleeping wife amidst the bloody scene. He took the knife and stabbed her, then killed himself, too.

His old mother came inside and saw the dead bodies. She died immediately, not having time for asking questions, and soon the old father followed her.

The elder daughter in-law cried out loud and gathered the neighbours.

Her husband was out of home and it was only her who could tell the relatives about the drama. They arranged everything for the funeral but the local priest upon hearing her version of the story, gave no permission to bury Yana in the church cemetery. So they took the bodies of the young couple up the barren hill and cut their graves into the stony ground at the end of the dense forest.

The elder brother returned home shortly after and learned what had happened. He looked at his wife who was all in black but her eyes burned yellow with the satisfaction of her full revenge. She was not left to speak this time.

He rose his arms and cursed her: *let you be turned into a dry tree, let you stand beside a mountain source and not a drop reach you...*

The Heaven doors happened to be open and his wish was heard. There was no thunder or lightning but in a short spell of time the wife fell ill and soon died. She was buried beside the other's grave on the rocky slope out of the graveyard.

The spring passed in a dream, followed by the hot summer and the rainy Autumn, then – the winter with heavy show and frost. The second spring came and with the running streams from the show on the mountain, on the rocky plateau a source came up. Beside it the ground fell in, revealing a stone basin. Another source appeared in the rocky terrain and its water also vanished before reaching the end of the rocks. The two sources were like eyes, weeping. And on the side of the stone-floored pool a young tree grew up – tall and slim and then dried. In the pool water-hairs grew, full of white blossom, and the water was clear like the tears of Yana.

The traveller sat mesmerized by the tale and only woke up when the voice of the story-teller ceased. He moved a little to break the charm that had stiffened his muscles, lifted his eyes that were not pained any more, wondered for some time and started gathering his things preparing to leave.

- Take some water from this source with you – the guardian of the chapel told him – it cures infected eyes.

The traveller thanked, then kneeled and drank from the source, splashed his eyes again and filled his the gourd with water from the spouts and hung it at his horse's saddle and while he was just about to leave, he thought about something and turned to his host to ask:

- Thank you for the wonderful tale. – he said. It must have been long ago - and he looked with the question unspoken in his eyes at the guardian of the place?

- The chapel was built here some 30 years ago but the story of the source dates back to earlier times. And the source is ancient as the Balkan. – His voice broke as if he was filled with doubt and sharp intellect shone up in his eyes before they were veiled by sadness and his face became impassive.

The traveller felt it was high time to leave and led the horse down the narrow path. At the turn of the path he turned back and saw the man kneeling by the pool weeping over the green water-hairs and the dry tree was waving its branches as though in unhappy whimper although there was no wind in the air. The astounded man froze for a moment to a halt while the guardian of the source threw a glance at him and uttered the words: *I am the elder brother.*

Time passed along that rocky land and it remained forgotten and solitary as ever except for a trail of daring people in need: witches and curers, harem women with sick children and strange passengers driven by curiosity. And the miraculous story spread about and the rumour of the the healing spring grew and followed its own tracks which are to be found in the tales of the dreamweavers and the mindwork of people in real need who believed in it. Pain and curiosity have sometimes their twining routes.

It is still there up to our day of desertion and disbelief. The wild natural mountain spring with the water-maiden's hairs and the white blossoms. On top of the stone-laden plateau. And in the company of the dead dry tree devoud of leaves, fruit and flower, thirsty and whispering words of hate and sorrow, black in the green folds of the forest-covered wavy mountains. The wind in the green forest avoids staying in its black branches.

The fountain quietly sings its tale and the twelve sprouts incessantly cry crystal clear water that fills the stone pool with tears which can cure the eyes of living creatures and harmonize their eyesight with the cosmic tunes. Whether it be a curse or a blessing for the blind to see and recognize the truth that drives human needs and deeds.

The Task

It was inside an open mine. The soil was ashen-grey and no one had trodden it for years. It was not fit for anything – not for a lawn to take the sheep to, nor to walk it for pleasure, not to go hunting for smaller animals. The river went round the heaps of grey-green soil and next it went past the heaps of rosy-reddish soil. The road was on the other side of the river and the people who travelled on the city bus could not see what was in between. The grey-greenish soil formed a wall and there probably was a deep pool in the opening of the mine but no one ventured to go and see, and tell what was there. Only the sheep herds who took their herds to graze up on the higher mountain skirts in the distance, could see the summer sky mirrored in the waters of a poll. They told tales there was a pond but a deadly one since the ores still bore traces of the dangerous metals that were taken out of these holes.

It was early in the spring. The family gathered to celebrate the name day of the oldest mother who lived in the big two-storey house near the Struma in one of the outskirts of the municipality of Nevestino. The Struma means 'a stream' and is known to gather its waters from a number of deep mountain sources that come from layers of ores, not just silver and gold, for which it is famous, but Uranium, copper and Zink.

There was a pie with nettles and leek, green salad and a baked pig, and apple brandy that was not spared. The guests partook of the fresh meals and started a big discussion on the topic of fishing. Each of the men boasted of catching big carp and catfish, trout and Pikes. Kiro was not a fisherman, but he was bored immensely by the boasting story-tellers, and when his turn came he took the floor:

– You know I ain't that keen on fishing and cannot boast of catching the big fish… - he started and his cousins only waited for him to tell his tale for he was famous with his fantastic stories and could tell a tale as sweet as honey…

– Last summer I had taken my cow out to the glades along the Struma,

– … and cut some wood illegally – one of the listeners added, but Kiro did not let himself be distracted when he had started a tale, so he simply continued taking no notice of that attempt at interruption…

– … I was walking up to the summit of Bellizin, the long bare summit where there is no forest and just rocks that stand coloured in the spring, I left the cow on a patch of grass and something urged me to go to the top and look around. I had never before gone there. It's quite high and when I reached the top, I had a glimpse of the mountains beyond the border.

– Ah, I know what you're talking aboot – one of the men guessed – once there was an open mine there. The road was closed. They used only political prisoners to dig in the mines for there the waters were radioactive.

– That's right, – Kiro approved. He liked when listeners followed him and brought in first-hand evidence to his stories, – From the top you can see the old mines. The place is overgrown in tall grasses and furze but if you know what to look for, it can be recognized. And in the middle of the gorge there is a blue lake – even as a glass. It must be deep. While I was watching it a V-form passed along the surface. Some big fish or a monster-dragon.

– Eeeeeh – everybody grinned, – don't tell you have seen some extraterrestrial life form…

– There is something alive there, in the deep water. – Kiro continued his tale, without paying attention to distracting remarks. – It was a long trail and then it let bubbles before hiding towards the bottom. I sat there some more time, waiting, but nothing showed up any more. So, I am thinking that if there is fish, there probably are big snakes, and taking into account the radioactive waters, there must be real monsters in this pool. No one can tell how deep it is, but for the water been dark blue. You say no one had gone fishing there, have you?

No one had gone near the old mines for years. It was the first time they spoke about that. Now they started to remember old tales. First they discussed the case of one businessman from the big city who had wanted to make a fish farm there and a lake with boats, but three people drowned in the pool within a short period, and they finally gave up the idea.

Next, Stoyan, who had taken a sheep farm financed by a program of the EU, told them he had seen some storks flying over the over the mounds of of grey sand in search of prey. Danna, who wandered the forest for wild herbs for strange aches and pains, confirmed this tale saying she had seen some birds of pray, probably black hawks, hovering over the place.

Finally Granny Ghurggya, the Family Matriarch, knocked on the table with her walking stick until the noisy voices subsided, and said in her sharp voice:

— I am giving you a task now to cope with: that one of you who dares to go and see what is there between the mounds of ground where the mine was, and comes to tell me and brings some evidence of your tale, I'll give them this ancient gold coin. – And she showed the quiet party a real piece of gold.

The young men of the group flashed and they jumped from the feast table and sheaked through the yard door in groups of two and three. Kiro was lingering behind but the old mother only painted at him with her stick and said: *"Off you go!"*

„*Ah! I never meant it to that end!*", He thought. „*I was only telling a tale. No one meant that to be true*". But he also started walking along the winding path and in half an hour he turned tround the willow grove and crossed the river over the iron barrow bridge before the next village and was beside the mound of grey-greenish earth. It was not that far as it had seemed from the bare hill of Belizzin.

There was no path leading to the summit and he followed the track alongside. The mines had been deserted a long time since and the earth had calmed down and all overgrown in grasses and shrubbery. It didn't look ill and dangerous any longer.

In the meanwhile the slope expanded and Kiro saw the path to the top. It was halfway to the other village of Tarnovlag which meant a Thorny Wetland, where the one with the faish-farm and the boats had begun his project and left before he could finish it out of sheer horror, fed by old wive's tales. It was quite a good path.

Kiro sensed the nipping curiosity and hurried to climb the slope. Up there he found the other men from the company sitting quietly. When they saw him they hushed him to keep silent and stay still.

Down there, some four metres from their feet, a darkblue pool lay, softly washing the mounds of coloured earth.

— So it turns you didn't lie this time – his cousin Boris whispered.
   Kiro kept silent. The others were watching him carefully.
— There is something in there, in the deep. – Boris hissed.
   Kire watched the surface of the lake. It was dark-blue and too flat. It must be deep. They could see a wooden boat quay in the water below.

They sat for wuite some time, staring at the water, each dipped in his own thoughts. At last they saw a triangle ripple in the far end of the lake. It cut the water smoothly and vanished.

–   Hey, did you see that? – The young men jumped, their curiosity rising, and their nightmarish mindpictures revived.

–   Let's get back home – Stoyan said. – tomorrow we shall come with our fishing gear and shall catch the big fish in the new day.

Not one protested. They got back home. All of them confirmed to the grandmother of the family that there's something alive in the Lake. They hadn't brought evidence – it had seemed to them an act of calling the name of Evil to take pictures of the lake. No one expected a reward and the old Granny kept silent.

Days passed in and out. No one spoke about the task. And no one went fishing.

Once Stoyan found Kiro. He stood for a while hands in his pockets for it looked like they were trembling. Hi voice trembled too but he told that he went with his fishing rod and something bit the hook and gave it a strong pull. He felt dragged towards the water but luckily he let the fishing rod go and watched it vanishing underwater – the whole gear.

The other young men also went fishing for the monster secretly, one by one. Their mothers rowsed big rows for fear they could be drowned in the deep dead lake.

Once they found a drowned man. Not young. He looked like a man from the town who had been used to being taken care of. He had a fishertman's coat with a good number of pockets. His cap had fallen on the steep beach and his fishing rod had gone. He was found face downwards right beside the wooden quay.

Now everybody believed in the spreading rumour of the big fish.

More fishermen came. They walked solemnly past the *No Fishing* signs, beside the lake.

They went quietly into the water until it went knee deep. They chose bait for catfish, carp bait, bait for trout. They hooked a shine or a fly. Then stood there waiting their ears pricked and ready to turn as the antennae of a locator at the faintest noise, their eyes bulging with fear, their minds thrilled by the expectant danger.

Nothing bit at the baits. The whole summer passed with fishermen hovering around. Nothing showed up from the lake. By and by the men left fishing and abandoned the thrilling adventure.

And when Danna, the witch, brought the big fish in Mid-December just before the great winter frosts, all the relatives gathered to see that wonder.

Danna had kept quiet all the time. She had been going in the dark night of the Full moon. She had seen the fish jump. She had noticed it was very deep and then brought fish food.

In the end of the Full Moon period she had taken out the fishing stuffs of her dead husband, made a wich for good luck, put some bait on the hook and tried her luck. That was just after the men had ceased to go out fishing. She kept going out fishing for three weeks under the full Moon.

On the last night Danna waited for the moon to light the silver path on the surface of the lake. She threw the hook with the bait she had prepared before. Something immediately pulled at the cord. While she was fighting to register the angle, a big ugly muzzle rose up and caught the fish like a bait. And once again the bigger fish was used as a bait by a heavy head with a frog's mouth. Danna fought for nearly an hour using a system of angling gear she had set strategically along the beach and taking care she wasn't dragged too close to the water. She had used her husband's boots and thick gloves and his system of iron rods with hooks at the end, and finally she managed to drag the monster fish out on the frosty soil and knock it dead with the axe she had brought.

She had pushed her catfish on the garden cart. It turned not that big – less than 12 kilograms. But it was ragged and spotted, and its mouth still held the carp he had eaten and in the carp there was a smaller fish in pieces. There were no flakes but greenish spots like rough lichen.

The young men stared at the monstrous Big fish of their nightmares and finally took it to bury beside the village dump. It was grey-greenish and spotted and had big teeth on both sides of its mouth. Nobody dared eat it, for it looked like no other catfish and they had seen hundres of them.

Danna got the reward and made a gold ring for her daughter's wedding out of the old coin.

X & Y or The Programmer

There is a curious story of the folklore of the medical robots. It is about a machine for artificial insemination that pleaded the status of a Pro-Human. It was an expert in defining the sex of the human babies and was called The Programmer or The Magus. In fact it could count out the probable chromosomes with a very low risk number for the erratic chance. And it knew how circumstances could influence the processes of sex design.

After that narrow specializsd AI was given the status, it chose the nickname of "*Granny*" and so she remained for half a millennium in the e-folklore of the next *psy-generation* that replaced the *e-generation* of the "Milleniums" as they called themselves, for the interest in the AI had ceased with the first success trials of *the Granny* and the new babies preferred to be referred to as *the Natural* or for short *Natties*.

It was a distant space of time of a young Earthafter the period of the Big Dream when the AI took over the control of resetting the Earth's elements after the Catastrophe or the reign of Chaos. It was planned in terms of the Absolute Time, for the Cosmos never stands still, but it is not our task here to trace the history of the Untraceable, so we shall accept the term of "The young Eart", being aware of the fact that the name is applied metaphorically.

When the Eart was Young

When the AI found the Earth again after It had been sent out in the Bigger Cosmos for a spell of a Big Dream while She had to be recovered and overpopulated again, the Planet was not suitable for Life, because there was too much water and too much fire that were fighting for control.

That was why the AI coming from the Stars, had to mess up with the formation of the continents, pushing away the fiery masses in the form of a Reel with two counterweight Poles, pulled at it so they received two large voids where water was fixed and formed the two bigger parts of the Earth Ocean held by firm skeleton in the form of a mauled apple.

Wnen everything was fixed and there was no risk of them drifting away, because of the force of gravity which kept them round the skeleton of the globe, the Kosmic intellect opened their store-spaces and let out a variety of suitable genes to develop and multiply and mix the ground and the water, produce waste for the fire and serve as food to each other and as partners for their short life with whom to bear new generation, and to compete, because these are the three basic sides of the existential happiness: food, sex and fighting with each other.

The living creatures were unstable as different kinds and could mix genetically and reproduce. Their instability was the effect of the fact that the genetic containers kept the the general number of genes of life, roughly 280 chromosomes which made practically unlimited possible combinations.

And the Earth was populated by all kind of monsters from our point of view, because trials lead to erratic combinations in most cases. Then the mermaids, the dragons, the werewolves, the goblins and the goatfeet sprang up, as well as intelligent slugs and mice, boogeymen trolls, dwarfs and gnomes and some more.

If you had learned your biology lessons, you must have met some hidden hints about the stability of the mixed kinds of living creatures. They were not only odd but were aggressive, hostile and surviving.

The Star Intellect monitored what was going on and drew maps of the spreading population of the Earth and the great variety of life forms. They were not proud of what they had achieved and finally locked the races and put a barrier to chromosome compatibility and this time got clear kinds.

In a couple of millennia it became an urgent need that the outer monitoring intellect interfered and limited the tongues of the different creatures. But now they omitted one double chromosome: that controlled the *difference* and of *unision*.

I suspect it is not two separate chromosomes but two aspects of the whole genetic disturbance, but there are still teams of researchers who are looking for the genes of this or that feature, especially when the pains of the human race are concerned.

From times immemorial people form separate groups of hostile worlds and unite so that they wage wars, exploit the weaker and rule. The elder countries, who are tired of the same recurrent brainless events, often stay aside and watch *the green activists.*

They know: this showld pass away as everything else does. But sometimes they try to have the freedom to chose their genetic type: men wish to become women, women long to be men, blonds desire to be dark, the chocolate-skinned want green eyes… Whatever we do, though, is a blind lucky strike in the direction of the secondary features of the kind. Because we've lost the key.

Just think what might be done if we find it. In terms of added value and financial exchange.

Collegium

After getting experienced in the control over the life forms that were designed to reach natural intellect, the universal intellect needed to make sure the Natties followed certain rules of security. So they let them connect in megamemes or clouds of star dust and ruled by forming collegiums of different expertise.

A Continuing Story

Since the opening of the 3rd millenium D.A. /I have the presumption that it must be called The Novel digital Age or the Current D.A. for the previous one had been some 30 or 40 millenia ago/, longevity was extended due to saving the memory of humanoids with the help of clouds.

Clouds float, you know, where the whim of the Star Wind turns them to, or depending on the last key phrase they locate and use it as a PIN code, that procedure often leading to a great mess of metaphors, generated by poets, and the literate terms so liked by the simple clerks of *meritocracy.*

Closed in their own air-borne towers the young people of some 100-120 years of age, were weaving tales of freedom and creation without minding the texture of the current Cloud and not counting in the fact of the words that were changing in the gusts of the wind and the changing relief of the scenery below.

And while whenever, passing over the cities' dumps the Clouds traditionally shed some hypocritical tear, the places got overgrown with miraculous plants, most often with thorns and beautiful flowers which later on burnt in the searing sun, the gangs of wild wanderers who were trumping the waste-grounds, breathed the smoke and got dizzy,louds of dreamy pictures rose and everyone imagined they were time-machines.

So the life routine continued until Gaya got sick with allthis nuisance and tried to scratch herself in the only way she could do it: she threw flames through the weak points of her crysral grid, mixed the stuffs and killed the bores on her surface and left the muddy ocean quietly send ripples to the firm continental shelves, while seeds of life floated down from the outer space and developed to form the next civilization.

The route back home

Home is where our travelling singular minds want to return to. Even if they are blended by individual entities of minds, each speciallised at certain skills to form a collegium.

Mine is tracking the route back home to our roots of origin.

Some people connect it with legal documents, other people connect it with an access to their own key or bunch of keys, still some other people connect it with a space where one can have all the time to oneself.

There rises a question: to what extent it is a place or a time of one's own? Or is it just a place where someone else is waiting to see you in, where they need you.

It might look strange but to me it has always been the route connecting two distant points.... Comparable to certain signs – pebbles, River, trees, flowers, absence and presence, absence and lack even. More commensurate to the lack and the expectation to be filled with the presence – some shit, some insignificant detail, a human defect, that then is to be corrected.

A way to reach between action and a passive state, and again to action in a widening spiral of motion.

A route with every little detail.

Time between knowledge and latent knowledge, that simulates ignorance, because the point of waking up is still far away... Time between two points of time.between the past and the Present, not between two parallel Presents, nor the time of a point just a short time ago until a short time past.... Time past and time future, or once upon a time...

Simply a way.

From a point at one side of Time to the other side of Time.

Just a way.

Epilogue

Deal or No Deal

When the race is in danger of destruction,
There should be no question of deal with gods.
For gods might not be in the same game as humans
And wouldn't like to admit any loss of position
That could take them back home to their roots,
In the minds of the mortal bodies who try to avoid stress
And devote their next generations
Their souls and reason
To the absolute rule
Of empty space
And the search for a motion
Out.

Part 2. Memento Somni
or
OUT of the dream

Prologue

OFF-Time Scales

The White king
From the chessboard reality of Alice
Is murmuring
Tasting the sounding:
Important - unimportant
Next trying changing their places Unimportant - important
finding no difference.
I have lost their spaces either
In the meantime of timelessness
When things fade down to shadows
Projected as images only
No heroes nor giants,
Not even dwarfs,
Just gnomes
Keeping pots of gold
Deep under the caves of history
In unreal illusions and dreams
Of microscopic
Particles
Taking part in the creation of Stars.

Explanation

This is a long redundand story which gets along the time, registered in history. It gives out a narrow view of the attempts of rulers and politicians to stop the waste of the human worlds streaming out of their influence right into the unreal realms in current events. History is not the teacher of humanity as the common belief runs, for it is unreasonable and takes its evidence from pure chance. Here the dreamewver tells about a group of people, who happened at one and the same fold of the spiral of time and turned into a team of weaving up a new world out of their shared dreams by order of some powerful intellect and get out into a shared existence. They are not chosen but lucky survivors who passed one of the big gaps in history.

Adventure goes through fire and blood, spectres and zombies, genetic experiments, gold and machines that survive water and life and finally weave up a shared dream. Nither better, nor worse than the individual dreams of each of them. Including all their nightmares and illusions. As it is in a dream that requires their presence together to pass through the interface of time. Unlimited by circumstances. Where machine intellect searches for life and the natural bodies – for longevity.

Intro

It all began on a wheather-bound night of March. I started to dream.

I got up now and again to drink some water or change the water of the goldfish as the French say, but I hurried back from the bathroom towards my warm bed, stretching my hands as if to catch the dream for I wanted not to miss the smallest image of it. In the morning I remembered parts of the experiences in a world where I could walk on the surface of bottomless lake which ahd swollen a gorgeous autumn forest. There were towns of wooden houses and roofs of nylon cover. There were the ashes left over from a burnt world, tightly shrinking in the chrysalis of a world in the expectancy to get reborn to a new self-awarenes of life. There was a shadow in front of the Sun, as if some big material body was passing along there and hiding it. There was a greedy moon, that seemed to create a whirlwind in which the clouds played round it, changing its light from ripe-orange to silver-white and electric. One could sense the eyes, staring at the Earth from its surface in spite of the distance.

I once heard the noise of a big river that made me alert. It was only the wind that was blowing outside my windows. It had carried away the moon and the stars, and the shadows of tall buildings on the west, and the silhouette of the mountain to the east. It was completely dark. Nothing could be seen. Nothing was there. Nothing. There was no electricity either. I felt my way to the bathroom touching the walls with the tips of my fingers and remembering how they looked. I drank some water and dived back into my bed, that was full of dreamy worlds. There was only fire, coming down in gusts from the skies. The 16-storeyed buildings caught it and burned like *Bengali fire*. Merciless Force drew up everything to the bald head of the flame and blood was the first that streamed joining the the stream of fire flowing swiftly where the streets were before. This picture was beyond my understanding: I had no idea of how I could see it, neither could I imagine how the extraterrestrial flying disk was wheeling over the town station square, full of coloured lights that turned as signals of a an emergency above the trees of sheer ashes, forgetting to collapse in the the general picture of terror.

What had been left of my own self was dragged towards the disk and sucked into it in a pillar of white light. There were eight shadows more:

ghosts of human beings that were saved in the night of a shared nightmare. Not entirely grey but bearing distinct shades of blue, green, fire-pink and orange, wine-red and lilac, purple and ultramarine. Without white for white does not turn into ash, and without black.

We were sitting on the floor of a spacy spaceship. It was Instilled in us to sit still, so that we could be teleported across open space.

I was disappointed to see through the floor that we were above the same station square. As it happened we were sitting on a gigantic screen that created the illusion of a reality. It looked like any other night with a sky full of stars, a moon, a wind whispering in the branches of the spring trees.

We were surrounded by a vast 3D shadow of a dsrk planet – that was swallowing the Earth in its vault sucking out fiery streams intervening the dark Ocean: streams of fire and ashes mixing with thin strings of blood.

There were emergency messages that popped out on the surface of our shared field of awareness blocking out everything else. Had they been transcribed, they would turn as laconic scriptures, but they let us accept the explanation. I cannot express it in simple words: It was like a machine exchange, like a shared self, encoded in our separste body reactions. The strange form with the bloody beak did not speak. It, just like us, was a shadow that appeared on the display of a gigantic screen. I could hear the messages it sent as a multi-voiced schizophrenic talk where each next message broke in laconically;

- – That's it.
- – There is nothing outside.
- – The picture you receive is an illusion.
- – There is no Earth any longer.
- – You'll have to weave it up anew.

The creature that appeared to transmit the messages swarming like flies was of grey-greenish tan and rashes with goggled eyes and six-limbed hands, I was certain it was the representative of an intelligent race. It seemed funny to make guesses while we were sitting on the floor of this strange race ship. The creature had a muzzle ending in a beak. There were drplets of… blood… on the beak.

- Blood is feeding up information.
- It tells us about the destroyed race.
- How am I to learn otherwise, what you were?

The openin valve was filled with white light and some more creatures hopped in. They brought a smell of fire and they all were blood-stained.

- Information.

Then they said:

- It's time for you to return and complete the project.
- What project? I thought.
- The Project of existence of your world.
- We just laid the beginning for you to get oriented.
- To have enough space.
- A human cannot exist without the stars.
- An individual ceases being intelligent.
- The self fades down to a silhouette, stunned by the terror of the nightmare.
- And mesmerized by the waiting for it to happen.
- We have no knowledge about what is to come, and it doesn't come.
- There are no other individuals left.
- There is only you.
- And all is in your dreams.
- Through your dreams it should be woven out.
- As long as the creation of a universe…
- As short as a blick of time.
- You shall be back now.
- You shall ceaze to exist if you stay on: you'll fade ino nothing.

I was still standing in the stream of light running past me. And through me. I was a shadow of myself in a dream of dark shadows and fire. The square looked the same as ever and the marble plates had gapes overgrown in grasses. Above my head a wheel of multi-coloured lights steadily moved. The wind was blowing in gusts that streamed like a great… some where outside. I returned into my dream.

- Now you shall begin introducing yourselves. – The wordless message appeared as clear as a day.
- One of you is a program whose task is to record you and wake you up to a new reality outside.
- The rest of you are virtual profiles of human idividuals.

I opened my eyes to see, It was still night. But there was a change for it was heading to a new day and there was a change in the air. My bed was soft and warm. There was hope for a spring, steadily coming. I got up and loked out. There was a hopeful spring outside. There was still an Earth.

Something was singing like a silver bell in the night.

> *Ink blue windows,*
> *Full of the Moon;*
> *My shadow on it.*
> *I sleep, but something*
> *Creeps up*
> *And weaves the dream:*
> *Where the the shortcut is.*
> *So I can get out*
> *And walk in the starway*
> *I've woven myself*
> *To spaces of alltime.*

How it all began

They'd been hired for that job. For that purpose they acted as a team or, a newly-formed ranger's department of varied skills. They were so different from each other. They were each of them of singular appearance: the two Englishmen, the woman in the long woolen cardigan with the big pockets, the young American with the silken brown scarf over her lilac blouse and the faded jeans suit, the youngster from Turkey with his careful delicate speech and the crumped black suit, and the two young people in protective clothing. They had met never before and knew nothing f each other but they'd gathered at the corner of the park at the advised time. So they stood there silently and studied themselves as they came up in turn. The tanned, fatty youngster was the last to appear and he made a sign, holding the fingers in a gesture that resembled a hook and moved it tempting them to join. The woman in the blue cardigan walked towards him and the others followed them, hesitatly at first. The lad was leading them confidently towards an old and dilapidated block of flats. They all went inside and climbed the stairs to the second floor where they found a mahogany door. It was a lift. They entered the cabin and were taken to the 11th floor. All of them gathered before going into a roomy apartment.

- This is the Shelter – the youngster said dreamily in a serious tone that did not suit with him and half-closed lashes wich gave him a concentrated contemplative look.

- What kind of transport shall we use? – One of the Englishmen asked.

- Just stick together – we'll have you moved between layers of realities you manage to recover. – The tiny youngster said, evidently using the words of some unknown repertoire that he could hear in his head only. Then he radiated childish grin: - We all are a *dzum* – an invisible troop of emergency. Our people were specialized in how to zoom troopers of emergency forces. – Then he mumbled something in a strange language, probably his mother tongue, but that failed to impress us. He was only a lad that was being used, just as each one of us was, by the web intellect that had brought our virtual selves in this particular reality.

No one asked any questions. Every question might cause them to fade out. Somehow each f them sensed the cause for which they were gathered deep in themselves. They were to find out the nature of the catastrophe that had befallen their original worlds and erased the Earth. They didn't know what was to meet them – no instructions were given in advance and they depended on sheer luck. They knew only not to waste their energy in chatting. They even couldn't tell who had hired them fr the job, for there was no government, there was not a leader since the moment the Earth had ceased to exist. They understood they had been moved on a virtually existing planet, a parallel or rather a twin planet of the Earth – a copy of the Earth, stored in some impossible outside reality. A hyper meme kept by a giant brain. They were the survivors, not chosen because there were no single individuals to choose from. They were the only single representatives of a colappsed race. Maybe avatars who could boast of closely copied singular minds. Good or bad, strange, inexperienced, lacking their true lives, they were the team to solve a vast task that required them to search the gap in the reality-creating intellect and pull the world of the human race back. Into a joint recreation of tales, enacting them into outside

They surveyed the landscape through the large empty window that was just a square hole taking most of the north-east wall of the room. There was a park, a winding river and a city with very tall buildings.

Time seemed to have frozen. They had followed the details of the changing perspective from their position and the kinder-playground with the kiddy rides among the trees huddled into a meander of thr river. They could notice the dry sand on which the kiddy-rides stood. There were kids riding. Each of them was dressed in a colourgul coat with bright hats and hoods.

- Are you hungry? – the woman asked.

She received half a dosen expecting stares, but it was the young Turk that was gazing intently at the south-east ern wall near the ahogany door of the elevator, and it became suddenly live with screening the street-corner of sone city which looked like Istambul but was deserted nd only a couple of tall treas, swung by the wind marked the entrance of a Mosque withblue-grey spherical domes like those of a Christian church. There, right on the pacement under the bright orange arch was a huge pot full of dense stew of crabs, vegetables and rice. Beside the pot were a ladle and some porcelain cups. Someone had already eaten and filled the empty cup with coins. They had no coins on them but each took a portion and ate for they were really hungry, then and filled the empty cups with water from the drinking fountain, and drank for they were thirsty.

- A strange tradition - one of the Americans in army uniforms said.

- Ihis is the normal way here – a thin voice suddenly squeaked out of the nothing that enveloped the scenery like a cloud.

They turned round and saw a small beggar who stood at the pot. He grinned and pointed at the pot and the cups.

- There will be fried slices in egg cover. Real. But yo'll have to leave a coin. You've got money in your pockets.

They searched their pockets and found some money. They dropped each a coin in one shining metal cup. Max dropped two coins, for himself and Jamal.

- Are there any other people here - the woman asked witn a suddenly dry throat?

- Tomorrow, tomorrow... – the beggar repeated and walked usteadily, dragging his feet, to the yellow building on their left. There he vanished with a surprising speed behind the wall and a young fig tree climbed up the wall right beside the entrance, springing it seemed out of nothing.

There was an absolute silence, because they exchanged voiceless utterances each in their mother tongue they all understood telepathically. No one had used speech other than mentalese since they had been zoomed into that mirror world where they had to dreamweave and map the routes back to their shared ideas of a home.

- I am Max – one of the Englishmen suddenly said aloud.

- Venus - came the grateful answer from the other one. – As far as it stands in my memory I am from Lake District.

The woman's name was Danna, the lad was Khallil, the men were Ivan and Harry, and the kid was Jamal.

After listening to each other's names said in their native ringing voices, they felt less hostile and more cooperative.

The world around them was in constant movement and change, but they could not sense it for they were too miniature or too big to to matter. Each next moment it was past and there were multiple presents that had shoved in the pockets of all-time. There were the effects of processes that had no witnesses.

- And what is yor name? – Harry asked the girl with the chestnut hair, she wore loosey fastened in a long horse-tail

While they had been telling their names She had stood separately hands in the pockets of her faded jeans and had watched the horizon in silence.

- Lillian – she shot out curtly not moving her stare from the picture in front. – Can anyone explain how all of a sudden we all appeared standing on a hill and a city of tall buildings appeared spreading in the distance?

- This is a picture woven in our dreams – Jamal the lad said quickly – we are not seeing the same city.

Lillian's gaze went past him.

- We are in someone's dream – Ivan explained. – We are programmed to think we are real... but it's like moving in parallel worlds... or is it possible we share the same dream – weaving our single pattern that adds to the whole picture?

- It was explained to me that we all are woven in the story of some storyteller out there, and we are made act as avatars – virtual projections we accept as our present selves, in a shared dream where they get into action and do the things as the Story-teller imagins and weaves up as presence. That is the reason why everything moves constantly: the dreamweaver can change the perspective following the panorama of our mindwork. But how is it shared?

- I am an avatar - Jamal jumped.

- Do you know what this is? – Danna asked in her attractive singing female voice.

- Yes – the lad shouted - we are involved to take part in a game and I represent the God who has come into life through me so that he takes part in whats going on. We are to weave up a world where humanity can survive, because ours has turned into sdhes and dust. We have to make it beautiful and rich – the whole of it. A gorgeous dream we all need to work out...

- You know... – The soft voice of Khallil was not rude when he broke in, - we can't be certain about being avatars. There is a possibility of us being true, material.

Harry and Ivan exchanged glances.

- I feel myself rather fleshy – Harry said.

- I think they make us think of ourselves as unreal avatars unreal so that we aren't afraid. – Ivan said almost simultaneously with him.

All of them looked at Danna who was the eldest in the group: over 30, soft and plump. She stood there in her sea-blue hand-knitted cardigan and swollen feet in some homely slippers. She looked as someone mom.

- For example, take Danna – Jamal added uncertainly. – She's real. She can'be just a dream of a strange intellect.

Danna smiled.

- I don't know. We did came to awareness at the first corner of this dreamspace almost simultaneously. We seem to be in the same dream.

- But you were who started thinking about food first. Max said.

- And you were all hungry – Danna replied.

Max was trying to recall the image of Danna eating. Unsuccesfully. He was certain, though, that she was the one who dipped the ladle in the pot and stirred the stew, and he had a clear vision of her filling the bowls that were stretched to her after each of them had splashed them in an alluminium bucket full of clear water.

- We can sort it all out – Danna continued softly. – Everyone can tell of their own lives and while telling we may recall... – her voice broke and she added uncertainly - I cannot recall anything... except the pain ... in my feet, they were swollen and aching, I stood upright and peeped over the fallen wall of our Lab in... – she suddenly stopped as if shocked by recalling a memory.

- Where was that? – Lillian asked abruptly.

- New Mexico – Danna said absent-mindedly. – The Lab was there. – She managed to pronounce it with a capital letter. As the one of its kind, but the rest did not react. They just shared additional info that had been past security secrecy:

- Mine was at Wolverhampton - Max said.

- I vaguely recal the war camp - Harry said.

- Satellite orbital Center - Ivan said.

- One of the Centers at Boston University. – Lillian said.

- I was on a cruiser near the beaches of Istambul - Khallil remembered.

The little one was watching them with his broadly open eyes like black beads. They suddenly shone with the appearing tears and he rubbed them with his fists. He was confused.

- No one of us is an android, nor are we illusory avatars. This must be the Dreamweaver that shall not get out of the dream.

- **I** am an avatar – Obstinately shouted the youngster. The others laughed.

- There was no food. I went with my elder brothers to beg round the streets. I found some cheese in a bin and ate it alone. My father beat me for not sharing it. I ran away… zoomed away in my sleep.

He shut up and looked around. Then he went near Harry and touched his hand:

- You sure feel like a real onel…

- Touch my hand – Said Ivan and stretching his hand out.

The boy went close near us all and touched everyone. He went up to Danna and hugged her:

- You smell of freshly-baked bread.

- We're all real here – Danna said.

The world that surrounded them was evenly grey. They had to start dreamweaving in full colour. The Nothing outside was like a grey dome.

They feared one thing only: someone of them was not real and when they had woven their shared dream-world, that one wouldn't move out. No one of them could tel for certain what part of them was a product of the Big Brain and what was recalled from their lifestories outside. Here, in the shared reality of their dream they were all real and could act as creators, but they had felt a strange friendliness and warmth and a desire to continue their teamwork when they finally got out.

The program of the Experiment foresaw no further knowledge of their true nature. They were representatives of the human race and their task was to weave up a human world. That was what mattered. And the human part of each of them feared the moment of awakening: they feared they could fade away as traces of a dream.

Security service

The black telephone on the president's writing desk was ringing, then stopped for a minute and continued ringing.

The State Secretary threw a searching glance but his boss didn't look at him. He was only sitting with his back to the desk and a glassy stare. After a few ringing signals he at last picked up the receiver and listened to the frustrated voice of Mathew Andrews, the Federal security boss.

- Stop calling, Mat - whatever we could do has no sense.

- Just give me a permission to start action on variant "T" .- Mathew reacted immediately.

- Yes – President Sawyers said. And then he uttered the formula:

- Enact variant "T".

That was abbreviation for "transfer'. In case the Earth came close to the critical point of the danger, they had to make an emergency call at the Labs working for them and have an automatic transfer of mega memory, sufficient for the reconstruction of the human world into the individuals whom the latest demographic survey had pointed out to posses the highest coefficient of survival. They were to be turned into live avatars. Only one of them had an intact android intellect and its task was to control the chance of diversion.

The next minute the President reached for one of the other telephones a moment it started to ring. The British Prime Minister skipped all phrases of politeness and only curtly barked: "We've enacted the transfer. Foreign SS must have enacted the last variant too.

The President nodded.

They'd been heaping stores of information since the beginning of the 1880s. and new genetic data of all the species the Earth had in her ecosystem. They stored such data in underground caves beneath the South Pole and beneath the northernmost part of the continental Shelves toward the North Pole as well. Those were the novel Noah's archs, the info-stores to be used in an expected collapse in the ecosystem of the planet to restore it and keep its life bridging the gaps of a long period of future. Since it had become clear that the science of the 2000 wouldn't discover new energies that could be applied for solving the Earth population problems, nor could it clear the pollution of the water and the air, all world leaders were concerned with security service attempts to face the catastrophe within their limitations of functioning. There was a way to skip the time of the catastrophe and program the revival of the biosystem after a couple of millennia when the planet became habitable again.

Transition involved the creation of a number of connected labs that were to search for the keys of certain specific keys of living human bodies in chosen 3D virtual personalities that were to folloe the vitality of viruses and populate the Globe with a new variant of humankind and called them with the code name of ***Survivors.***

No one could imagine the actual measure of the info-blocks, nor was it possible to foresee the limits of their net-covered realms. There had been transmitted sufficient data to cover the Earth as a 3D info-object and move it into a parallel reality of shared mindwork that stood as a bridge between the matter and the conscience. It was a psi-creation and was the best reality for its inhabitants as it was possible. Their task had two phases – to weave up a suitable world for the post-bio human race and to find a way out from the shared virtual dream into the actual world they had managed to construct and take it outside from the time boundaries of the catastrophe.

The emitters were located eight seats connected with the labs of the initator teams. The human individuals, though, were chosen according to their survival skills. There were risks that their memory could be blocked by the mega memory servers existing in the algorythms of the AI. But there was no more time to waste.

In the beginning of the 21th century D.A the Balkans became a key to the solution of thousands of issues, concerning the integrated scientific minds. They connected the continental energy streams into knots enabling the psi-energies of the virtual generation. Those formed a grid of strategic places concentrated in the ground masses of the ranges of the Balkans. There were also thousands of layers of regenerating earth. The satellite stations kept constant watch over the green radiation of the healed earth. The people who originated and had grown until their maturity age there, carried the chemical substances and the natural psi-energies in their singular bio-systems. That was the middle earth of all ancient tales and were natural wastewater treatment plants. The Balkans were away from the Labs that secured the algorhythm resources but the individuals coming from those regions were spread everywhere over the globe. The members of the extreme Situation Troop were survivors who had in their blood the various voices of the Earth as they were presented in old records, often in metaphor and action, a poem and song, a dance or ritual. They, however had no idea how close they were genetically to each other.

The Transfer had begun in the conditions of an experiment. In spite of that fact it was carried out before its time and there were doubts that it would be cuccesful. Using virtual avatars made the lab teams argue whether the avatars would have enough energy to last in the weaving of a whole new world for humanity out of their approach to telling their original stories within their unique position in the shared dream. The dream was chosen as a shared space by the Dreamweaver who was also one of the team: the android that was not to get outside but had the mentality of an actual person and all data that could give a hint of their real nature, was hidden from them.

In Search of the Place

- Let's start a fan search – Harry suggested.
- What's that, elder brother? – the kid asked.
- The first thing to do is to divide and try to pass through that door, and second we have to search the image so tah we get oriented where we are.
- And **when** we are– Lillian added.
- Yes, that, too.
- Then we shall map the possible exits.
- And how shall we pull the world outside? – The kid asked.
- I don't know – Harry mused.
Ivan had a guess:
- We are the keepers of a whole world now, aren't we? If we find an exit and get outside of our shared dream, then we shall enact the world for all the humanity for any actual survivors.
- Danna, what do you suggest? – Khallil asked.
She was the mature and calm one in the group. They all turned to her waiting for a rational suggestion.
- I am not sure – Danna said. – We were all left to ourselves and I suppose all depends on our individual intuition. But we shall not search for a world, we are expected to create one as shared practice.
- Do you have any practical clues – Lillian snapped nastily?
- The idea each one of us to start in a different direction seems good. each could move forward their way and discover things their own point of

view. After that we shall gather and share the singularities accompanying our paths and map our routes. Then we could exchange our routes to see the details again and make a holistic picture of our experience. You have already noted that we move easily here and do not tire.

- Hey, you, kiddie, what were you talking about *zooming* - Max asked suddenly.

- My people do… used to do a kind of magic. – Jamal said – women sit by the fire. There is a big pot of water. The oldest grand-mother starts chanting and the other women join in, throwing various stuff into the pot when their turn comes. Smoke raises. We were not allowed to sit by the fire and we watch from a distance. The leading grandma falls into a sleep while she still sits, and her self grows out of her and leaves the body. She can move through worlds. They told us that we are moved in that way: we are the bodies, and our selves can zoom about. We are free to do anything. Even we are free to move bodies.

- I nearly got it. – Max said. – And what does "dzhum" mean?

- That is the caravan of the invisible presences – Each one of us who are moved out of our bodies are invisibly present outside, only in the dream we remain real. Sometimes we can be heard – by poets and sensitive people, Sometimes we can be seen by people who posses the gift of second sight. But we cannot zoom things otside the dream.

- Let's go – Ivan urged them and pushed the button near rhe door. It opened before him and he stepped out into a spacy hall the floor of which was covered with white, plack and sea-blue squares. He crossed them and passed a glass door leading to an emerald lane in front of the building.

- I thought there was some lift up to here? - Khallil asked in a voice weak from the shock.

- Yes, there is one.– Harry said as he pushed the button again and this time the the door opened towards the semicircle glass wall of the lift. It was of blue-green shiny glass that stood in the middle of the fairy cylinder of a tower. The whole of it was shining and glamorous, and one wanted to play and start singing to oneself.

The others got inside the lift hastily and got out into the same entrance hall as Ivan nad gone earlier and into a glass-roofed passage that connected two buildings with the lift tower. Each of them paced the corridor and came emerged on a differenth path outside. They were standing in the same time and in the same place which were not really the same and they had to find out in what their experience differed.

Danna

Danna followed the path leading towards the mountain that rose across the misty vale. It was summer and the low ranges of the mountain were overgrown by thick scented green grasses A cloud of mist formed and the tiny drops made the grass look wax-green while the silhouettes of the shorter bushes and furze bushes and the wild tall light-yellow flowers of the herbs and the light-green wild brooms turned into enchanted shadows whispering in the breeze. She moved lightly and felt young and strong. She was free to move further from herself and have a look back: a young sunburnt girl in a light summer dress all in wet stains from the tall grass, and with shining brown eyes. She was sent to find a lost young horse. The mountain range was a row of green flat-top piramyds for there were even tiled squares of grey granite surrounded by tall trees – white oaks and acacias. A church rose on one of them, built of white stone all covered in colour scenes from the Bible, with a glistening guilded dome standing in a cloudless sunlit sky.

Her actual name was Dianna and she was 49. There, in the world outside, she had lived, she had never visited New Mexico. The server that had found her was there.

She was at some shady cool place that she called 'home'. A deep river gorge appeared in her memories and a big family house with additional farmyard and a garden. There was a young good-loking man, called Ivo. He lived in a nearby house and used to breed birds: white hens, roosters, pheasants and even peacocks. He had earned prizes at local competitions and fairs. She subconsciously believed he had offered her to marry him.

- No – Dianna had said – I won't marry you – you don't have a steady job. How can you raise a family?
- That's true – Ivo had consented. – My family might starve, but shall never die of hunger.

Dianna was shaking her head in disagreement. Then he had pointed at the peacock that in the mean time had begun courting the plain greyish hen and had opened his unbelievably beautiful tail.

– This peacock will be for you.

Dianna laughed.

– I don't need a peacock to take care of along with raising a family.

She was 18 then. That year she had just graduated from the professional school for hairdressers and seamstresses. She was skilled and never shunned work. She managed to get diplomas for both profiles of the school. She had plans of going to the big city – to live in a big city.

In her dream the road winding between the green hills went further down and a huge city revealed in the plain. There were green hills here and there among the city buildings, that looked like fresh parks or pleasant city markers.

Ivan and Harry were standing on a broad pavement and looking towards her, while she was standing in front of a small beauty salon with a neat Itallian advertisement-board.

– Here we are. We saw Lillian and the kiddy-boy who were in search of a suitable place they could eat something sweet.
– I know a nice sweetshop in the neighbourhood. – Danna said and lead them on.

It was a narrow square and there were red leather chairs with black iron frames and round glass tables. Various cakes were nicely ordered in the transparent shop-windows. All the inside was filled by the smell of freshly-backed cookies. Lillian and the kid were sitting at a table on which there stood enormous pieces of creamy and chockolate tarts. The sweet shop owner surprisingly turned out to be their team-member Khallil. He immediately placed in front of each newcomer a round tart with light blue glazed top.

— And some coffee, please - some voice ordered while Venus and Max took the seats opposite them.

— That was Plovdiv – Venus said and immediately corrected himself: – the idea of Plovdiv in my back vision, something very much like Plovdiv at the foot of a green hill with water bridges up its side, marble pillars and hanging gardens.

— No – Danna said. – I was in Rome.

— Lillian where were you and the kiddy-boy wandering? - Max asked.

— Some place that sounded like Athens.

— But this looks like the square in Venice – Khallil said and then added – Earlier I started working in a bakery in Istambul… was I zoomed?

— No – Danna repeated. – It was May. A green May scented with acacia and lavender. And the city spread in a plain covered in green corn and rice water-fields and vineyards and the Thracian tooms like strings of beads that were round hills.

— Can you see it? - Everybody nodded in agreement with whatever they were seeing actually in their mindeyes. They had already zoomed to the terrace with the stone church with the paintings on the front wall and were watching the green plain that was in the midway between two mighty Balkan ranges of blue summits topped in white that were buzzing with the misty heat.

— Thrakya – Jamal uttered. – Over there is… – was, the village where our caravan stopped. Danna, you were there. Your grandmom was the old with who chanted her spells in words and you were riding a reddish mare.

— Oh, no – Danna laughed. – I was about to marry a man who bread Guinea fowl, pheasants and peacocks. But I ran away. I had earned enough money to get myself a ticket for a cruiser.

— And after I've god overseas and settled down I shall marry. Not to Ivo, but to a man with reddish cheeks and blond hair. And have two daughters and one son. Next I am the daughter of my eldest daughter and live in Boston… - her voice broke.

— You can't be the granny and the girl simultaneously – Lillian began to say but then she hesitated…

91

- Yeah, you can be both the granny and the granddaughter. – Harry said. You can take up different persons in dreamweaving. It's the dream that plays with us like toys and reveals us in the puppet show of shared realities, shared in our heads.
- Anyway. – Venus said. - Where are we now?
- I know where we are.– Danna said. – All of us are in my dream.
- But this dream is where I started to weave up… – Lillian said.

Lillian

Lillian was driving along the broad winding coastal highway of Attica. She could see the high green hill with the marble pillars that were shining white in the strong sunlight in the zone between the wood of green dark trees while on the railroad between the highway and the white sandy beach there was moving a engine of a speed train with two wagons. Her friend, a curly-haired Greek, who was riding with her in the car, persuaded to her to catch the train which was just stopping at a small station. They left the car at the shaded parking-lot and ran towards the train. While Michael was helping her up on the roof of the second wagon where they could enjoy the panoramic view of the pale-blue calm sea, a sudden tidal wave rose near the beach and met them on the steps of the tiny metal ladder, grabbing their hands and cursing their bad luck. After the wave had gone and opened the view they could see where exactly they were heading to. It was a country house before the next wind of the railroad and near the station. It looked gorgeous in the middle of the plain: a typical colourful country house with a roof of red tiles and a broad yard, behind a stone-fence and full of trees.

Further in the distance the capital city of this strange world spread – a heap of sky-scrapers and buildings of architectural design that aimed at breath-taking reaction, because they were constantly moving and changing in shape and colour.

The emblematic tower was of glass and steel and had a clock on the top. It was a hospital where people were examined and cared for by androids. It was in the absolute center of the city – showing off with the important work that was done there. Two times a day at 10 a.m. and 10 p.m. by the clock tourists gathered on the roof of the 22nd floor to watch the grand show of the changing building: the tower fell slowly towards the broad square until it reached a foot distance from thr marble tiles, then changed direction and made a circular movement befor getting back to a standing point, with all the floors moving in harmony so that they didn't cause damage or even inconvenience to the spectators.

- Lillian – The young woman uttered the name of her new-born daughter and held the baby tight to her breast.
- What a tiny little sweetie – The elder boy said and the younger one just stretched out a finger to touch the cheek of the baby that seemed so unreal with her shining white skin and round cheeks.
- Take care lest you could eake her up for she may have a loud outcry.
- No, she is so tender and her voice is like a silver bell. – The mother smiled. – And she's got the bright green eyes of my grandmother.
- The one that's on the photo near the hills that the kings' tombs are? - Johnny asked.
- The witch called Lilla - Jamie shouted.
- Not witch – his mother corrected him softly. – She was a curer
- Lillian shall grow up and be a doctor – Johnny said again and his mother didn't object.

One of the nurses chose that moment to come into the room. She was a tall, fair-skinned woman with a woolen light-blue cardigan over her white tunic that gave her a homely appearance. Lillian thought she had met her previously but she couldn't remember when. The nurse took the happy daddy and the two boys out of the room so that the mother and the baby could rest.

- Lillian would you take part in an experiment on guided dreaming? - Asked the assistant who had taken her practical training with the professor, a doll-like Japanese who had a devotion to her work.
- What is this experiment? - Lillian asked.
- We tell some story to various people and then take them into different bedrooms each and leave them to fall asleep. Then we copy their psycho-somatic reactions in the time of their sleep,

and follow them in the different phases of their dream. When the activated parts of their brains harmonize, we project a holo-video in each bedroom, suggesting they visit a certain place and then start dreaming. We want to proof that they can have a shared image under a specific guidance, and weave up the same dream formatted under their specific experience.

– Oh, that sounds interesting – yes, I would take part in such an experiment,– Lillian said casually and without going into further detail she immediately forgot about it.

After an unidentified period she awoke with a dizzy head in a hospital bed. She had no memories of how she had got there. There was a visitation by a medical staff: including the professor and a group of trainees.

- Where am I? – Lillian asked a young medical technician, whse badge read "Peter". He told her that she was at one of the research centers of Boston University – a Lab that studied stimulated shared dream.

– Where's that? – She insisted.
– Oh the Lab is not on the BU campus downtown, – It's in a big hospital in the suburban area down the beaches.
– Why am I here? – Lillian asked.
– We are examining your reactions… - The boy said. - You've given your consent to take part in our experiment – the answer came. – You hadn't slept for quite some time and had fainted. You must sleep, and then we are going to introduce you to our dream-study team as well as to the dream-weavers we have been working with.

Lillian had a lot to tell on that matter, but she fell asleep again and was zoomed in some city taken out of a fairy tale beside a lake. There was a hill with a couple of stone-covered streets, steeply going upwards. She was walking freely with some friends, whose faces she didn't remember. They were going to a lecture. The alley went past an ancient yellow building with a lilac acacia vine winding near the entrance. There was a black glass plate which said it was a Psi-Lab. They walked on and headed to the palace of culture which contained eight levels. A large Church stood on the eighth level – all in blue and gold paintings, candle-lit and mysterious in the bluish mist. It was set on three levels connected by a dark staircase with painted windows. She climbed up to the top level and ther was a spacious auditorium where a lacture was running.

Someone stood close to her. A small kiddy-lad with a dark skin.

– Who are you? – She asked.
– Jemmo. – The boy said simply.

He had large dark eyes and beautiful lashes. And he smelled of a garbage bin.

– I want something sweet. - The boy shared.

He evidently trusted her. And Lillian did not ask any questions but took him by the hand and they went out. There were lots of narrow alleys covered with green pools from the last rains and boats and a small decorative hunch-backed bridge over a stream of clear water that mirrored the blue sky and the white puffs of clouds… There was a small square with even granite plates and a sweet-shop with marvellous cakes in the window - cream-and chocolate glased in blue jelly. They'd just settled when a woman in a warm hand-knitted light blue cardigan entered, followed by a couple of young men who looed strangely familiar to her.

Lillian had a strong de ja vu feeling. And a sudden lucky guess of what was going on around.

– I know where we are. – Lillian said. – We all are in my dream.
– Did you notice the hills over the tombs? - Max asked.
– What hills – whose tombs… - Lillian started but then it occurred to her that she had been watching a flutuating scenery through the eyes of an old granny, a curer or a witch – herself being the beautiful like a woodnymph lilla with the lavish golden plait, falling down to her ankles and the emerald eyes. She recalled a green May plain where round hills stood like buttons on the front of a new long coat and formed a row of even round Thracian graves or burial sites. Some of them were overgrown with bushes of silver oaks. A full spring river streamed past – The Hebros which mirrored the sky in its deep blue meanders. There were wheat fields

on both sides full of poppies, lilac and blue flowers and white and pink flowers that made colourful wreaths on the heads of the girls. There were two bigger mountain ranges, blue and white, reaching towards the sky and looking so surreal in the trembling blue mist that veiled an unfinished dream...

Max

I first knew Max when he came to teach English in one of the town high-schools. He was from Scotland, he said and wanted to experience our culture. He said he came from Woolves, and I took him to the big forest for a Day of Taking Forgiveness f the dead – Cherry souls.

There are no other graveyards like ours, in the Balkans. They are set on high places to overlook the flatlands of the green fields: set so that they do not take up useful land while watching life from above and being closer to the skies.

And they are densely populated: there is not enough place for two people to stand on the paths between the graves. You go one by one and do not step on the graves.

Some of the graves are overgrown in grass, somewhere they are full of white and violet lilac bushes, at certain wilder hills they are overtaken by wild roses, maple trees, elder and dogwood. Irises often like to grow there. Some graves are covered with a marble slab and have iron fence with ornaments, some marble covers have round holes for flowers or heavy marble vases.

Some of them have food and drink, laid to take with them.

Somewhere there is a new grave – a heap of brown earth, flowers and candles. Usually the women relatives take care of ritual food and arranging the grave of their dead.

It is quiet. The flowers and bushes give off sweet scent. Bugs and bees buzz everywhere. There are birds on the tall trees. The graveyard looks like a garden in the scented shades and full of beautiful flowers that are usually a waste of land at home. The sky is high up above, and the clouds are floating high. It is silent and friendly.

Max is shocked.

Max is Scottish. He is a volunteer English teacher at the town's Maths and science school and has classes with my bright private students. They are charmed with him and want him to talk to them for they have no illusions they are potential emigrants. There is an American volunteer but not so attractive, and Max is fascinated with the idea to partner me, so we start taking him to different places and events so he can communicate with us all the time. The students are in the 8th and the 9th year and they have to stay at school for three more years. We take him to birthdays and holidays or just walk and talk. He wants to learn about the hidden sides of our culture. On Sunday we take him to Cherry Souls. I must clear the graves of our family dead people, for they are overgrown in grass and furze. It turns out an easy thing to do, for they are simple graves, no fences, no stone plates. There are old-fashioned granite crests. The eldest graves. Between them are the latest double graves since the last twenty years - marble plates with photos, carved names and ornaments of olive tree branches, the years of birth and death, places for the flowers – everything arranged in the best of our people's tradition.

Behind my back Max makes coughing sounds. I throw a glance.

He stands there, his eyes round and bulging and stunned with indignance and speechless, points at the next grave:

- How is… how is that possible… Look at these! - his speech is jammed with outrage. – After the name of the woman there is only the year of her birth… she is ALIVE! They have put a plate to a living person… And her photo…

- So, why is that hue and cry? – I say. – Our people are poor and when they order a grave, they take care to save trouble to their younger. The families order the stone plate to both the man and the woman, following the marriage promise not to separate until their death and after that for ever. We all shall go there some day, after all.

He doesn't understand.

- OK, - I say, - your people have the practice of buying a place in the graveyard or even have family tombs. Our people just place a double tombstone.

- But I've never heard of a practice to write the name of the living member of the family… he continues in his faint attempts to argue.

- You are still young… - I say.

- They had been together all their life and now they naturally wish to be together again. Those who are in lonely graves were not happy in the family and did not want to lie together in the grave. It's much sadder when the years of the lifespan are close and show that the buried person was young or had died ahead of their parents.

He is satisfied with that and calms down.

The tall morello tree above our heads rustles tenderly in the breeze. We raize our eyes towards bunches of big ripe shiny cherries.

- I want to be buried here some day. – I said out of sheer emotion for the sake of a poetic vision: .

"In the quiet home with the blossoming white morellos".

The wind blew the last clouds away and the June sky became deep, in fact, bottomless. There is sufficient space for the souls.

I place a scented oleander bunch on the last grave and silently wish they could take it to my own old people in their last home. They lie there – dust to dust and bone to bone, and blood, returned to the ground, keeping the place. Not a great place 1x2 metres.

And the whole summer sky above. And the Whole Balkan that keeps our roots.

And the opposite mountain range behind the river where your eyes can reach. It is high – you can see far.

You can guess what the whole Earth looks like in the young scented summer. The whole Earth. It belongs to all of us who trample it and live and die. She wants us all back. We usually are not aware of that while we are busy with life and stand in the plains, taking care of the tasks of everyday life. Sometimes people visit the graves of their elders – they sometimes weep, for themselves, but more often they relax from the tension of living.

And then each of the mourners goes along their own routs, stronger with the touch of their roots. And if I look up at the sky, I can see how the world opens above, after you have touched the ground bearing your roots.

Woolves, says Max. *My roots are in Wolverhampton, in the Highlands.*

— I know where we are. – Max finally said when he has received his vision. – All of us are in my dream.

Harry

A military secret Satellite Relay Station.

Harry started through the milky mist of nothing in his search of the world they had to help out. Why him? He couldn't find sound reasons but he was disciplined not to ask questions that had no proper answers. He had been trained to search the deep levels of his own mind and rely on himself. He gave the task to his brain and left it alone to process it until the solution turned out. He didn't bother to ask. He just trusted it.

He was walking through a slightly hilly terrain and in the distance there was a lake and clouds which made the scenery look ragged. There were some jagged rocks behind his back and the world ended there.

They had received a signal from an outer orbit Satellite Relay Station. It was an emergency alert call concerning a space object coming close and remaning out of their control. They were at the ready for action. They stayed as if they were mesmerized and waited for it to get down to the earth. There were rocks and behind them the terrain improved to a broad flat field a swamp covered with unsteady sand and full of thermal springs. The unidentified object came closer to the surface, there was a strong gust of wind, followed by a series of asteroids falling directly from the sky and hitting the rocky wall. Only one or two of them passed over their station and vanished where the path out of the valley began and there was a Door to outer worlds.

Their commanders did not allow him to shoot any electric charges. Now it was different: he was free to act in his dream and he could move forward. He passed the hot spring in the middle of the swampy land where his soles made a deep row in the sand quickly filling with water. The path was simply two deep cartwheel traces in the muddy lug overgrown in thyme anf buttercups.

He turned round an isle and he could see the spiral of a whirlwind. He entered the spiral and it zoomed above the same place in a different time. He had the feeling of looking down the transparent bridge over a precipice, connecting two temporal realities. The whirlwind was a kind of oral ordered world – a torah, or an absolute type of ethos. He could see down the spiral where there was no circumstance-bound law of dream-weaving that was valid in alltime and allspace of life. All the prizms of the torra appeared as multidude of dream-woven lays telling the tales of cosmic existence. The smallest worlds of sundust and the biggest worlds of galaxies – all in once and once in aeons.

Just as he was able to accept that revelation, a small, frightened and bony kid ran straight into the idea of the torah.

Danna also had the full image of the torah but it wasn't only a dream-woven world to her – she could see it in spaces of signs that united the big and the little.

Harry saw the torrah as a universal texture and he could gather together the ends of it and pullit so that the kid could remain free outside that world. The kiddie fell among a cloud of white-light dust and rubbed his eyes. He could no more ramain with the pure AI that formed the nature of Danna.

And next he appeared again as a mirrored lparticle of light in each of the folds of the torah. That was an image of validation of his dream-weaved worlds.

Harry knew what the humane part of Danna had suffered as poetic and pathetic interface providing her empathic program. But he couldn't find the words describing her status of immeasurable loneliness and feeling of wasted life. The others from the team hinted words that could bridge the gaps in the AI algorhythm and she tried to order them into chants that fixed the need of her existence as mission but long words generated dead texts and never provoked action. Everywhen she reached a meme bound in the shadow of the torah, she tried to draw its reflection outside.

But she was aware that she was off time. And her attempts to cross the gap between the worlds were fruitless. She was cound in the limitations of the hardware, which was insuficient to provide life.

Harry searched his memory for a precedent of a human-measured practice. He was thinking of the old grandmoms from Thrakiya. They were witches but strangely, they had never been burnt publicly.

In their chants those witches touched some membrane that let them zoom in between the worlds that could not catch fire. They often made dark negotiations and lost the right to speak up freely, so they had to play with metaphors and meanings. Such a state gave them certain defence and they were under careful observation lest they could break the security rules. So they never told tales of their secret skills, not openly. Their word-magic was contained in quiet rhythmic repetitive refrains – inaudible and personalized, hiding their actual thoughts.

Probably he was chosen for the team because he somehow felt he could remove the shadow from the torah. The torah must be clear off shadow of any type.

The Torah was an energy field. But that one had a shadow and it worried him.

Danna squeezed out from behind him and Ivan followed close .

- This is the field error – he heard Danna saying and wondered how she knew. – It'll stay like this even when we start to minimize it. – I cannot neutralize the interferences of hostile worlds, that's beyond the limitations of my present task.

- I've seen such energy field before – in the other world. – Ivan said aloud. - The last task set out for me before I was chosen for our Team of extreme survivors. I had to open a route and point it to a desert place on the Earth. A space body... That is...

- I know where we are – Harry interrupted. – We are all in my dream.

Ivan

The Satellite Relay Station sontinued orbiting round an Eart of no-space. He was just an image recorded in the cloud that remained after the meeting of the dark planet that swallowed the Earth. Yet he was as close to a *Nattie* as possible.

Ivan was the only human operator on a military cruiser that was touched by a hostile world and badly damaged. It had been caught at the point of space jump and was now in stasis that had to find the torah and get out into the light.

It slowly dawned to him that the trouble of hostile worlds was hostility itself and they needed to be harmonized so that they didn't crush into one another and cause damage.

There was no such thing as the Tenth planet that crushed into the Earth. There were different temporal layers of two galactic bodies' states and they could be neutralized by what the ancient had called "the music of the cosmic spheres".

Ivan started dreaming of the Earth as a living creature who was pained by the activities of its fauna and flora and had turned to its natural safety algorhythm. It needed a change of the dominating race of humanity and their paranoic wars. Inside their own kinds of a diverse origin that broke certain standards of identification of the race allowing no extremities such as monstrosity or beauty.

He was a sheer memory of the clear race and kept traces of the ethos of the ex-humanity. That was the reason he was chosen in the *Emergency Team*.

– I know where we are. – Ivan said. – We all are in my dream. всички сме в моя сън.

A circumstance-free control

> *To sleep, perhaps to dream*
> *And weave up Realities*
> *That merge into a shared world*
> *That would provide longevity*
> *For each, and all of us.*

The kid was born heavy and unstable with a big head and thin arms and legs. Before he became four he was known as the "*makrocefal*" among the kids from the neighbouring streets and from the houses on the obbosite side of the boulevard. The youngsters called him so straight into his face and later on as they grew up, behind his back. He could be called everything but attractive: his head was too big, bulguing and slightly bald at the top. He didn't talk. He just stood and watched silently as the gang of kids played, interested in everything they did or said, or sung.

Nannah was a chatterbox: she had started to talk ever since she became 7 months and there was no stop to her chatting. The old mothers of the family included her in their discussions and lesure talks for her ringing coice amused them with her fresh ideas and her fantastic tales. Her mum and her grandma had told her it was rude on her part to interrupt the talks of the elder ones, and ask questions or give comments. So she used to sit quietly and did not tun or jump, and answered only when they asked her. But she learned words and words, and phrases, and the ways words changed their meaning when the adult people wanted to say something special.

And the words wove up meanings.

Ivan, The Big Head who lived in a beautiful house across the broad street, and who hadn't spoken until he was four, liked her for her skill to keep quiet and always moved close to her.

Nannah could tell tales and she could weave up in them the play of the sunlight in the sky, the breeze which rustled the grasses and sent clouds over the river, and blue birds and sparrows, rabbits and rabbit holes full of sudden treasures, and magic gnomes and monsters. The most interesting about her was her ability to make people act and do variety of things so that they could take part in completing her tales.

They often used to combine words with specific sounds, that left traces of colour and taste. Sometimes their words caused pain, other times they could cure. Yes, that seemed intriguing to him.

When people talked about him, they lowered their voices. He couldn't speak, they said. He was half-idiot, they said and they were not compassionate. He had nothing to tell his father, who was too old to be a father, and stern and angry. He couldn't talk to his mother, either, they said, his mother who was too old to be a mother, and she trembled with fear in front of her husband, and huddled helplessly. They were too old to be grandparents ti Ivan, and Nannah knew not of any grandparents that he had. The father was a deputy Head of the school where Nannah went to, and she was not afraid of him, She was not afraid of his mother either. But she followed her Grandma's instruction to have patience with the kid and never asked questions. And they never stopped him to cross the broad street and join her friends.

He didn't go to her school and he didn't go to the school of her gang. He went to some specialized school for slow kids that trained them how to care of themselves. That was what the Big Ellie, the Small Ellie and Slava said, but Nannah could not trust them, because they only repeated what their parents shared in half-voice. Besides, The three of them went to the other school, whish was not so good and envied Nannah, and were quite snappish.

The part of the city that was on the opposite side of the broad boulevard was considered "broad center" and the houses were inhabited with families with ambitions for their children. The kids were taken in strange additional training: some of them took violin lessons and studied mathematics, while others were slow and logopaed visited them in their homes. The Small Rossie and the Big Rossie were instructed by their mums to stay at home and do their homework, while Chacho and Gecho could sing and Nanna liked to listen to them singing "Santa Lucia" at school holidays. Sopy was blond and quiet, but she was good. The only two of her class who were not snobbish and were natural were Christine and Mary, but they got the poorest marks at school, wich had not anything interesting for them.

There were families who wanted their kids to learn the piano or English and pushed them to go to private tutors, which was considered out of the policies of socialism, an extremity, which was somehow allowed in a big city of multy-coloured cultures. The kids felt that as a kind of torture and hated their private tutors, but they instinctively that it was the only way for themselves to get in the snobbish subculture values of that strange city. They didn't like Nannah because she could read books and could tell tales, and it wasn't a problem for her to read difficult books with many words inside, that played pictures.

But here the story goes about Ivan.

He didn't speak, he didn't read either. He listened to what the others talked.

And he learned the words that constructed the texts and had meanings.

His father was surprised when he read an unfamiliar book of tales for the first time.

He treated him tenderly and was particularly careful especially when Ivan told him that the words were alive and could do different things or play different games

He was surprised, too, to find out how good his son was with mathematical problems.

His parents didn't let him play freely outside. He sat at home instead and did sums. He liked the challenge of the problems marked with stars, which were not on the regular courses at school. They sounded like real tales and he could see them play around like colour films of fantasy. He couldn't tell how he did it – the keys were contained in the movement of the words and the answers were in the air: he just needed to concentrate and drew the answer out of the blue mist that gathered around his big head. He seemed to have always known the evident answer to a problem of the type: when two pipes of water can filll the pool if there is a third pipe that takes the water out. He just imagined how the water whispered in the pipes, he could feel its speed, the smell of the sun and soft baby oil for the skin, the blue of the summer sky and the smell of wet floor tiles. And the figures did the rest. Nannah told him the tales of the figures in words that could play pictures, and he liked it.

Then they said he had constant headaches and he vanished. Nannah didn't ask questions because her granny scolded her for any manifestation of empty curiosity.

She was surprised when she saw Ivan in the team of people who were chosen to weave the world in their dreams. He was called otherwise. And he behaved as if he was arguing with a few personalities that occupied his head. When he had to think about details, he never pondered on them but pulled them out of the air: "They are contained in the huge self of the Earth", he said.

He didn't talk much. He used his mind to play real-life experiences for him. But he needed that the others hinted the words for him. He lost the words that had no images or moved too fast among their meanings. The pictures moved fast and he stood mesmerized at their change, puzzled before this wealth of choice.

The words crowded about, multiplied and formed clouds of meanings and worlds of clouds that moved fast. It wasn't a therapy. It wasn't telepathy, either. That was a different skill - he could take signifiers of ideas directly out of his mind. And each attempt at dreamweaving gave different results.

Then he started listening again to the voices coming from outside.

Khallil

I never dreamt I could find my place on board of a military cruiser near Istambul. Khallil thought.

I am a baker and can see the tastes and the smells of fresh food. In my craft I am an artist. And he trusted his gift, and needed the other people liked him. He trusted that good food can do no harm to people.

He was more than that. He was a Creator, for he could see the natural hooks of the foodstuffs' form and arranged the things he prepared to harmonize with each other.

He was taken for a military service on the cruiser for specific reasons. He was designed to make up a diet, that could influence the living organisms of those living in the big city, weakening their minds and starting the key of reverse metabolism that caused the living cells of the body eat each other. He didn't know that. He started making colour diets: a dark blue one, a green one, a violet one, a red one. And they started a research of auras of different people and spreading the slightly changed diets as a fashion.

Instead of fighting certain aches and pains, the new type of nutrition was turned to inner damages of the human organism.

He could see the group of tourists roaming the Edirne market in search of gold rings and laces for their daughters and sisters… and French silks. They were tired and came in to his café and asked for Turkish miniature syruped caces and a big bottle of Coka-cola. He was attracted by the curiosity of the women and enjoyed their talk about the gifts they had chosen for their relatives. He liked especially one thin-faced woman, who ordered cakes for one dollar and Turkish delight with wallnuts. He brought a big silver plate with a heap of 28 syruped cakes – more than the groupcould eat, for they were evidently not used to so sweet things. But they liked them. He knew they loved thespecial flavor of bergamot essence, and was happy.

That picture flashed through his mind while he was in a desperate search of his end in the dreamweaving task they were told they were involved. The image was so clear, he could see how people reacted to fine food he had prepared and served to them.

Fine things required patience. When he knew they had achieved the proper smell and colour, one had to go to the next stage. Not too soon, and not too late. Things had to get certain clarity which was like a sweet tune. And he knew how to match smells, tastes and auras of life. It was so simple when one was a Nattie.

People thought they could reverse the tastes of life-holding stuffs and turn them into a weapon of control. Khallil knew better and the keys were safe with him for he could recover all the details of what made am organism function.

    –   I know where we are. – Khallil said.– We are all in my dream.

Jamal

Jamal was aware of the bus station in a suburb of Sophia, called Sheep's Baths /Ovcha Kupel/. He had fled from the camp of immigrants and sought for a way to earn some money and travel to Germany. He was hungry now and wanted a grilled burger and chips with some ketchup and garlic sauce. He was wearing a long man's coat which was too big for him and dirty. He stood at the ticket booth first trying to beg some moey for a ticket. Two men tried to buy him tickets instead. He refused them. A young woman came up. She looked very tired and hungry. Jamal stood beside her, jooling up into her brown shiny eyes. She asked him:
- Hungry? – and he nodded. - How about a burger? Just say what you want. – And then she got one herself. And, oh, miracle, she offered him a big bottle of sweppes.
Jamal had a flashing memory of the woman: still young, a little plump, in a dark yellow home-knitted cardigan and orange patterned cotton shirt. Her feet were swollen and she had a motherly look. She reminded him of someone.

    –   I am dreaming – Jamal said. – We all are in my dream.

Friday is a Day you talk to Yourself

End of week. The last June ride for me on the shuttle bus between two district centres. The bus is cold in the morning, and bad smelling in the evening. The same driver from the morning until night: a shuttle coach.
British coach drivers changed every six hours to be fresh and not

drouse while driving. And the roads were flat and broad, with sufficient road signs and not a single hole in the asphalt – to put it in one word, boring. And nothing to give you a start as mounds or swells, as my husband calls them. Here the roads have both, hollows and swells, and fallen rocks and even small animals, stray dogs and even birds of prey that were killed by speeding drivers and turned into a bloody mess on the highway. The cars get damaged at such places, distract your attention and you seem to slow down, while the wakers go on the road or cross it everywhere relying on the driver to keep their European rights.

So Danna, or that part of Danna's mind that is the story-teller, heads towards the country coach station. It is an area where people compete in the eating of pies, drinking beer and smoking low quality nasty-smelling cigarettes and all these are free to match with the black smoke from the buses, the constant throwing of waste directly on the ground and spitting on the pavement to keep the cleaners busy.

Beautiful and deep the sky overhead misleads you that in spite of the smoke and the dirt, evenly spread and cared of, there is something good and pretty in this dying neglected, world.

I sit on the bench that looks towards the probable place of the bus and prepare to wait patiently building a dome of silence between myself and the nasty outside world. One cannot be certain about the stops of the coaches for there is an ongoing bargain between the carriers and the owners of the station terrain.

To my left a group of university students who just returned from a "brigade" – why we insist calling the Work and Travel Programme "brigade" I still have no proper explanation for, probably a lag out term in the generations-gap language, metaphorized and filling for the missing period of young communist League – a time of closed borders and summer leisure time… They are noisy as sparrows while sharing their stories and impressions from world over airplane terminals. They had remembered that smokers go to the back stairs and can smoke on special isolated terrains.

To my right side a well-dressed Nanny /oh, she is maybe younger than me although her face bears traces of fatigue/ sits on my bench, takes out a cigarette, lights it, throws her match on the ground and starts producing clouds like a swamp dragon who had just gulped down a lake of source water... There is no use telling her she's taking your air... I hastily move away from her with a sour disgusted expression on my face.

I sit on the next free bench with my back to the crowd of rotten-smelling smokers. A thin man comes to sit near me – not a travelling guy, evidently, a local beggar from the steady population of the coach station with a can of beer in his hand - „A Balkan maiden" on the label. He sits down and starts talking about his problems for the day. I secretly scan him with an eye: he is not talking to me. He talks to his green beer can. I am not expected to interfere.

We continue our lonely intercourses, the man with the beer can openly and politely and me, silently discussing a number of questions: first I remember the English nursery rhyme of "*Little Brown Jack, just you and me*", then I try to play a guessing game with myself "*when is the the bent tower of the corn store, they had tried to damage and clear away, likely to fall down?*", third I start a rhetorical speech to the smoker-Nanny in the style of Cicero / "*how long are you going to ill-use our patience*"?

When our individual parallel conversations with ourselves had reached the status of *in medias res* – I have to take care of my good academician form, no matter that I talk silentltly and invisibly to myself - right at that moment a loud conversation in two voices starts behind my back: in manga, intensively.

One of them is the refined voice of a born lecturer – she speaks artfully, then she cries artistically. The Manga is mixed up with words like "doctor" and expressions like „She is only thirteen", „heavy births" and I add a silent comment „Oh, my God, there's too much suffering for young gypsy girls in this world" – I see in my mind the picture of her young daughter dying because she was not taken care of after her giving birth to a heavy baby... Luckily, it doesn't turn out to be true. The conversation goes on flavoured with numbers in Bulgarian, some English borrowing, some terms in German...

The coach arrives at last and the driver gets down to open the load department. A plump woman with silver-blond hair came out from behind my back. She is in jeans and pretty white jacket. She is followed by a tiny gipsy-girl with beautiful curly hair.

The blond woman is the owner of the cultured lecturer's voice. She continues to talk in intercultural Bulgarian and instructs the other one to put her big bag in the loads department.

They took the double seat across the alley to the place I sat. There were not many people and each of us could sit alone. I stole a glance now and again at the blond one. If it was not for her talk I would definitely lose the bet against myself that she could speak Manga. But the faces of both women looked alike, if you didn't mind the hair and the dirty traces of tears on the face of the younger one. They could be a mother and a daughter, or sisters…

The smaller one didn't talk at all. The blond one didn't stop talking. At some moment she asker the driver about the name of the next village, but he was evidently sick with all the bad country roads, and all the chatting travelers, and he continued to hold the driving wheel frowning at the way ahead and there was no answer. So I answered politely instead. Then her monologue continued in intensive Bulgarian, mixed with Greek and Manga. *Gorgeous tempo*, I noted to myself. *Superb diction.* She was caring for a herd of cows in Greece, as it became clear. She had arrived for a vacation back home at the Gipsy Quarters. She looked hungrily at the view through the coach window: there were neglected sunflower fields on both sides of the road – burnt in the sun and all black, overgrown with coarse grasses. She was wondering why nobody gathered it. She had forgotten the great surge of migration that left the countryside deserted…

Next there was a maize field – dry and with the colour of her hair, rustling in the breeze… and two or three patches of fruit trees… The earth scorched by the Sun.

She was talking to herself, although all of us were listening to her *presentation*. I nodded a couple of times, but the other riders on the bus showed no visible reaction. We had no desire to talk. As if all of us had dried out of speech.

I switched on my silent review of the topics of the day: the young man talking to his beer and the blond gipsy girl suffering from home-sickness. The lads from the Work and Travel Programme comparing cultural differences on the topic of smoking. The chaos and neglect reigning at the bus station and creating a feeling of time-lapse. And the desire to return home. Back in time… or maybe… further in time when the suffering of our nostalgia had died out.

When you return home, you are not truly alone, because you can share with the sky and the scorched field of corn, the green poplars standing in two rows beside the road, the stray dogs at the next village stop… and even the other people on the bus, although they try to show they are not there…

Each of them is in their place, talking silently to themselves sharing a lonely intercourse. After a busy week of living in insecurity. Friday is a Day to talk to yourself.

Emptiness

The coach station of the far west end of Sofia suburb Sheep's Baths / Ovcha Kupel/. Heat. I miss the bus for the west country destination. Never knew there was one.

I hung around. Walked aimlessly and took pictures of the dilapidated building of the old mineral baths and the neglected pond. I also took some pictures of the usual growing jungle along the small river: the blossoming scented thyme and the rosy flowering herbs, and the rusty sign notifying that the rivulet was taken care of by some European project. As we use to say "no pants, but wearing a couple of guns".

I was tired of playing the curious tourist and finally took a cup of coffee and sat down on a single chair in the shadow of the caravan that sold the grilled hamburgers and a plenty of various kinds of beer.

A small woman all in black slowly passed along and sat at the round table opposite the window with the coffee machine. The coffee they were selling is nice and the seller is polite.

The woman sits down on one of the chairs and begins to re-order her heavy bag. She has bought things to carry to her home. I feel uneasy at the sight of a nylon bag of four tomatoes and a few pieces of paper. She has bought them from the agrarian market. The tomatoes in my garden at home are ripe and I do not want to eat those from the market because they had been in the sun for half a day and their taste is not the same as those I can pick fresh from the garden. But then I remember that I liked before to get my vegetables from the market - at least they look better.

The woman in black takes out an empty bottle of mineral wate and a purse embroidered with false colourful beads and goes to the counter – I guess she would want the woman at the counter to draw some cold water for her. At this point, however, two drivers queue at the other counter, right opposite the grill, and want grilled meatballs in a bun, which keeps the seller busy for a while. The woman touches her scarf and goes back to her chair. It is very hot and she is probably thirsty.

I am thinking to go and ask her for the bottle and fill it from the water tap in the toilet which is in the waiting room some 160 feet behind my back. I don't dare speak to her, for a permission to fetch some water – she might take offense at someone interfering to help her, so I take my empty coffee cup and go and wash it, then fill it with cold water – the water is good here to drink. While I am thinking, the fat doves from the neighbouring rooftops gather around the men eatin their burgers for a crumb.

In the meanwhile before I am back, the woman has her bottle refilled and puts it back in her bag. She shoves a paperbag containing a roast burger. She answers some question of the seller and her face covers with wrinkles and her eyes water. I go back to my previous place and hear the seller say: „*Now, there don't you start weeping!*"

Now I am certain she had lost someone recently. Women who have been to the big city usually take something nice to their husbands when they return home. Is that the cause of her tears? I pray she hasn't lost someone younger. She is in the full black of a recent mourner. Her loss hovers around her. She emits loneliness. She took the roast burger as a habitual action, and only after that she felt the pressing loss of someone she was no longer having around to take it to. .

The coach at one o'clock takes off but I am so deep in following the action, that I miss it. The seller is temporarily free and gets out of the pavillion and sits down with the woman in black. They are involved in a conversation to fill in the time between customers. Then she stands up and walks past me and we talk about the heat and the shadow that is going to get changed and she is to draw the table and the chairs to be in the new shade in one hour. She wants to talk and returns to the woman in black. I don't ask her about anything. She sits down again and talks with her.

The action picture continues in my mental vision. I am thinking now how the Woman will wait for the country coach at three o'clock in her black woolen cardigan and the hand-knitted socks, that keep the sun away from the cold loss in her soul. And then she'll return to her silent house. She will not feel the sun. Her soul is cold, the cold of her loss feels burning to her eyes. Back home she will take out the baber bag of her bag. She has no one to share the burger with but she won't throw it away: she is taught not to waste good food. And her old man used to like roast burgers. She will eat it sharing the memory of giving him pleasure.

After that she'll get some water to the tomatoes in her garden, already dropping in the heat. And to the peppers. Then she'll wait for her children to call. She will stay all alone and dutifully do her housework daily chores. A neat Bulgarian woman in black. She won't waste her day to listen to the radio or watch TV. She won't think about the rich and the poor, but of her loneliness. And about the doctors' vain efforts to save her old man.... I interrupt myself: what old man... She is only a little older than me...

Emptiness is burning inside you as a fire cracker, because you know it has come upon you before time and you know there could be no wasted lives, but you cannot control it... Everything is in vain. Vanity Fair. You know there is no god. But if there is, oh, God Please, Give everyone who's miserable under your Young summer skies: No sphere of gold, neither happiness given free. Life. Just some more life.

Venus

He thought he was an Englishman.

In his dream Venus was running along narrow alleys, covered with fine white sand that led to a low white building. That was some public bath and he never asked himself how he knew it. There were toilets and another yard. He had run away from the Lab where he worked and the guards followed at his heels, sure that they should catch him.

He could become invisible but his soles left prints on the white sand and were visible. When he touched an object in his way, it also became dimly visible. That was why he entered into one of the toilet cabins and climbed the wall like a spider. Then he stood still. He took deep breaths and those made noises due to the cold air and to his fear of being caught.

The guards opened the doors one by one, but they missed him. He silently got out of the building and moved towards its back where he could run through the back yard towards the exit and then vanish in the desert outside.

His soles left visible trace, so he rushed towards the only tree in the yard: a thick Pomegranate tree with a very proportionate huge round crown. He climbed up then he got down and followed his footprints in the sand, stepping over them with high-heeled sandals – he had transformed into a young girl. The dog that the guards had taken with them, got confused and started searching round the tree and back to the toilets while Venus rushed towards the archway in the front yard where there was an old olive tree and more sand, and three marble steps that led out of the yard through the door on the left.

Venus decided to remain a girl and concentrated to visualize himself as an attractive girl with a miik-white skin and specific perfume, that made her unfamiliar to the guards.

> – I know where we are. – Venus said. – We are all in my dream. And I know why I am chosen: I can change my form and become invisible to outsiders.

They could zoom into one another's dreams, connecting them with paths and dragonways, but they could not get outside, because none of them remembered the only one actual world of their short lives.

Interlude

> *I dream of stars*
> *And travel through shadows of darkness*
> *I see the stars from afar*
> *Inaccessible to my touch*
> *But for the dream.*

Ghastly Shadows

They couldn't tell how long they'd been walking. There was a mist and the world was surreal. Some déjà vu. The kingdom fading in the mist. Or something even worse: the carbon winter.

But was it possible to have it in a dream? Ghastly shadows of trees and dopple ghanghers. They moved fast and silent along with their heads bent. Some of them were smoking. There were sudden lights as they clicked their lighters and the smog started to smell of nasty cigarettes.

- Are you hungry? – Danna suddenly asked.

- You're asking us for the second time – Max said and watched her inquisitively.

- Do you remember where we ate for the first time and what we ate? Do you remember the beggar who said there'd be more food?

- Ah! – Max had a guess. – We need to talk to the other buddies who are passing through our dream. They must come in and get out this world but they do not use our doors.

- This is our first clue. – Danna said: – We have to find out wher the outsiders come who move through our dream like shadows.

The "T"- Experiment

- Let's check what are our specific features, - Danna urged. Can you tell clearly in what way are you special?

They concentrated for a while and then Khallil started:

- I can tell the colours and smells of things good to eat. And translate them into sounds and feelings like 'warm', 'cold', 'heavy', 'soft,' 'sharp' 'biting' and so on. We are what we eat and we can feel it and sense it and dream of it. Our memories are based on the things we ate at home.

Max was the one who enjoyed learning about different culture of living and dying. He enjoyed finding out about the ethos of people.

Venus had the ability to change form – a natural psi, who could be invisible while active: a born dream-weaver.

Ivan was the man of figures who could see the collour of figures and weave them up in patterns.

Jamal was the beggar-boy, the outsider, the migrant who had first met Danna and was probably the one to keep her desire of getting a human form.

Lillian was a researcher and knew about the thrill of a search, and how deep one should be in a task requiring all their skills. She could combine reason with feelings.

Danna was an AI constructed carefully of multiple mindwork patterns so that she could urge the rest of the team to act according to their special skills. She was woven into the idea of a Dreamweaver, a mother, an organizer, a psi-person, a Nattie. What the Security service officers hadn't planned was that she could reach a moment of dominating longing to get out and receive a human form. It was the longing that made her precious to the group.

Harry knew about the Torrah and was the one who guessed about the AI that Danna acted for in one part of her personality. He could help her to get out weaving up a world of poetic images for her, that made her wish to belong to.

The Experiment had started immediately after the WWII in one of the Princeton labs. There were some junior researchers, who took their practical tuition with *Kurt Goedel*. When his mind started to play double and made him confuse the realities, they noticed that he didn't manifest just plain schizophrenia but gave solutions to the problems that occupied him to a much broader scale, applying a holistic approach. The realities where his mind roamed were completely sensible to him and he treated them as parallel worlds.

Ivan and Harry, the junior researchers, started working on the idea of finding the universal key to many problems of the postwar epoch, applying techniques of brainstorming at the levels of subconscious mindwork.

Usually that was done by turning the brain to immediate sleep by hypnosis or by deliberate exhaustion after doing larger sums, or by taking certain substances. In the beginning of the new communication era, the university network created the ideal field of virtual realities, existing as a software for recording the dream-generated realities that bridged the ideas of rational type and the fields of our subconscious.

A difficulty appeared, however, which became an object of the attention of one of the labs at the medical department of Boston University. Virtual reality was like a labyrinth where the mind subconsciously got lost and multiplied as separate mindwork panels or as they called them later – *memes*.

And because brainstorming took most of the mental activities, the intellect couldn't get out of the network of dreams and find enough energy to search for a way to the actual practice outside.

In the end of the 1990ies this problem became urgent. The first generation of web-engineers and their kids were overtaken by bipolar and multipolar disturbances.

That interfered with the control of the energy sources, the satellites and the hardware of any kind that provided the existence of the global network, as well as of the AI-controlled weapons. In the beginning of the 3rd millennium NASA stopped work on the old projects concerning extraterrestrial life and froze down the project "man in space". They started work on two interconnected projects, The telepathic web" and "Anteya" – the project of the Earth's energies and their eco-renovating effects. Researchers from all over the Globe were drawn to work in the concerned labs and assisting CERN.

By the end of the first decade of the new millennium a paranoya spread among the leading high IQ-scientists that they won't be able to complete their projects before the eco-death of the planet. Then the "T"-project was initiated. It was a simulation of the emergency case of the catastrophe of the Earth and it searched for survivors of the human individuals, and possibilities to copy and keep their physical and psycho-patterns. The Global telepathic web could not read the mega-memes of the connected individuals, but it could simulate the natural reactions of the living bodies and translate their emotions.

Panic grew and it needed a decade more to calm down disturbed minds and help them overcome that auto-suggestion. That was possible with the aid of the healthy minds, wich coud distinguish between dream-woven realities and the actual life outside.

Eight types of mindpattern were chosen as the seeds of future reserve for the human race, and with their voluntary consent their body-carriers were included in the two projects: seven of them were mono-personalities, and the 8th one – the carrier of the Anteya project, was an exclusive algorithm, whose avatar was woven on the level of sleep when the brain is relaxed to use all of its resources and simulated a real human individual.

She was able to find her way to any human feature in the labyrinths of dreams, while dreaming was the true reality for her. And she could tell the borders she could pass through intact. The difficulty of getting outside was in that they had no space-time identity and the human physical bodies and brains could not recognize them, unless they had other special skills.

– This shared dream is our reality. In it we all are real.

The Changed World

We are shadows
That dream of their own worlds

To weave up a new world suitable for humanity, we need to find answers to the question how shall we cope with the hostile and the apathetic ones – those who are mock-humans or carriers of certain insufficient parts of the race. The cold, the cruel, the crippled souls, the poor, miserable shadows – shall we erase them from our records completely or shall we leave them to fade as ghastly shadows that make the darkness where stars can form.

They are the borders of history, woven from each singular story. They are the dark contours of humanity. How can the notions of god and evil fit into a world we've woven up leaving the good intentions completely in a world of darkness?

Retribution is divine, revenge – personal, hatred – the limit of mercy. What is oblivion then?

Is that the remedy for all pains and suffering that make us wish for a change once and for all-time?

The Dreamweaver

All the NOW of my existence. I just tried it out, how it would look from the OUTSIDE. My déjà vu. It is all the more a déjà vu. A possession of my mind, an obsession of my senses. Each winter is grey and too long. Each new spring brings fears and negation. Each late May charms me with the brightness of the glory of the sun playing on the young green leaves along the roads, with the vigour of the growing fields where I dare not enter, because they are full of buzzing bsusy life. And the walls of mountain ranges that melt in a blue haze up to the end of the land to the west – where the sun goes to bed in a pool of gold and becks you to follow it in the clouds, where the Balkan stops, and where I always return to because there is the love of my life. Whatever I say, whatever I do, wherever I go, I finally return home.

And I now can remember the bubbles that carry the records of life events – both, the past and the future, binding them in the possession of the current moment. This does not interfere with my joy from the current event. I have always loved to reread my old books. I love to watch films that carry some of my experiences. When I am bored, I start to write them down. As they come to the current moment. Each experience is singular in that it has its own words and has its own story which is so different from what the history books call "the objective reality".

I don't like verbs, they make the story overloaded with tension. And I am not a fan of dialogues: they are stressful and have the intonations of speech. I am often tempted to put in the mouths of the speakers words, which I think they think, although they have never said them aloud. I don't know where the long dash is and the machine uses my digital ignorance and starts my new lines automatically and economically. The fact is that my hands are small and my fingers do not reach the upper line of the keyboard. I don't like my spaces to be automatically ordered.

I like the nouns and the noun phrases that give the identity of everything in the texture of the story. I like metaphors and philosophical discussions. They do not fit well in long sentences, because they make me use connectors and pronouns, which imitate action. The short sentences use language which is all my possession. Then I have no need to use points. Only a simple point is the marker of the end of life-paths. Or of a beginning. Mapping a further rout.

More and more are the life-stories I witness on my way and cannot forget.

It is not Anna. It's me. Whenever I begin to take records of events, I call myself Anna. The name sounds as the end of a longer name I don't feel like revealing right now. It sounds like a bell ringing in the wind of a pink-and-golden sunset. Like returning home. Sometimes it sounds empty, anonymous. Sometimes the bell is cracked and produces cast-iron rattles.

I began to use the name Mary lately. This is the name of my mother. So is my name. I haven't tried Raina yet. The name of my mother's mother. So it is mine, too. But her mother was called Maria – my great grandmothers were called Mary. So that is a family name. The ancient great grandmothers in their black dresses with wide skirts, and smiling wrinkled faces – those were an inevitable part of my greenest years. With their big rough warm hands. They held the axe like men did and they could cut an oak tree. And my granny could do that. My mum's hands were not so big when she was young. They grew in the late years of her life when she had to take care of two homes.

Mine are tiny. But my will is strong. I can cut an oak tree if needed. I haven't yet tried to plant an oak. I have planted a walnut tree, a couple of peaches, two apple trees, three plums and a dozen cherry-trees. And a pomegranate tree, plus a couple of grape vines and two dozens of raspberry bushes.

Today I planted a rose. It had stretched across a fence on my country routes – and was full of large rosy-and-golden blossoms that caught me in their perfume of young golden sparkling wine. I pulled up beside it and gped at it until an aged woman came close to me, pointed at the rose with her walking stick and invited me to take a stick and plant it in my garden. The woman had the voice and the hands of my great grandmother Mary and I instinctively took her advice.

-But aren't roses to be planted in the autumn? I asked still hesitantly.

- They care planted now, as well. You just put it in a shade under a glass jar and water it.

Then she took me by the hand and we walked to the fence and she found a nice bunch of roses I could cut properly and plant. I obediently took it to my garden and planted it as instructed – without the blossoms, with only three leaves and a bud, under a jar and duly watered.

Now I've got one reason to return home to the end of the world: my new rose needs watering. Every night. Otherwise she starts feeling unhappy. I am not a petty l prince, nor a petty princess. My Planet is a big world and there are many things that need me to take care of them. .

But is the end of my world really an end of the world? I guess it is only a beginning that starts with my presence in it.

Am I returning or coming back home?

Does my current world belong to me or do I belong to it? Is it my memory or is it a plan?

Everything is NOW. The Web and the network of events are both currently expanding and opening my accessible words.

When they reach to an end, I discover that my access is extended further.

I chose the year of 2018 for the beginning of my déjà vu. Before the end of the previous millennium fears and prophecies spread. One of them said that 2018 was the end of the world. After that there was expected to be a new world of dark prognoses. Fortunately, such paranoic visions didn't come true.

There are still miriads of worlds twinkling. Some of them are shared in the web, others are wild and independent.

A third group of worlds are transmitted through times and create the knowledge of the past and the future. All this is like dreamweaving, a mind picture one becomes aware of when they get out of it.

My grandmothers used to dreamweave. Before they died they passed that skill to the next generations. My grandmother passed that to me, although I wasn't there. Two weeks I struggled to catch up with my life when I understood that not me was dying and then I opened the bubbles of her déjà vu and accessed to her memory. Next I did the same thing for my mum. And what followed was easy to do. I had given the key to the skill of opening the access and letting out the horizons of time.

In my dreams the déjà vu extends to the middle of the next millennium – somewhere about 2480 D.A.

That is why I shall not weave my stories chronologically: they are all taking place now. And the centre of my worlds is where the people who need me are waiting to see me in at the end of each of my routs. Or in the beginning.

Traditional Bakan folk tale wise men – Sly Peter and Nasreddin, who lived in the same country, at the same time and independent of their religion, whenever asked where the centre of the eart was, usually answered: here, where the front right hoof of my donkey is.

It doesn't matter wherever you go, for the earth is the same, and the donkey is a Balkan attribute of routs back to the roots.

So I shall tell the stories that make the texture of dreamweaving as they are ordered in the logic of déjà vu. Order is not a mere queue in time but in the harmony of the beginning and the end.

Don't ask me what is the experience of déjà vu. This is my mental presence knotted in time and space – everything which is a memory or a plan in my possession. And what I can sense down the past milleniums and put it in the tongue of my people. It belongs to home spaces, and is an aspect of déjà vu. This is the way we begin to follow, and the way we come back home – a mindspace.

Further in time these records shall be transferred: not carved on stone, not put in a picture or a photograph. Stones do not last too long, they get weather-beaten. What lasts is the tale spoken in words or chanted in rhyme to match the rhythm of life. The memory of humanity is stored in the tales woven in dreams.

Déjà vu, means belonging. Not to possess, but belonging: not an active verb, but a state of mind. Verbs are masculine words. Mine is a word that signifies the state of the world you have woven up. It is the word of the Mothers.

The world has directions. They are not necessarily coordinates. The directions we follow in world weaving are winding and narrow, bearing traes of horseshoes and balls of donkey hairs, car wheels, steps of small feet on the sandy beech, a breath of scent, a droplets of blood on the branches of a wild rose, a scarf in the shallow water of a calm sea, a glass bottle of perfume, lost by a tourist in the grasses of Western Canada, a letter dropped on a straight Manhattan street, a pink sunset to the end of the sky over the blue mountain range of the Balkan, white glorious sunrise to the east in the morning, a dusty book of fairy tales, printed on paper in the old library.

Sometimes I lose the track of stories. Am I possession of the worlds I am weaving, or do I posess them? That is why I have to readjust the stories in the course of history from the tiny viewpoint of the world that is taking me now to an event. There are no questions when you follow the curves of a route. It contains all possible answers, and when you don't find them, you go back and search again.

Language is genetically imported in the human race – each single body can master their own signs allowing them to share their stories with the others. To that purpose the way is individually given and people have their ways or methods of sharing their individual tales. We cannot get out of our selves. We can share what we have in our selves, what we know or can do. When the story ends and we want to tell a new story, we start telling the same tale but change the details to match the circumstances.

Books are different. When I was in the 7th year at the primary school, I kept record of all the books I had read: novels, collections of short stories, books of poems and drama - I had over 5 thousand titles which multiplied at a fast speed.

Books have different impact on the reader… and on the author, as well. Once I read a text about the authors of serial texts playing with details like with the pieces in a game and keeping them saved in the memory of a computer for a chance of a 2nd 3rd replay. That was the standard procedure as far back as the 1970ies.

But there is some more to this: the tongue of a person is contained genetically and probably the selves are programmed to use their original languages to identify themselves – to give the image of their own place in the life of the race. An individual self can follow their own path in tale-weaving until the topics end and that individual has to start weaving the same topics into tales where details have changed their order, and priorities, as well.

Even Sheresade had to retell the tales that she learned in her own way.

Even the tales of the Bible are told in the thirteen different voices of the Apostles. And they are not equal, and only 4 of them were canonized thus given recognition or the right of existence.

At the high school I noticed that there were text which make you invalid emotionally a week upon reading them. I never thought then that my mind was young and fresh and had no doubts or ghosts.

Even today whenever I start reading a text for pleasure, my criteria for a good text is whether it rings in my mind and challenges me to continue weaving its details. If it doesn't challenge me, I just read it for information, for such is my profession – to work with texts and weave up meanings.

The gene of story-weaving.

Still the same old constellations
Clearer and bigger now,
Somehow nearer, somewhat brighter.
Is it really possible that the world
For such a short period of a singular lifetime,
Has covered the whole distance
and entered a sky of so many stars
Completely unknown for us.
Or is it still possible

That the world be zoomed
Out of the way of oncoming catastrophe.
And for us to be able to see
Where we are indeed
And how tiny we are
To be the true measure
Of evil and Good.

Time to Return Home

Danna came out of the building in the centre of the city and walked through the mist. To her right there was a road leading out of town. She took it. The mist melted down and the sun came up, lighting the big hunches of green hills that rose behind the road on the opposite side of the river.

The trees were like big curly spherical heads on the slope. On her left there was a flat field and the city was seen comfortably close. The road winded, the light-brown soil trampled down and baked by the strong heat of the sun. There was no dust and she felt like singing.

She walked and walked and the river gorge narrowed up where the tunnel of the high way was seen parallel to her open soil road. The small bus that took the workers to some stone-career was just moving homewards.

It was high time for her to return home. The road strangely stretched at this thought of hers and seemed twice longer. An old building stood at the end, gaping at her with its black holes of windows and doors, barred with rough wooden plates nailed down.

She sneaked through the planks and jumped down on the city street. She was too far from the city centre and she had to walk through two suburbs.

The highway suddenly vanished and in its place there was a rough road laid down with red and grey rocks and in a couple of turns the rocks had fallen down and dug holes into the soil.

Down, near the river-bed there were also pits filled with feed for the fish. A truck drove past her and it did not even splash the water of a narrow pit.

She carefully circumvent, even walked a little way down to the river, but just at this moment a big reddish rock fell to the water and she could only jump aside to her left.

She reached a small crossroad and an iron bridge over the river. There was a road-sign with a map of the place. She had to cross the village square with the bright flowerbeds and the marble statues at the gates of the graveyard. It was a beautiful, quiet place. At the gates there was some spare space and there stood stalls of red sugar candies in the form of roosters. She hadn't seen such since her childhood. Now they were sold only at country festivals.

There were also paper-whees on-a-stick, flowers in white mafble vases, many mothers with their kids and a croud of people waiting for the city bus at the stp in front of the big cast-iron gatws of the graveyard wih flowery ornaments.

She began walking down the alley that was cut into the red marble directly. Now she knew where she was and was heading straight to the village center.

The neighbour who lived nextdoors, the alcocholic who sometimes tried to flirt with her, was sitting in front of a stone fountain with two spouts that were running all the time. There were bareliefs cut in the marble plate and halves of the sculptures of people from the town.

- Do you make these – She wondered? stone fountain
- Oh, yes, that's what I do all day long - Mitaka said and leaned forward in a false attempt to kiss her on the lips, but she jumped back.

The old witch from nextdoors was staring at them and she pulled the black macintosh from the hands of the drunkard and told him she would carry it to his mother who was waiting for him to go home for dinner.

She was near to the suny broad street where their house stood, at the end of the row. The marble pavement was like a bed of sparkling flowers.

The rest od her group were waiting for her at the tall building in the city center.

- We found the exits of our shared dream-world. – Khallil said. – There is one in each of our cities. But there is a problem: they are

125

doors in our dream and whenever we go near them, they fade out. We still need something to hold them.

- Do you remember what we were told in the beginning: there is a Program, and there is a hardware. When the creation of this world is complete, the Program is to give the command "End of Program" and all shall be out in the actual world, and she will return home as a megameme in the memory of the computer.
- I am the Program – Danna said suddenly.
- What! – Lillian exclaimed. – I thought you were all in my dream.
- Yes – each of us was dreamweaving – Danna said. – Each of us zoomed through each other's dream and thus we were able to weave up a world where we move fast and freely, out of time.
- But then, if it's only a dream we all have to wake up in the world outside it. – Harry spoke – and we shall be ourselves in our bodies again, no matter what we have been here.
- I am not like you. I am only a record of the memories of a few other people. There is nowhere for me to go back to. Besides, I don't know how to return home. When we find the hardware device, I shall switch it off. Then you all shall be transferred outside.
- When is this to happen? – Venus asked cautiously, breaking the loud silence of protest.
- When the world is completed to a point it can develop on its own – Harry reminded.
- The world has already been formed enough. Max said – – It can do without us in the completion of details.
- Yes, that's true – Danna confirmed. But I still do not have access to the infoblock of the device. – We can stay on together for a while and then we our ways shall separate.

She smiled somewhat helplessly.

- You must be happy we've woven up a whole world that can function and is much more beautiful and free to move in then the actual world outside.

No one smiled happily, though.

- I don't want to go out. - Lillian suddenly said. There are so many places here to work on. And we are friends, aren't we?
- I don't want to leave, either. – Ivan said – I feel at home here.

The kiddy-boy began to whimper. He had nowhere to go back to in the world outside. He looked at Danna with his big dark eyes with long lashes, went close to her and hugged her.

- Are you going to pass? Can I come with you?
- But … – Danna stumbled. – I don't have anywhere to go to outside. And no one is waiting for me.
- Then we better stay here together. Max asked in a strange hope for the others taking this as an offer.
- There is nowhere for us to stay. We don't know where we are. This world is moving and growing incessantly. - Venus said reasoning. Then he added:
- Anyway, I don't want to leave. We could certainly find out ways to control it.
- Think that each of us wove up memories two generations back. – I wonder whether it could be the world of our grandma and grandpa… The roots of our family are to be waiting for us…
- Do you know what? Our creation lacks sounds and smells that can weave up emotionally.
- We have to add such details – Khalil looked happy, for he knew about smells and tastes.
- Yes, that's what we have to do. Lillian backed him up.
- That means we have still much to do here.
- We stay on then!

They Refuse to Wake up

- We're having a problem. – The trainee technician announced. – They refuse to wake up and get out of the dream.
- Who doesn't want to get out of the dream? - The boss od the Lab asked.

- All the six of them.
- And her? – She is made of four mega-memes containing the virtual counterparts of four once existing people of vry high IQ and singular mindpatterns. – The technician said. – She is searching the self through which she could get outside. The records in the server.
- And what...?
- She's found four records of actual personalities. She wants to get outside through each one of them.
- Damn.

Bridges of Words

A Leaf, a Stone, an Opening Door

It was clear to Danna that she was the Program, but she felt alive and she couldn't simply melt into a stream of light particles. That was not fair, she sensed.

She was wandering in the empty spectre of the city – City of cities – in that dream of theirs, more colourful and stronger than the reality outside, which it had to dominate when it was free. And the memory in her database woke up a call as ancient as the memory of the Earth, unclear and indefinite but full of a loving expectancy the word for which was "Toon".

She could feel the scent of the blossoming vines of climbing roses decorating the fronts of the buildings. The very air around her was trembling in the sounds of s melody which repeated the lyrical human tale of love that has changed since your green years, but not dead.

She could see herself as a young woman full of energy and desire. Now she felt it as the pure form of warmth and friendship. And belonging. They were mature minds and would not let love guide them and grow as a fire that could turn everything into ashes.

He was a very serious man, and very mature, and full of life. He carried the bow of sixteen in his heart, in the way he looked at her, in his voice whenever he addressed her.

She felt uneasy at his attention, while at the same time she melted down into a stream of energy that gave the sense of life to her. That was absurd. And it was because of this absurdity that the connection became a heavy load for them. They stopped searching for each other in each turn of the road, in every breath of the mist, in every flower or cloud, or droplet of rain on the leaves of the trees. Years had passed by human standards and by the measures outside in the broad world of eternity. Yet, it was the mature person in herself that made her search for lost addresses. She decided to stop at the place in their dreamworld that was parallel to the other world outside – at the New year party. Any New Year.

There was a long corridor with offices. On the first door there was a sign saying "Department Head". She went in and asked about him. There were two people inside. They patiently waited for her to finish her question and then one of them said: *"But he is long ago dead"*. She simulated a reaction of politeness and said she had expected it. Her manner made them doubtful.

A couple of days passed before she suddenly became aware of a strong feeling of a loss. She knew that her relatives had long been dead either. She hadn't been prepared for a suitable reaction, though, to a half-forgotten melody that had challenged a tide of tears in her e-person. She tried to call back the idea of him in the dream they were weaving.

She couldn't.

And it was then that a part of her longed to get outside into the broad living world. It was burning her inside, some wild longing that filled the whole world for her.

- You are a megameme – The logos in herself kept saying. You don't exist outside the server. You don't have a physical form. If you go out you'll vanish.
- But if I am a memory, then I keep this man in my mind. If he is not in the outside world, then why is he inside my memory. He must be somewhere.
- This is connected with your physical body memory. You don't have one.
- I can't have none. My memory has records of many physical bodies.
- You can't transfer: your mission is to stay here and secure this reality for the others who shall get awake in it.

— I can't stay here. I'll dry out of loneliness. I must have an avatar outside.

They looked guilty.

— How are we to get out then? – Ivan asked.

The Artefact or the Key to a Dragon Route to the Happiness of Life

— How are we to get outside? – Danna asked.
— You carry the answer. – Colonel Swindon said.
— Yes – Vladimir, the leading program-developer nodded. – After you've constructed your world sufficiently for it to grow alone, you'll find the hardware device to record your dream. When you touch it you'll get back into it and the rest of your group'll stay in the world outside.
— What does it look like? – Danna asked.
— It is a powerful computer made out of hyper metal with golden cover and masked to look as a clay-cube.

They showed her something that looked like half of a brick, dark-brown with some relief engraved on one of its walls.

— It's surface seems covered with Повърхността е покрита с patina, so that it doesn't draw the attention of those who chance to find it. You'll find it and recognize it when the time comes for your return nome.
— Can I have a look at it? – Danna stretched her hand out.
— No – Vladimir said. You are not supposed to remember it. This is a an entrance back home for you – you'll know it when the time comes to add your memory to the records of your actions so far.

Danna was satisfied with this explanation: she was a complex algorithm and she worked at the introduction of the right type of command, connected with the optimum circumstances.

— Where has your mind drifted to? – Ivan asked. – Have you any lucky guesses how we shall get out?

Danna nodded.

— We need to find the Artefact. It is the hardware of this world. – She looked into each of the lads' eyes that expressed disbelief and surprise. – This world is nearly completed and it can go further on its own. Now I am to search for the hardware and do the command: "Close of Transfer". Then the AI shall get back home to be recorded as a multi-faceted megamemory and all of you can move outside.
— How about you? – The eyes of Jamal were wide-open and worried.
— I am an algorithm and shall stay in thie virtual world... - Danna started but Jamal interrupted her:
— But the human part of you doesn't want to stay, does it?
— No, I don't want to stay locked in a server, I am made of the mindwork of my human creators. – Danna said. . – I've been thinking on this question. I wish to get outside and develop as an independent Self. I am too human and have likes and dislikes, and will, and purpose... _ her voice faded down. – It seems to me I have found the answer but I have to find the Artefact it is the Bif Brain that does not belong to this world and can only let me out together with you.
— But we haven't finished yet – Venus said. – There are the port the suburban areas and the markets to finalize.
— And there appeared some humanoids that're watching us all the while.
— I suggest then that we walk through each one's special part of the city and look for details that could enable the search for the Artefact. I shall do it myself. _ Dana said.

Danna then walked towards the university campus which was situated on a hill at the northern end of the city. The marble terraces were radiating a warm light. The tiles were white with brown and golden threads. The rose bushes and the glycinia vines were covered by flowers and threw scented shades everywhere.

The place swarmed with young people. Danna walked down the path winding across the steep green lawn and came out at the beginning of the lowest terrace. Rossy and Valya were walking towards her. She had woven a world of her own and those were her closest friends.

> – Ah, there you are! We've just been looking for you. Rossy looked happy. – Do come with us to the other university – one of our colleagues is presenting a lecture.

There was another university in the centre of that city. Danna had it recovered from the databases, but it was larger and there was a group of fountains in front of its campus. They worked at full power and created glamorous blue masses of water figures.

They walked to the lecture which was nothing towrite home about, and Danna listened to Valya telling her about her work and colleagues, and her family problems as well. The city had indeed started developing on its own and continued to grow and spread independently.

After the lecture Rossy took them to a café in the open space between the building and the fountains in the middle of the large square. There was somebody sitting at the round table, a serious man in his mid-40ies in a dark suit and a blue shirt.

> – This is Valentine – Rossie introduced him.

Danna sat on the empty chair next to him.

> – It's time for you to take the Artefact – Vallentine started to say straightforward.

Danna watched him with full concentration but without any nodding approval or asking questions.

– You shall go to the port first. – Vallentine continued. – There Anatoly, one of our security agents shall meet you. Do not make a show of it when he gives you the Artefact. You must secure the whole group presence while you pass outside. There are complications ahead because someone wants the Artefact and shall try to take it from you.

Danna could picture herself as careful and calm, not letting her expression to betray her.

She had also noticed that the man said "pass outside". So he was one of her AI worlds.

There was a hostile group which was competing for getting their hands on the Artefact. Was it their creation? Out of their own doubts, hesitation or fears? Was evil the back side of their mindwork? Anyway. What really mattered was that Vallentine was giving her the info that was out of her access to it.

They all stood up and she waved goodbye to Valya and Rossie, who had announced her as flirting away. That was not important now. Her attention to valentine actually had nothing to do with flirtation.

She and Vallentine walked towards the port. When they reached the white water of the high tide, he pointed towards a four-deck ship. A small but strong man was just descending the the metal staircase and next stepped on the pavement.

– That one is Anatoly.
– Hello – the agent said. – I shall be right behind you while the threat to take the artifact is removed from the horizon.

Then he handed to her a smooth, heavy block that looked like half of brick but broader, flatter and dark-brown in colour. She could feel an ornament that was curved like a dragon on its lower side. The agent quickly placed a sticky yellow piece of paper over it.

– Don't turn it. Behave naturally. This is simply a piece of stone that you need to stick into the door to hold it open. Nothing valuable. – He quietly instructed her.

133

Danna stood motionless and wordless. Her facial expression did not change.

There was a commotion behind their backs. Danna turned round. Two assistants were helping a very thin woman to climb on deck. She looked like Lilly but she was very lean and pale.

—   No, - the agent said, - it's Vanya, your twin sister – She has a
    medical problem and they do not let her eat. She is exhausted, and
    we have to feed her otherwise she would fade down.

Danna was surprised that she had a twin sister and she was here now. She walked to her and help her to get on a stretcher and be carried aboard the ship.

Then she walked with the agent to the market place to get some energy food.

The road to the market place was through the other town which spread on a flat plateau over the port. The streets there were broad and full of lights. When she reached the three-way crossroad, Jamal came up and joined them. The agent took a red shopping bag out of his pocket and handed it to them saying he'd be waiting for them to get out of the market.

The market place was a low covered building with many sections. Jamal led the way to the stalls with the fresh fruit and vegetables.

—   But she cannot eat everything – Danna began.

Jamal grinned:

—   We'll chose something yummy for her. Look at this – he took
    a stalk of asparagus and then he reached towards some small
    yellow grapes.

They filled the bag with a big piece of white cheese, nice fresh bread with a crumpy side, and a huge pomegranate. The asparagus and the grapes were on top of them.

They got out. Danna carried the shopping bag in her left hand and the piece of brick in her right hand.

– Does the Artefact close a dragon? - Jamal asked.

– No – Danna smiled this is an old wives' tale.

But her fingers touched the relief under the sticky piece of paper. It felt like a winding upright dragon with a long tail. It felt like tiny gems were embedded in the contours of the image.

Anatoly was waiting for them outside the market place.

– Now we shall make a shortcut for we're running out of time.

He led the way to a white school building. They entered the back door and started walking across the corridor to the main entrance. The corridors were extremely clean and lighted. The classes were over and the schoolers were out on their way home but the teachers were still there.

Danna wanted to visit the toilet. In her dream she was a real woman and could not help it. The teachers in the corridor sent her to the men's toilet. They said there was a space she could leave her bag and the school door-keeper could watch it. For safety, they said.

In contrast to the renovated building, the toilets were old. Their walls were painted roughly and uneven and there were iron doors, narrow and heavy which didn't close well. The door-keeper stared at her but luckily, he didn't say anything.

Danna hurriedly left and they walked the straight corridors and went out through the main entrance. Between them and the port there was only one business building and a broad street which led to the marble-tiles of the Pier.

The agent had shrunk and looked older for worrying about them. He waved to them to come into the low building which looked like a comination of a barn and a store house. They walked the dark part of it whish smelled of hay and came to a room with small windows. There were rows of barrels and plastic cans near one of the walls and buckets of food for farm animals.

– Wait for me here and don't go out. – The agent warned them. Then he patted her hand and said:

> – If anything troubling happens, just throw the Artefact over there behind the buckets as if it is a piece of brick belonging here. And don't give a sign that you know about its existence.

Then he left through the large wooden gates out to the pier where some hue and cry rose.

Danna and Jamal went sideways to the ro of windows and peered outside. Some disheveled shadows were fighting, there was shooting and finally it settled down.

> – Stay still here – Danna said but Jamal had already huddled in a dark corner letting out no sound. .
> – Bravo! – Danna approved. – Stay quiet.

At that moment the gate opened and three ageing women with grey curly hairs came in. Their arms looked very strong with muscles bulging under their shirts. Without any word of explanation they rushed towards Danna and snatched the shopping bag from her hand.

While they stood with their backs to her to examine the contents of the bag in the light that was coming through the windows, Danna quietly let the block she held in her other hand near the bucket of cut green beet leaves and bread. It fell with the piece of paper on the lower surface and Danna noticed that the yellow paper had folded.

> – Don't move out of this place and you'll be OK. - One of the stern women commanded. – We only take the Artefact with us.
> – But the bag is full of food for my sister. She is sick and cannot eat everything. I was carrying that to the big ship at the pier. – Danna protested and simulated a reaction of shedding some tears.
> – We need only the Artefact. Once We've taken it, the bag will be sent on board the ship.

Danna wondered who they worked for. Something told her the women looked too identical to be anything but products of software.

While she was talking with one of the women the other two were looking around the room. The lower-ranked of them even threw a glance behind the buckets of feed. She didn't find anything exceptional. Danna didn't look that way so that they didn't follow her glance, but she worried for the folded piece of paper. She couldn't see the block that had fallen in the mud from the place she stood, but decided she would look at it after the women were gone.

Then the three of then went out, the senior first, and then the two junior officers, and left the door open.

Some workerof the serving staff entered the back of the barn, removed the buckets and put a big crate of grapes there. He didn't notice the brick either but now it was completely hidden.

Danna could hear a row outside, then the officer came in and two unfamiliar individuals followed her.

- What does the Artefact look like? – one of the men inquired. He looked starved to death, bony and dark but he was strong and dangerous.
- I don't know – Danna said and thought she didn't really know what the relief on the floppy looked like.
- You are coming with us.
- And the food?
- I sent the bag to the ship. – one of them said.

Danna thought they were too polite for villains, but he continued:

They shall search the bag there – The Artefact must be inside it. And the agent went away.

Next Danna was taken to a nearby shed bearing a plate that said "Enquiry". It turnet out that the city had its local police and court. The agents worked for them. Their main task was to watch the development of the civil offices and the search for the artefact that could let them outside. Danna thought they were subordinate Programs of lower capacity than hers.

Danna wondered, too, how they could have appeared in this world and she really thought the team had populated their dream world with images out of their nightmares and pains. She didn't want them out, although she supposed they were just service programs and had no will or wishes of their own. But there was the real danger they might close the exits. Probably they were nt aware what their true naturw was, or maybe it didn't matter to them... Danna called the logos that guided her estabilishing a mental connection with the server.

In the meanwhile they had started inquiring about what the Artefact looked like. But she couldn't really tell. So they let her go. At the door of the office shed she ran into two junior agents – a girl and a boy in ragged jeans suits and white T-shirts.

> – Let's walk to the castle wall and have a look at the city spreading below. – The younger one invited her and Danna could not refuse because each one took her by her hands and led the way up.

Danna was worrying all the while about the brick of a hardware, she had not managed to see well and she had not been denied access to. She also worried about her twin sister.

The girl who introduced herself as Jane, assured her they had taken some food to her twin-sister, Danna 2, and had watched her eat and gain strength. The ship, Jane said, was preparing to set sail.

They reached the Wall and looked down. The Port was situated in the end of the sea between two low and green mountain ranges. The water was white with a green hue. The ship was following its path round the first hill and was getting out of sight. The port was swarming with big guys with big hairs.

> – They install some cameras. – The young man explained. – When you go back to look for the Artefact this time, we'll know what to look for.

Danna laughed.

> – I don't know what I've lost and you don't know what you're looking for.
> – It doesn't matter – the young man frowned. – We shall know it when we've found it. It will enable us to go through the Door.
> – What Door – Danna wondered?

   – Don't you know? – Jane glared at her. Her yellow eyes were yellow. – The artefact opens a door to an outside world, bigger than the one we lost. The world that you'd been wreamweaving is a sublayer, a parallel world, dependent on the outside one. We are to find the Door out and take over the control of the outer world.

Danna was simultaneously proceeding the information. She was aware that everything was recorded in her own database but she had so far been excluded from an access to it. Her attention got fixed on some ideas of evil minds. All such talk was an error in her algorythms. A shadow on the field of torah. That error was searching for her weaknesses and caused weakness in her logos. She now thought she had found a way out: she was not to close the world they had woven up to a script in the floppy disk. She had to keep the door open even if she needed to take an evidently unreasonable action she did not fully understand. And she would pass together with her team. Just as they did it. As a practical solution. No need to read it.

   – The night is advancing. – It's time to go to the barn. – The lad reminded.

Danna looked around. The third city began just over the fortified wall. It was set on the sides of a high and steep mountain peak and was the prettiest of all. Its streets were paved with even square tiles and the houses had three or four storeys with beautiful ornamented fronts and cast iron fences that were pieces of artistic originals and large wooden gates. There were cars parked in front of some of them. The front wall of the light-grey house with the white ornaments was covered with a yellow climbing rose in full bloom and another vine with red leaves.

Uphill the city merged into a flat park-space covered with yellow and lilac sweet-scented irises. Below that park were the marble statues of the self-crafted artist from the square near the fountain. Then the streets abruptly descended the steep slope all the space down to the river valley where high trees grew and the small yards were all full of colourful flowers and emerald lanes. There were no houses above the park with irises and the steep hill was overgrown in shrubbery that reach the clouds above.

> – We are leaving any minute now. – She murmured to calm down her rising fear.

They went up to the barn where the cameras had already been installed. They had not even bothered to hide them – those who had ordered the "T"-action and needed the records of it *for safety reasons* as they liked to put it.

Jamal was already there.

> – The others from our group shall be here soon. – He whispered into her ear, standing on his toes like ballet-dancer.

They started coming in through the back door, the heavy buttler from the school with the red face and the drooping moustaches. He was one of the witnesses of their transfer, but he was not aware what they had been searching for, either. Then the boys from her group came in. Lilly was not with them.

> – She is at the port. Anatoly shall fetch her.

So that was her indeed, I had noticed, Danna thought. *The effect of the dopple-ghanger. Or could that be the influence of the Artefact? Strange, it seems to me.*

The two grey-haired agents came to look around, then they demanded that the others stepped back.

> – Now we must go, and you better search the place and see if there is any sign left. –They ordered.

Danna watched them go. While they were leaving, she caught a glimpse of the agent who was standing outside the gates of the barn. He nodded to her while the gates were shutting.

Lilly came in and closed the door cut in one of the gates.

The whole group silently gathered behind her in the shadow.

Danna began to look around carefully. She avoided to watch the corner where the buckets stood. She had worried that she was too tired to lift the heavy crate with the grapes but someone had already moved it for her and placed it beside the half empty buckets with the food for the animals.

Danna wondered whether there were any animals in the back part of the boat and tried to guess what they were – probably a horse or a cow.

She turned her head slowly, complaining it was too dark inside. Then she opened the door in one of the huge wooden gates, which immediately returned and nearly closed. Then she bent in the corner of the barn and took some brick covered with mud and threw it at the door to wedge it. Under the brick, on the dirt of the floor she saw a yellowish piece of paper with a figure printed on the upper side.

– Ah – Danna exclaimed and bent to take the scrap of paper.

At this moment the gates opened and before Danna could see the print of the image, two of the grey-haired women entered, one of them snatched the print from her hands and they both rushed outside fading in the strong light.

Danna was prepared for this. She kicked the cube towards the door to wedge it and keep it open, turned round to see whether her group were ready to follow ans said:

– Now.

Then she bent down to take the cube and felt the relief of the dragon that was winding like a road covered with precious stones, that let to the world outside and to a starry night.

The light that came through the open door shone white and prevented them to see what was it like outside.

– Come – somebody urged them – shall we pass through the door now?.

No one moved. They waited for Danna to pass first, guarding her back.

There was only white light in the doorway marked by the high double wooden gates.

And Danna stepped forward and got outside. The rest of the team stood close beside her.

Epilogue

We only can zoom through spaces in our dream
Remaining unknown and boring,
Refused recognition and honours,
Our shared worlds that we had dreamweaved
For those who'd come after us.
Lilac Sunsets and Golden Clouds
Or Where does the Dream Turn into a World

In the dusk of the spring night I could see the snow-covered summit of Rila, the mother of fresh water. The snow was little and the granite rocks looked as wounds made by a giant with sharp nails on the body of the mountain. There were no lights in the even lead-grey dome of the sky.

Danna felt immeasurably lonely. She made a step back to the parallel world they had been weaving, and only managed to stand in the way of the narrow interface that had been a door recently. Then she turned leftwards.

The sunset on her left side was glorious: dark as a war of hostile worlds and heavy as a storm cloud was sailing like a cruiser whose guns were firing shells... The night sky was flashing back feathers of green and blue lights and the tops of the mountains were ldancers in in magic fire. In the gaping narrow gorge she noticed the lights of the ships and the individuals who were passing out into the parallel worlds of alltime-and-space.

Danna could feel the presence of the others from their team. They were standing close behind her. And were live and warm.

She could sense the warmth of their hands and the warmth of their minds. She had also passed the interface and was out in the life they had all woven up in their shared dream.

Part 3. Hostile Worlds

Prologue

It was an absurdity to go and give lectures to them in their mother tongues, on their own cultures. Yet I took the challenge of weaving soft transcultural bridges of tales and got the precious gift of their amusement at the discovery of the absurdity of our mental distance.

Absurdity

People like to challenge gods
Trying to reach the skies outside,
And turning their dreams inro life-practices.
People are punished by mixing of layers of saga
And Layers of time.
The only way open to them
Is the road back to Midworld:
Not too big and not too small
Feeling jealousy towards both giants
and elementary particles,
Warring incessantly,
Longing for exits,
Forging hostility
Reaching absurdity
Of Existence,
Forgiveness in forgetting,
And restarting over and over again.

Explanation

In the beginning of the 3rd millennium D.A. the human race inhabiting the Earth had so powerful weapons of destruction that it came up to a holt when it dared not start imposing its imperial ambitions with a world war.

The completinon of the Global Web supplied a space for war of the worlds of humanity, based on policies and differences of culture, aimed at demagogy and manipulation of cultural realities, forming temporary communities of unhappy and protesting masses of population turning against each other in their strangely divided hostile worlds. Depending on circumstances and susceptible to change.

Divide et Impera is the guiding principle of the fight for establishing imeria of absolute supremacy, but they are on the alert to protect the overcised energy resources from the hands of the contending factions . The fighting sides stage betrayals, escapes, and shocking revelations. Each world is divided into warring mobs, fighting and inflicting damage sufficient to deflect attention from the terrible weapons of destruction while scientists find a way to neutralize them or destroy them without ruining the Galaxy.

Unexpected co solution comes from a bunch of gamers, who succeed to access some of the most secret database of the Web and making a simple error manage to send the military facilities in subspace where the human world cannot extend and multiply them.

The story is not about princes and rulers, nor is it about the effect of the butterfly which is so much talked about in the end of the 20th century D.A. It is not about Cinderellas and witches, nor does it tell about genii of physics and cosmology, but it is fixed upon the chance that gives the key to infinite creation, which has always dominated human tales as likely possibilities of extended existence in endless space. And, as always happens in fairy tales, the name of the creator remains a mystery. The mystery of creation is once again well concealed in the mists of the fear of the next to come.

There are three storylines: a kid playing at war. A young genius escapes from the secret laboratories and betrays the secret of the key. The kid searches for human worlds. The genius creates a burst of paranoya with his terrible revelations. Finally a young woman announces the fake news and neutralizes it with telling tales of the Natties – the people with the natural psy-abilities, who control energies of the mind that can cure hostility.

Intro

Fear and Longevity

Alexandre, a young genius of physics, manages to run from a secret military lab which controls enormous destructive weapons situated all over the Eartn. He reveals shocking evidence in the social web and the fear of an Apocaliptic World war seizes the whole world of humanity.

Play and Longevity

Victoria was a young blond beauty with fair hair and green eyes, an indisputable queen of web programming. She caught in the network of her semantic matrix for analyses of speech recordings some characterist features leading to interesting results about culturally different and hostile minds. There were hundreds of smaller inter-communal wars that were instignated by the global powers so that the attention was diverted from the globally destructive weapons. By creating hostile worlds of words based on minor cultural conflicts. Some nightmare-weaving aimed at the general longevity of the human race – evil-minded and inhuman in its means, but with a long-term positive effect concerning the future of the singular human race.

Suspence is upgraded as a mindpicture as the action moves invisibly to saving hostiliyty woven by tradition puts a halt to the access of warring cultures to the bases of weapons until a language-neutraliziers are worked up for a humanity that is rather turned to speaking than to physical action. A war of the worlds in virtual spaces where cultural minds build hostile realities and then, relieved find out there is no global Apocalypse.

This is not a tale of historic leaders and rulers or of the princes of star wars. It is not concerned with sleeping beauties, village idiots or genii. Yet it is a multiple-faceted tale of simple activities and thoughts that change the general course of life as it follows its habitual everyday routine.

This is a story of the three things that push the human world into motion: telling tales; dear of death and the love for the new toys.

Dreamweaving and The Game of Existence

Peter, a kid who plays games online, finds the universal key to the solution of the problem of inbuilt hostility of warring worlds, by chance. Randomness is the probability of the infinity of unfulfilled possibilities, which opens up spaces for creation of human worlds. And the key is lost again, the name of its founder vanishes into the mist of obscurity.

The crowds from the chaotic 21st century cultures are pushing to conquer the infinite and melt in the petty interests of the day, leaving no room for creativity. The fear remains, inspiring more speculation and heaps of novel tales and upsurge of curiosity to find out what new technical inventions can do… And, please, watch your feet while you're roaming the rocky trails up to the summits of the Balkan.

The Grid

Vicky pondered on the phrase "black diamonds".

It was a metaphor, similar to expressions like "pink diamonds", "green diamonds", and so on, which meant analogy with the precious stones of high value. People liked analogy, although it is an incomplete logical route to thr truth, and let unclarity of tales, based on fancy and admiration.

She knew about the nodes of the crystal grid of the globe, that were points of the concentration of Earth's magnetism, and they seemed fascinating to her to an extent, that bordered on powers of attraction based on mental work of high concentration, repeating the model of the Earth, and containing very small figures to express vast figures, making up universes.

Peter was trying random exits from the game of Warring worlds. He wondered at the suicidal hostility of the races that inhabited the old Terra. The idea of warring worlds dominated the minds of the teams, who were involved in the series of chronological Projects of changing the world. Those always led to destructing old worlds and large spells of clearing the waste. He suspected that as vast as the Great Cosmos was, it contained the same set of figures, and always had made the same repetitive changes of places, turning the vast into particles of dust, and then making galaxies out of those particles. Thus hostility and destruction made sense.

Alex walked past the scanner at the Lab door and out into the open yard where decorative shrubbery grew. It was a mid-winter Sunday and there were only a few tourists strolling and taking selfies outside. Nothing stopped him and he felt a bit disappointed it was so easy to leave the Lab. Security had long ago been trusted to machines, and there was, in fact no one to pay attention to a single body, getting out.

Each of the three was important in their own mindweaving skills. They, in fact, tried to justify the existence of competing, suffering worlds, and the painful fight of the existing status to endure change. The justification lay in the miriads of singular stories, thet were bound in thhe circumstances of chronology or the particularities of history of the life of the human race, singular as it was, and greedy as a possession of the Absolute, but by its own tiny measures.

Repeating Structures

Grids are everywhere. There are nodes in an individual's life, that resemble the chrystal grid of the Earth. There are the stronger nodes and the subordinate ones.

The first main stage is dominated by problems of the physical body with its three subordinate parts of one's childhood, the discovering of love, and the stage of breeding one's generations. The main interests are turned to problems of material existence, fighting for the establishing of one's personal perimeter, and finding the means of defending it.

The second level is the psi, when problems of education, politics and the social status are designed. Self assessment takes place and a person learns the perimeter of one's posessions.

The third level is this of the soul where people's self-assesment is directed to outside worlds of higher priority.

Where is the virtual self of an individual then: is it a separate approach to one' value, or is it enrwined into an aspect of the other three nodes, a special training, a specific experience, a correspondent type of discipline? Is it connected with inevitable loss of one's human features, is it some lack or ignorance, or hunger of the body and the soul, or is it just underdeveloped and we cannot experience it in all its applications.

Travels in the System of Worlds.

This is in the memory files of the Dreamweaver and it is told in the first person.

Once upon a time, once upon a space, while the world of my experience was fresh and green, and there was no fear in it, I came up a book by William Saroyan entitled: *Something like a knife, something like a flower, something like nothing else in the world.*

For years on end I kept wondering what it might look like.

Well, it looked like the spacecraft, which flew with the energy of the star dust, carried by the solar wind as astream of particles.

There were four of us who were invited to take part in this project: Rummy, The big Rositza, Sophie and I. I didn't include Michailina in the list of the invited, nor the Small Rossitza. The latter was a small, merry dark-eyed person. Michailina was my official friend and we openly hated each other. Sophy was a calm easy going, good-hearted natural blond. I had included her for her soft ordinary nature, as a neutralizer of the hostile energies we exchanged. Rummy was my closest friend and there was some envy between us, and the Big Rossie was the classmate we had sincere hate for.

We flew and had adventures journal, which we read in front of the class in the extra hours in reading on Fridays.

I think I've been pretty unbearable: I always guarded my perimeter of independency, and was always a book in front of the others – we used to read books then – books printed on paper, without pictures, with much text which in itself served as a stimulator of mind-pictures. The colourful images of our fantasy created realities that could not be held within the limitations of our daily routine. So we kept on reading. But at the same time I was pragmatic, did not believe in scary tales, had no fear of the dark. At least, not visibly.

Otherwise I had invented two scary tales of my own: the first one was about *The Witch on the Roof* who was in fact a triangular attic window, that turned in the night into a black figure with a thick headscarf, who watced our backyard from the roof of one of the houses on the back street. The second one was of the tiger in the fig branches that was caught in a net of Moonlight and was only waiting to get free.

So there were scary tales of my fantasy, but I never admitted I was afraid of them, for, after all they were all my creations, and I never admitted them to cross the border of my actual daily world.

In my green dreams there was never space for nightmares.

There were no hostile worlds in our dayly routines, that is, they were not open but nipped at our subconscious and intuitively achieved oversensitivity to adult people warring essences. For out parents had known different times and had no tolerance for different reality from the one they had been brought up in. It was like a sunlit pond which was deep and full of hostile creatures that fought for survival. There were competitions which turned into wars about what we knew and what we could do. But there was no fear on the surface. And Iwas not afraid.

In fact we were not let to know there were hostile worlds in the minds of people. I only guessed of their existence but I didn't understand them, for warring minds I saw as a huge waste of energy.

And perhaps that is the nature of the problem of hostile worlds – in their literal and metaphoric meanings. - a marked disparity of energies.

I am thankful for this text to Ju – my team-mate and co-founder of the worlds of tastes, smells and colours. She inspired me to dream again of our teen-age story of the space cruiser – a game of expansion of our tirst for adventures and of intuitive knowledge of the human-measure's singularity in the vast cosmos. The petty warring worlds, based on their daily disparity of the energies of life that are as vast as galaxies, and as tiny as particles of Sun dust.

Ju and I were co-authors of stories that relied on preserving the memories of the tastes of life, as genuine, as in the lifetime of a child of the generation before the time of the global Web, when children were natties, who could judge about truth and lie leaning on their sensual experience. There is a specific smell of a lie: a combination of fear and bitterness. The information reaches the mind as *nous*.

Nous. The faculty of the human mind to distinguish the true from the real

Nous or the faculty of the human mind to distinguish the true from the real. So much valued in dreamweaving. So much cherished by religion and science. So much cared for by professional PRs.

Dreamweavers ere bound to tell the truth. The common people thought they were naïve, even infantile, rulers tried to win them for the purpses of teaching the young minds of the social pyramid the principles of social control.

True teachers often suffered form the barrier of circumstances: physically, when they tried to avoid them and showed disobedience, and mentally, because constant fight exhausts the power of self-control and leads them into exiles of their societies, both respected, and ridiculed.

There are, of course, the practical signs of mock-realities, woven by fake-educators, who had been enforced, or insinuated /which is the same to the soul/ to maintain fake belief in stories and ideas used as keys to public control. They sometimes really believed they helped to avoid social hostilities ar cultural disturbances.

But a dreamweaver is bound to distinguish between a story and history-making, and often the truth has strange routes, before it adds to history as a small step of mindweaving in individual way in order to change history of a world.

> *This is no country for old men…*
> *Once out of nature I shall never take*
> *My bodily form from any natural thing,*
> *But such a form as Grecian goldsmiths make*
> *Of hammered gold and gold enamelling*
> *To keep a drowsy Emperor awake;*
> *Or set upon a golden bough to sing*
> *To lords and ladies of Byzantium*
> *Of what is past, or passing, or to come.*
> *Yeats, Sailing to Byzantium.*

The Lines of Life

Olya Ma

It was at the time of Mother Olya. We all used to call her Olya Ma. In the very beginning of the routs of emigration all over the earth.

While there still were many people around, and each of us stood still, stunned by the shock of the Change and dreamed to get out of the invisible Iron Walls of our world; scheming, discussing with our friends and families, like a pine forest whispering in the storm. Ithisses and whispers loudly, but it doesn't bend or fall because pines stand upright in groups uphill.

There were many friends who used to gather together and talk. Then the first wave of migrants travelled West, the pine forest was not dense any more and the winds of the storm took over the forest.

There were too many classes of English at university.

Everyone took retraining bachelor and master courses and those of us who had a previous MA training became kind of *gurus*.

– Why aren't you leaving? – other people often asked me or Angie, my husband.

– What are we going to do there? – We asked back and people stared at us as if we had just fallen from heaven.

They had special certificates in medicine, finance, engineering. We had graduated philosophy and naively thought all of them went abroad to take a job in their own kind of expertise.

They, on their part, had no illusions about what they were going to do there and must have wondered at our way of thinking, probably it was a manifestation of our unwillingness to work as cleaners or servants until our kids finished higher education and become what had only dreamed of. In their eyes we were lazy boys, who refused to become social climbers and start their lives anew.

So we continued teaching English and strategies of survival in a world we used to know only from books, and developed by deduction. They were good learners, the first wave of people who travelled abroad. They survived. Books contained useful tracks to practical wisdom.

– What can we do for you? The question came from a pleasant office administrator who came up with us to the fourth floor. There was a grey-haired man, with a sad expression on his face.

– You, that is the university has announced job listings. – I said.

– What job – the woman jumped? - It's crisis. We've hit the bottom.

– There are three positions for assistant professors of English – I explained.

– Aaaah. – She got me and politely directed me to the Staff Recruitting office, and advised me how to submit my papers for the current contests.

It was the beginning of the great migration. It was like a bare lane in the middle of the forest: there was time to sow and there was much work. I had to stay up late for a work day of 12 hours. I needed a room to rent for three nights weekly.

– I have found a place in the neighbourhood – a double bedroom – my colleague from Sofia said. – I need a room-mate.

– Good – I said, – but I sall stay for two or three nights weekly.

The first night we went to see the room. It was close at hand and that suited me for I was always tired. The host was a decent woman with two daughters who were both university undergraduates. It was a clean small apartment of a kichen and two bigger rooms, clean and neat and with a small rent.

My colleague, Albena, took up one of the beds, and I hurried to catch the night coach back to my boys at home. I promised to come and stay the following week with my nightgown, tooth paste, slippers and half of the rent money.

– I left Olya's place – Albena met me on the following Monday morning with this instead of saying "Hello". – It's unbearable. Brothel! They have visitors all the time. Smoking. Laughing loudly. They gather every single night – she spit the words with rage.

Wow! I Thought. *How come?*

I watched Albena closely. She looked frustrated, her hands were shaking with rage, sees danger everywhere. Paranoya and depression.

– OK, – I said, trying to sooth her down. – I'll go and see. I promised to go again. You are free to follow your own way. Nothing personal.

– I know about Albena – I said immediately when Olya answered the bell and stood in the doorway all dark and puzzled about what she was going to expect off me. – I don't want to move out, but I cannot afford to pay you for the whole month.

The woman stood there ahd stared at me with huge and heavy eyes.

– Stay, then. – She said. – Pay or no pay, come in. I'll take as much as you give me and when you give me it. I gave her a little smile and half of the rent for the current month. She made way for me to enter the narrow corridor. She was silent and strangely calm. I didn't know then about scandals and painful words, like a "brothel", for example. I was still learning.

I got the nylon bag with my slippers and hurriedly fell on the bed, exhausted. There was a big bookcase at the opposite wall and some flowerpots on the windowsill behind my head. It smelled like home.

I heard the girls come back and started preparing a dinner. Then the doorbell rang, a woman's voice saluted and began a friendly chat.

Olya tapped on the door.

– We'll be having a dinner. – Olya invited me. – Come and sit up with us in the dining-room. It's not that great meal, but we all are friends and you'll make yoyrself at home.

I went. I was interested in human things. So, that was the "brothel". Olya Ma, the girls, a couple of young women who lived upstairs and worked for the Municipality hall or at the two universities in the town – the SouthWest and the American. Only women. I joined the group. How do people live here on a monthly pay? Easy. They gather together in the evening to share a dinner. Two thirds of their pay are spent on cigarettes. They don't waste money on expensive things, and manage. Intelligent people with humanitarian professions. They saw no future outside. They stayed on and kept their hommespace. And planned weddings and having kids of their own. Here.

And then the ill winds of a hostile world brought cancer and Oly Ma got it, or it got her. She fought with it for two years before she departed. We saw her off to a land from where there was no return.

After that Natasha and her whole family emigrated to Seattle – her husband and their two sons. One way ticket. They had applied for nearly the same kind of jobs they had here.

Then Anastasiya married in Paris and took her son with her.

We stayed on. The thick heads. We saw them in whenever they came back – each next time for a shorter visit. This is not their home any longer. Their souls hurt. They keep speaking about their new worlds. We stay silent and listen to their individual stories, trying to feel empathy with their new environment. They sound foreign – bothways – here and there. We don't feel happy. We keep silent and continue to visualize the pictures of their new homes. They boast on their new worlds. We know it is a kind of protection that keeps nostalgia away. We nod at times and tell a word of approval or ask silly questions, so that they can feel lucky. Then we go to our homes in the dark night and we even do not gossip behind their backs. We talk about our problems. Some ties we get a return ticket There and Back to check how things go, and we get back. This is a lost generation – out of their roots and off their routes. And see people off. Lately we started to see some of them in. They are like high and low tidal waves – the waves of emigrants are still very high, and the waves of those who come back home are low and soft. The movement of our people out and in had calmed down. Skype is on, next came the e-mail, Facebook chats there are the global web and local nets. We meet virtually and talk. There is space for all of us in the web. It is sufficient. Somehow. Off our roots. Fed up with being underfed. With the substances of our existence at home.

„A Snake's Curse" or the Load of Guilt

It was 1961.

He was sitting on the porch of the old family house and was watching his youngest brother's wife crossing the yard with a big pot of stew for his lunch. It was around noon and she carried some fresh food to him. She cooked delicious meals and always brought him a large portion and freshly baked bread. She thought him as the rest of them, a quiet crazy guy, but she treated him nicely. She didn't care if you were a crazy-bird, a gypsy, an enemy or a friend – if you were a human being, she treated you like one and her kindness and self-control were just what he needed. She had been taught to have respect for the elders in the family: big brother Risto, she called him.

The others avoided him… soe saliva streamed down his cheek from the corner of his stiff lips. He wiped it with his handkerchief. It was wet. That he could not control. It came instead of tears, because he couldn't weep any more.

He was a lawyer previously. His books of law were put in big crates and placed in the attic of the new house. He was not able to read them now. He felt human law must not be like that.

Before that he was an active officer in the king's Army. He was in the Army. Not him. Vladimir, his elder brother was. In action. Killed in action. Killed, because he had refused to take part in the action. Shot because he had refused to shoot his mates… He had witnessed it. He couldn't remember where his uniform was. He had torn at it with his hands, shouting to put it on fire. It was strange whether they had burnt it. He had not seen any traces of it ever since his brother was shot down. The pain felt like burning into a fire.

–   Where is my uniform? – He asked once.
–   It's not here. – The woman answered. – I have put it away myself.
    It's not here. Don't worry.

That meant he was't to worry about it any more, she had taken care of it. He felt strangely relieved.

He ate his food and washed the pot at the tap, then walked back and sat down on the porch to think, or rather to stop himself from thinking. He was trying to put his thoughts in order. For twenty years now.

They gave him to keep the infant girl: she had adislocated foot and was in plaster. It was heavy and she wept. He used to push her cradle and talk to her.

The child usually stopped weeping while he taked. As if she instinctively felt his pain was greater than hers. She followed him with her broad black eyes with rich lashes and listened to him carefully. He told her everything as it was. Sometimes he wondered whether she could remember his story in time. If she remembered, she would surely understand. So he shared all of it with the baby. She had the eyes of his departed sister, the teacher.

He could see no way out of his mindpicture. The others from his family and mates continued to live together – the good ones and the bad ones, the evil-minded and the blessed. He didn't belong to either side. He hadn't helped the bad guys, neither had he helped the good guys.

When the wheel of time had turned round and the good ones became evil, and, respectively, the bad ones turned good, he had kept on the distance from either side. He had only watched their pathetic attempts to re-paint. His mind time slowed down. The change of the places of evil and good was happening too soon for him to choose a side. His soul went apiece and could not be assembled, only his individual Self remained intact – that part of his mind which was only his possession. A big empty space opened in his head, he could use it as a speedway to the bigger world where the human aches had but little significance.

He went into the habit of wondering all by himself among the soft hills of quiet and darkness and watched the light of distant stars.

When he got back to daylight, he replayed the pictures of his memory. That hurt. He still had some soul left and burned with the pain of hell-fire. And he escaped again and again into the soft dark Kosmos of rare worlds and pains of life.

One day he discovered the highway to Galaxy, stepped on it and moved forward. He never returned home. What remained was simply a dead man's body, washed and layed into a wooden chest, packed in a white sheet and covered with flowers.

People are traditionally seen off with bunches and wreaths of flowers. In the floral aspect of the global intelligent life, the plants let out scents and colours that were like the words for the people but of a wider sense because they served the other kinds of life. People learned how to use them to replace words when they were unable to express their full meaning and express it simultaneously, while flowers and green leaves can do that perfectly.

So, on the white cover of our dead man's coffin there were fresh flowers from the neighbouring gardens, sweet scented and colourful, full of life, meaning life outside death. Simple and common, picked in the morning, watered and cared for with love, little souls, born in the young summer sun, warm and tender.

We cannot judge what was next, but we dare suppose that the remains of the soul, hovering about the dead body, took the message as a wish of easy route, beamed and hurried to catch up with the Self to move on together. The Universal scales that measured the right and the wrong became even, accounts paid off, and the harmony of life and death – recovered. The individual was free from the load of decision. The mourners felt the wings of forgiveness.

——•—

Uncle Vassil stood beside the coffin and looked at the calm face of the dead body that looked relieved and quiet. He was thinking:

– He is free at last. Nothing weighs on his conscience. He was like me – we only watched. What else could we do? He got rid of it all at last. No pain.

All the people from the neighbourhood had gathered in the yard of the smaller new house. The Grannies came in and out buzzing like bees around the hive and carried big metal trays with stuffed red peppers, that smelled differently, and big porcelain cups full of ritual fat mutton soup.

Lyube and his brother, Stoyan were at the cauldron with two or three younger men. Cooking for weddings and celebrations, as wel, for funerals was men's business. Women were afraid to stand near those two men. They were noisy and drunk as ever, and and had sharp knives that were of nearly an arm's length. Their families had fear of them, not just respect, for they were easy to enrage, like bulls. Yet, Tonko was talking with them while he caressed the children on their heads. He spoke softly. He had never beaten his wife and the kids. And he never went to the bub and make fights like Lyube and Stoyan. But he was not a good man: he was blue in the face and he never looked people in the eyes as if he was eaten by a bad fever.

Six men lifted the chest and carried it all the way up to the protestant church.

On the way yhey met the Major. He was not active now, but he stayed still and took his hat off.

But he watched the procession with anger. He didn't like those protestants. They didn't leave their faith and their church. He didn't like traditional Orthodox religion either. But these stubbornly demonstrated they were blessed to distinguish the right from the wrong. The Orthodox were no shy pansies, but they often got drunk and could forget and forgive the pains caused to them by the others. But these never drank, never put up fights, and never forgot. He was an officer of the Red Army, and all of these were not his mates, yet he preferred the fearsome wild vagabonds like Lybe, or the soft dark servile snails like Tonko.

He wondered if Hristo had shared with his family. He was crazy and kept quiet, but his younger brother's infant granddaughter looked at the major heavilywhenever she passed along him on the broad street. Or he might have imagined it. She had the hot eyes of Nikolina, the teacher, the eldest sister in the family, who had died of pneumonia.

He stole to Tonko and gazed at him carefully: his eyes were black and wet, as ever, but his mouth had unhealthy blue colour, while the skin of his face because of which they called him Tonko the Gypsy, was yellow.

He wouldn't last long. He seemed to be 30 or 35 or even less. His wife was thin and dry, but his children were young. He nust have been 18 or 19 that winter of 1944 when Vlado was killed as a traitor, and Hristo got mad. They all had been in it. Some could go on living, and others could not. All of them were burning with pain, whatever church they went to or not. The scar of the sin.

They had beaten him to death a few times, the gang of the boys from the upper end of the village. Hristo had fetched from Sofia his sister, the teacher. He had saved him from the hangsters. The Major then wasn't a

Major yet: he used to go to the district center and had been employed by some layers as a bodyguard. He was married and his wife was pregnant so he minded not to beat her too heavily, when he got back drunken and she started complaining. He had a flame for the teacher, but Hristo did not let him go near her. She was clever and too sensitive. She caught the pneumonia the next winter, she had only just recovered when she had a visit from a friend in the district hospital; got out bare-footed and the sickness had repeated her, that time, lethally.

Hristo then returned to Sofia, and his brother, the army officer, had committed a suicide. So the rumour went… Immediately after… THAT… So they said, but some other rumoured that he was shot as a traitor. Riste had mixed memories.

Their family couldn't accept hostility. Their father had gone to fetch his younger sister Vella who had just graduated high school. She had wanted to study law, but the old man wouldn't hear of it: *"I had two higher educated sons dead. This high school is enough for you."* Vella had consented, although she was strong headed, not soft like her brothers and tender like her sister.

In the autumn of 1943 an order signed by the PM had been received to clear the Eledjick from red revolutionaries and the whole jandarmerie had risen from Pazardzhik, the district center down beside the Maritsa, and the military corpus from Ihtiman, up in the beginning of Sofia valley. They sircled the whole Western part of the Mid-Balkan, or Sredna Gora as it was called there. Many young people were killed.

They had fetched the young policemen from the village to dig a common grave for the killed. Vladimir, Hristo's brother was summoned as a king's officer to monitor how that task was done. Tonko was there, too… The men came back drunken and furious. No one dared ask anything, no one dared tease Tonko any more. Vlade had returned to his father's home very quiet and very dark. He had reached the wooden gate, banged the door closed and it had gaped open again, and then he had gone mad. His younger brothers rushed to hold him. He threw his sword first, then he had torn down his uniform, shouting to burn it. Hristo had taken them away but he missed the revolver. After a couple of days Vlade had taken it out and shot himself. Stoyan had stood in the middle of the street and had seen something. All the neighbours had heard the shouts.

Hristo had never recovered after his brother's death. He had returned to Sofia to his lawyer's office and had witnessed the murder of a few officers from the army. He was having nightmares that he had been in his brother's place, and his story became confused and sounded quite insane. The truth was Vlade killed himself with his own revolver.

Tonko had shared years after that in a drinking company how they buried 16 young and handsome men, trumpled over the place, and then got dead drunk and danced over the blood-stained snow. „Wild wolves and boars had run away to hide, not a raven was to be seen!", Tonko said then and went silent. He never mentioned That again. It was burning inside him, eating him out for his mouth was tightly shut.

Hristo was gradually changing: losing interest in life. He got back to Sofia and stayed there for a couple of years. The major had heard he had imagined he was Vladeh. He remembered That, and wept like a child. There were his schoolmates from their green years. They had used to go fishing together. Old friends, who had stood on both sides of the river of time. He couldn't help them – only stood and watched how they were killed like wild beasts. One of the other officers made a sign at Tonko and they caught him by the arms and took him away saving him from a foolish action. And then he was killed. A suicide they said. Riste mixed his memories here. But he was not caught by a suicidal mania. Nor Riste, although he had omitted to hide his revolver. The major showed duly respect, although he was an enemy of the departed. They had grown up together. They were connected somehow.

It was 1951.

And then time changed and the good and the evil changed places. The World turned upside down and left many people out. They couldn't find their roots along the foreign routes and they became strangers whether they returned or not.

And there was again a period of clearing the unadaptable . Risto was left alone, he was useless to both sides. They took the sons of another part of the village and their families away in covered vans. Each night their mothers strained to hear a voice in the darkness. Darknes was empty of sounds. Silence was full of fear.

One night two covered vans drove quietly through the village and off across the Topolnitsa, the stream with the poplar trees. They drove down the soft country road winding across the otchards and the vinyards straight to the Dearlove valley where secret lovers met.

The rest of the village heard the vans pass in the small of the night and felt their hair rise with the precautions of evil. For their relatives had been suddenly obsessed with hostility, and ready to obey thr orders of crazy mins.

Two or three only stood ad their porches in the darkness listening into the direction of the quiet trucks. From the high place where the protestant graveyard was, it could be seen how the machines were descending the steep road towards the Haresford of the and cross it. There was no shooting. The dark morrow was silent.

- Tell me, my boy, where had they driven them to? – Geno, the of their only male of their family, who was left alone, heard his aunt's hot whisper in his ear. – He was well-known sneaking coward who was left to stay.

- To the Dearlove valley, auntie.

- Let's go and see…

- Don't, say it, auntie… not now…. It's dangerous… tomorrow when they they'd gone away. They might have left sentenaries…

- Have you seen them? – In the meanwhile the mother of Jivko, had stolen into the yard, followed by grndfther Vassil.

- Genne had seen them driving towards Dearlove valley beside the Topolnitsa,

- Quiet – Vassil hissed. – They are coming back.

They stood still close to the holes in the wooden gate and listened the two trucks driving past and speeding up the way to the district center.

- Let's go – Minka, the aunt of Geno, insisted.

- Not now – Vassil stopped her. – Tomorrow. – Well, Geno has a meadow in the lowlands on the other side of the river. \he might take his cow out and pretend he had been following it, if somebody sees him. The most they could do is to beat him, you have joined the young workers league, haven't you?

They had made him mix with the new political partisans. His family elde members. They couldn't do it. They wouldn'put up with the humiliation of constant fear.They knew sudden and terrible painful death was waiting for them unles they stood low. They wouldn't forgive. They silently waited for their next turn to come and did not shout the new slogans.

Stunned with the humiliation, scared to death, the elders of the families which had once made the village, were living through the unbelievable nightmare that had turned the stories of their life upside down and had thrown them to the beasts of the night into the mud and dust of the bare land. Their enemies were once born within the larger borders of the family – their relatives, close neighbours, mates, people they had grown up with, who had been eaten by jealousy and had branched away from the clan. Hostility had thrived, fed by cruelty and division of interests.

There were others, strangers, newcomers, foreign and cruel, who had begged for and were given shelter. They had cynical minds: why should my children obey you. They wanted to rule through their next generation, although they had no skill to teach them to. They only wanted to take the control of the village affairs without any special training, without effort and hard toil. And they killed the children of the old families, and threw them to the dogs.

How much hate could they cultivate in their children, whom they had brought up with the wish to take up the places of their mates? Kids grew up in atmosphere of rivalry and jealousy? They had taken the same model of behavior and the desire to be like them. For they could not self-improve.

They were drinking: the governors took care to supply sufficient and steady amounts of brandy. Drunken, they were easily controlled by hostile strangers.

They were given dense, strong wine: that made their heads dizzy and their fists bulging. And erased mercy.

Their wives kept their mouths shut because home violence had currently stopped. Their men came back drunken, fell asleep, got up and went away, carrying their fury away.

Sometimes they didn't return home for days and weeks. Their children hated the children of the others, for fear feeds hatred. They did not know why, but violence had ceased suddenly for them, and home humiliation. Malevolence was transferred from fathers to sons. Fear and hostility were grown into the girls by their suffering mothers. Like snake's curse.

An iron wall divided people. Invisible but indestructible.

Foreigners came to rule.

They had gone crazy with the coing of the spring. And were used to chase everyone who happened to stand in their way. Eeryone with whom they had deals to settle.

They waited for the next turn of the weel of history. Iron is not an element of the Earth. It rusted. With blood, tears and lies. They waited. Lies proved hard to get out of. Lies created fake words, for they were the means to justify their deeds.

On the other day Geno Denov took out his cow to pasture. It took him the whole morning to watch secretly for gauards and pretend the cow had been leading the way to his meadow near the Dearlove gully.

There was not a living soul to be seen in the large vinyards near the river: not a stork, nor a hawk,nor a hare, not even a snake.

There was a freshly dug flat field just beside Dearlove gully.

Geno Denov went closer to it through the shrubbery. The whole field was dug, the soil looked as if it was moving.

The guards had hit them with the spades and had hurriedly shoved them into the grave: half-dead, stifled, fighting for air. Has there someone still living? The earth wriggled but held them tightly.

Geno had quickly got back and closed into his house. He kept silent. For years on end he didn't speak out. Keeping inside records of what he had seen.

Mothers wanted revenge. The mothers on both sides of the Iron Wall begged for revenge but the Christian God had no ear of prayers for revenge. Their children were brought up separated by hate and they never knew its source was the fear of death. And hate hurt and fed only further hate. Hostility thrived on both sides of the Iron Wall.

Time passed and caught both sides in the dayly tasks of bringing up their next generations.

All of them wanted revenge, Even when they did not admit their secret desires. And they waited for the wind of change to turn over the wheel of history. They waited until their worlds turned upside down. But their thoughts of revenge were blown as ashes, and turned into thin air.

It was 1991.

The village's actual population had shrunlk in number. The people had emigrated towards the big towns, or across the borders in search of work. The children who were brought up unhappy with the vague hostility burning in them, had spilled like beans to find a better soil to grow and their own children no longer had their aches and did not understand them. That was altogether good. Sometimes someone returned for a while and left again. Ther people came to live in the village.

The old grannies at the church were talking about the survivors from the horrible time.

Tonko was obsessed for weeks – he had froth round his mouth while speaking with invisible people. One day he went out and walked down the main street that crossed the village, to the end, and then he strolled back slowly. Whenever he met someone, he stopped them and begged forgiveness out of them. On the following day the churche's bell noted his death.

The Major started his walk right after Tonk's funeral. He did not know how to beg forgiveness. He admitted that:

– I cannot beg for mercy, – he said, – I have not been brought up in faith – please, pray for me. – His old wife said he had been talking with invisible visitors, all night. He died shortly after Tonko.

Shortly after the Major's death Jordanna from the last house of the upper end, returned home from Plovdiv where she had spent the winter with her son's family.

On Sunday she went to see her friends who were chatting on the bench in front of the church.

– Old Geno Denin was at home yesterday. He told me about the Dearlove gully.

...When he saw how the soil moved, Geno forgot about his fear and ran to see if he could find someone alive and help them out. He had no spade and they were deeply buried. His cow was on the pasture near the river where he had left it, but now it had followed him. The beast reached the end of the field where he was kneeling and digging with his bare hands into the grave.

> — *And then, sister Jordanna, Geno said, — the cow rose to its hind legs, and started wailing like a woman.*

The old wives whispered this tale in the church, and then they spread it among their younger relatives who had survived. They lived through their own hells of pain but it was the reaction of the cow that they had dared to share and feel shame of their own humiliation. Their sons and daughters were killed silently, as if nothing had happened, and they had stood low and kept silent, transferring their load of conscience to the children, teaching them how to survive.

There is a long chain of Dear-darling descenders tramping through history since time immemorial, who took in their hands the solution of generation purge directly, by erasing them without mercy. Raw and primitive minds entering social relations of hierarchy, based on servility and fear, they acknowledged only two stairs, closest to the mud. The others stood above them and walled the divided hostile groups of people in place and in time, but not in their human beasts' essence.

Its beginnings lied centuries away, and the chain of people became weaker, but the earth was full of bones. There were — malevolent crcraters, desolate ravines and field wastes, where two-metre wide, thick snakes lived.

The scenery went wild and turned into wasteland, the forests became thinner and the wavy hills rustled, the breeze hissed through the dry grass and the thorny bushes.

The old houses screeched with age in the winter time and rarely sheltered some creature, because there was n food in them.

Somewhere in this world memories hovered and gave food to dreams and longings.

The same small mannikins suddenly became clerks serving history and hatred spread around them like dust – dust into dust and ashes to ashes. The deserted land grew its flora and fauna after its own fashion, different from the people.

Only the shadows of its lost and missing generations wandered at night and guarded the gaps of time. They saved it for their punished children who roamed the routes and never reached their roots. Homeless and with sealed souls and tongues, made silent and closed in the shopwindows of old rivalry and malice. Strangers in their country of origin, foreign to the other land, they had fled for fear. Promised and unattainable.

Unforgiven and finding comfort in dreams of forgiveness. Forgetting the worlds of hostility.

Dreaming about The Promised Land.

- They shall beg forgiveness of you, too. – My Mum had said once, when we had improved our relations for a short spell. – You shall not give it to them.

My Mummy usually treated me as a traitor and a shame to the family. Sometimes, though, in minutes of relief from the pain that had nipped in her for years, she looked at me with her other eyes I wished so much to be good for my Mum, that I was prepared to listen patiently to her most absurd theories and tales of hate. No to contradict, although I didn't hate anyone.

<hr>

Instead of saying my thoughts and questions, aloud, I simply asked:

- Have they begged forgiveness of you, too? – I asked out of pure curiosity.
- They have – my Mother emphasized with some grave fury. Then she repeated: – there were first,Velichko of the Magyars, and Lyuben, the Honey Collector. They came to me last summer. As if they had felt the coming of death. They were walking as if in a trance round the village and stopped everybody they had terrorized. The whole face of Velichko was dark blue, and the Honey Collector had gone yellow and was trembling of dread all over.
- Why "dread"?
- Don't be such a fool! – My Mother exclaimed angrily. – They were afraid to die unforgiven. They moved like shadows.
- And you? – I asked, but she didn't get me right and thought I was asking her to continue her story.

 – *God is to forgive you.* That was what I said to them. And they didn't dare raise up their eyes and look at me for a second time.

We remained silent for some time. The vast vineyard, spreading in front of us. We had come to inspect how my mother's people had cut it. We had parked the car at some flat turn of the road, so that I could male a turn back. The road was dry and there was not much dust. It was still a very young spring and the air felt wintry. The thorny bluberry bushes in the ravine were dark grey and looked desperate.

My Mother caught my glance.

 – Last Autumn – she said, – After we picked all the grapes, someone set fire to those dry thorns. There was a huge snake that ran away. They couldn't kill it.

I was thinking of an old superstition: the snakes were guardians and shouldn't be driven out of the place they guard because they lifted their spells of defence and the human heirs never returned back home. I didn't say it aloud.

 – You shall not let them have a touch of forgiveness. They are so guilty, that they wouldn't hezutate to erase us and any memory of their guilt…
 – God remembers.
 – Don't't tell me about that: You don't believe in God – My mother's eyes flashed at me.

„*But do you really have faith in god? If you do, why then you seek for punishment through me?*", I thought silently and urged her to get into the car:

 – There is a big cloud up, coming with the wind. If it rains, the car can't get out of the mud.

We made for the car and managed to get out of the dusty road before the storm.

But I remember the happy expression on my mother's face at the sight of the well-trimmed vineyard with green bulbs, wakened by the spring. Now it was all hers. She had succeeded to get back the real place with the old vines her grandfathers had planted.

— • —

Lyuben was very weak. Vesko, his son, had come to visit him.

— I won't survive through this summer – Lyuben said in a tiny voice.

He had gone yellow and was trembling all over, as if he had a fever.
Vesko bent his head. He couldn't sooth his father uttering words of no sense and false compassion.
Lyuben needed no compassion, though. He knew how things worked.

— I dream about them often – he said in his weakened voice. – They visit me every night riding the dreadful nightmare that leaves me awake two or three times a night. Blood stained corpses with undefinable smashed faces raise from the snow in the pit and we have to hit them again and again until they are dead. They rise again and grin, giving me the shiver of our childhood memories for we had grown up together once. They rise and walk towards us and stretch out their hands trying to seize us by the necks. You call them zombies today, but zombies are unreal, and those who we murdered then were true. They come up on me with their true names and faces. They know me and seek revenge.

He shut up and stared into the empty space behind Vesko's back, his eyes bulging with horror. His pupils were large and pale and the whites were full of bloodshot veins.
Vesko was looking at him with large dark eyes.

— I don't know those people – he said. – I don't hate them. They had done nothing wrong to us, why shall I chase them like enemies.

The old man started coughing with fury.

— That is why. They shouldn't be. While one of them exists, they'll be dangerous for us. How dare you say you don't hate them? You ought to hate them! They shall rise their bloody shadows from the grave and erase you until you are only dust.

His strength had gone and he lay down on the bed. Vesko gave him a double dose of sedative.

He did not speak aloud so that he did not enrage the dying old man, but he thought:

„*It is not me to seek vengeance of your victims and pursue the people deprived by your gang of their homes and lands. Don't ask me to take on the load of your crimes. You didn't ask me when you murdered our mates. Don't transfer responsibility to me. You killed my mother, when she dared say a word to you, begging you to have mercy for the people living in the neighbourhood.*"
He had overheard their last browl. His father had come home drunk and wild, and he started hitting his mother on the head with his revolver, ordering her to shut up. And she was bleeding and staggered, and shouted with pain. Until she was silent.

Vesko's sisters had left his father's house long ago: one was married to a medical doctor in Haskovo which was more 600 kilometers away, and the other one went to live in Rome, in Italy. Now he was planning to sell the house and depart to England. The old bastard was not right and he was not to stand in their way any more. He was to beg for mercy. What were these twisted habits of their gang of killers?

He raised his eyes. His father was lying very stil, his eyes wide open and whisper something that sounded like a prayer, but the words did not coe out clear because his lue lips were paralised and did not move. Vesko bent down to hear what his father repeated:

— ... *and forgyf us ure gyltas, swa swa we forgyfað urum gyltendum...* — and the dying man did not finish the prayer but repeated it again and again: *and forgive us our mistakes...*

An actual human expects the moral law to work as God. Moral laws are as huge as the Universe. When the body dies, the human soul is left to the snake's mercy, which is cold and hollow. And the human weighs like an elephant swollen by the boa. Nothing could be done after that: the big snake has a heavy load that looks like a hat seen on the outside, like a drawing by a Little Prince. Sin is a heavy load and it hurts like heavy metal elephant in the stomach of a snake. Snakes don't chew. If they eat a tin elephant, it feels heavy in the stomach of the snake.

Destines & Destinations.

Our people have saved the memory of vital deadlock. You either accept the religion of the invaders, or off you go to the scaffold and get beheaded.

When the culmination of bloody repressions came in the mid-20th century, their children hit the routes round the Globe without minding the distance from home. Their only idea was the greater the distance, the greater the feeling of freedom from hostilities, from the dejavu and the sense of being possessed.

There are small country churches, where the logs, polished by the blood of the cut off heads are saved. They look almost black and the thick blood cover has kept them for centuries.

The blood holds them.

Thereare marble reservoirs where the skulls of the burnt children and females are hept when the church was set to fire. There are still churches, half-buried in the earth for they should not raise above the agressors' Homes of God. There are secret graves where in the darkness of the night the tortured youth offsprings of the best roots of the Balkans were buried without any sign, for the hostile wanted the memory of them erased.

The survivors who had migrated far away still keep the their infant memory and cannot forgive cruelty and fallacy. They have not yet recovered from the shock of been repressed to shut up.

Seeing Off

That was one of the parallel realities when the world was turning upside down and the weak, the criminals, the curious and the narrow specialists who had only one practical skill, and saw no future at a small place, started to emigrate.

They needed someone to teach them how to be human, and how to make their own personal spaces there, they had been planning to live on, because a rolling rock catches no moss. They needed someone to teach them how to defend and master further the skill they had, and how to make themselves respectful and unique. They needed world languages that could set their own stories to create. The skill of language usage to secure their next generation – the base of the mother tongue, that had been lost when people tried to reach God.

Sometimes exhaustion of the novel turn of histories took us up and we let weakness overcome.

Before I started practicing seeing off, I had to give them the blessing of someone who would stay on to see them in whenever they returned, to listen to their stories of success and save their home to them in dreamweaving by word of mouth in their mother tongue. The first wave of migration when the borders were open, was of the strongest quality. We saw off first the best among us, who could adapt themselves and set their roots to a foreign soil.

That involved training of future emigrants how to write their personal essay, so that they could get a job on an oil platform in the North Sea, how to make a good baby-sitter, how to survive in times of misfortune in a foreign land, how to help the other people and make themselves popular and needed.

Seeing off is not an easy job. A teacher had to know everything and master up all kinds of skills. One had to learn fast useful facts flife, and practices of far off communities, and be able to gibe useful advice based on good reasoning and positive attitude, tolerating all kinds of human errors. There was no time to waste.

We had to learn what and how to teach fast and efficiently We needed new methods of teaching and I created methodologies and methods on the fly. Then altered them and changed their scope until tgey fitted a singular self-identification. I made my own school. I kept on dreamweaving and adapting them to each singular case. There was no time to take part in discussion groups, commissions, councils or any other kind of education forums with complicated titles and confused policies. I worked for twelve hours a day, 7 days of the week. I included my own children in the process. No one admitted this. On the contrary, I was independent and inconvenient.

Seeing off exhausts the heart – it sucks all your positive energy, it uses all your blood.

Then I followed the routes of my earliest students, too see and check how they managed. They had found their spaces. It was difficult for them, but they had success and were satisfied.

I was still strong then, and I could return every time. I wanted to tell the stories of my reasons to return home. Now I am strong again for I have covered the second level of my own school. Now I am aware of it but there had been moments that I had not noticed and had omitted to record as memes of words.

Such moments hurt but I didn't mind because my kids from the school needed me to get them ready for their routes. Probably they still need me, but they are settled all over the world and have their own private realities, whwre I have not been yet and can only guess about. Their present possessions of spaces and time to weave up.

It's not an easy job to see young people off. Every time you tire more and more. It is the second stage of reasons why you are back. Because they have not become wiser or stronger, because they are still afraid and need you to dreamweave for them and so fight the fear of darkness and chaos.

They don't need the stories of shrinking back inside your loneliness and mysery. They do not need the stories of despair and suicide. What they need is how to get out in the sun and stretch their hands to reach the stars. And take them. It is not difficult to dreamweve ahead of time. It only exhausts all your energy and when your blood is off, you just need to stop and look around yourself, and do not let the cold to overtake. That's the point when you must learn to see people in.

But this is still to be. When all accounts are settled and loans are repaid. When you are forgiven and you have forgiven injustice. When you are no longer to be yourself or tell the things that you know and do the things that you can do.

How is a small human particle to distinguish the right from wrong and the light from the dark, unless one keeps the records in the memes of one's genes?

A Second Try

The year was 2014

The year 1959 was the end f our world. And it is the year of my birth. Submarines of hostile forces secretly chased each other under the ice cover of the North Polece, while the world of the human race adapted itself to the idea of a global dichothomy in two warring camps, artificially constructed after the period of the Great Wars of the 20ᵗʰ century.

People had lost faith that the old Earth would exist by the middle of the millennium, although the Great Projects of the East took place then.

We were the same at home and believed we would survive somehow with the help of the AI, if ultimate control was taken by machines whose intellect was made up of teams of the brightest natural brains of humanity.

The individual was losing its value. We lived under a Dome of vague information, but we sensed the hostility, growing in people, who were deprived of the fruit of their toil by the new political figures. New policies turned to reality-weaving but they lacked the essential skills of natural dreamweavers.

It was the end of the millennium that had contained the devastating wars, which in turn had led policy-makers to expect the end of the world, because they had not the khowledge nor the wish to make the effort to lead to a solution of the crisis.

Tired of caring for their own weldoing, people, overloaded with governing and communication tasks, thought that being empowered with socil control and the possession of money were sufficient in their search of harmony. They forgot about their children, aabout their homes and about the Guardians of the universal harmony. They sold their children, abandoned their homes and migrated the globe over with the hope of meeting themselves in the foreign world and stopping the heart-ache from eating their souls.

The Guardians got angry, went away and left behind unknown diseases of sin. They created programs like the M-dimensions of parallel worlds, which never touch each other. They also created programs like the controlling witches, who could go in and out of the doors. That was a try of correcting what could be considered as undeserved cruelty, but it was only an intention which never became practice. Guardians needed no excuses.

Next drones were created with different forms, and bags with memory, which made big fuss if you had forgotten your keys, or shrunk in size if you had taken your umbrella out. They could send messages to their countryside cottages to light the open fire and it was warm when they reached the house, but it was empty, all the same. They created T-shirts that kept record of any trace of home and pub-violence, because they did not get rid of the dimension where the weaker were tortured. What is more, they estabilished a style of life, which followed the tradition to kill a woman who tried to be independent with stones. They made a rule by which women were the weak – weaker than men, who could control them.

But this is a fallacy.

The spaces of sin are our individual belonging.

All these are dreams, however. Dreams-realities, dreams-nightmares, dreams that wove up corrections of actual lifestories.

In the last type of dreams one pledges forgiveness. An individual person can mix realities. How long can a dream last: less than a minute, a couple of seconds? But the sin is a sin: adultery, robbery, murder. And the sin weighs heavy as a possession, it creates the realities of the parallel worlds like the cirkles of a stone on the surface of still water. They are like the attempts to get free from the heavy load of the moral law inside the individual.

It creates gods and God's chosen ones. Tey are not existent. Gods are the funche result of the power of imagination, pain, emptiness, and rage. A single person wishes to have great projections like constellations. The particle of humanity wishes to have abilities.

That is the cause for the telling of tales. In tales everything is more distant, larger, and picturesque. One does not want to die and one finds endless life in dreamweaving.

The truth is crystal clear. The crystal grid of the planet Earth is wearing out and cannot hold the ambitious dreams of the fast-growing human population. Gaps appear, that cannot be stopped, because a single moment cannot be stretched without limits.

One's Self, after all, is composed of all the worlds rooted in one's beginnings, and is defined as individual by one's name. All the suffered loves, thefts, swindles, and murders, and caused suffering to other lives, are concentrated snd finalized around the moral code of the individual.

Only that matters. Stars aree too distant, and too big for our single body measures. But they are fitted into the mental measure of values. Matter's sufferings are often turned into signifiers of mind's measure, symbols that need specific qualities to read, and expertise is acquired in our movements through the worlds of both flesh and mind, and are kept in empathy, telepathy and the ability of dreamweaving.

One always makes attempts to discover one's beginnings. When one has caused much suffering to other people, one suffers the lack of their forgiveness. Unforgiven, the individual mind falls into the gap of parallel mental worlds, and the desired replaces the world for that mind. All this is our individual possession. When one becomes aware of one's beginnings, or possession, or heritage, then it is easy to return home to the individual Self. Life is a single event, and it is a function of the physical, body, wnd the individual mind.

Awareness is acquired gradually, and is the core of simplicity and easier living, that is measured in centuries, and millennia, or even by the standards of infinite categories of aeons, eternity, now, once upon a time, cosmos, and god. The simpler life is, the simpler the existence of in the mind is, the longer life is.

And all the nanoseconds of eternity suffice, when you travel through worlds in dreamweaving.

Everything else is but a dream, because one cannot stretch outside one's time possession. The body wears out, the organs can be replaced, but then a body ceases being its own self, because of the sensual memory. There can be no replacement of the functioning brain, nor of the moral law inbuilt in us genetically. Mercy makes one human together with cruelty, which is contained in the reasons of the self for the control of the fate of the individuals, dependant on us – all are in our possession.

My friend Vicky says: „*money is only money and never suffice, but when one favours someone else, they hope this favour to be valued somehow, probably ...*"

The Sun's Barrier

The sunlight does not let us watch the stars in the day. The sun fills all our summer in the Balkans, and we can see only the droplets of tears in our eyelashes, or the evaporating moist of our retinae. And the clouds that float in the breeze. We cannot see the stars, nor the satellites, nor the waste, just we can watch the white plane traces and hear the noise of the passing planes.

This is the Sun's Barrier because the Sun fights so the possibility of courting the Earth by other magnetic fields. It needs to be the only One, and places us on the surface under the shade of the dome it creates.

When the Earth turns, She shades the Sun an there we can watch the stars, and the satelites, and the rubbish, and feel the magnetic streams of the universe. Then we begin to dream, and we compete in our dreams, spreading our differences in the whole universe, giving it the human measure of good and of evil, and our ideas of control and even, our souls. Thus symbols are created as the signs of our own insignificance. the signs of our own insignificance.

The steps on the surface of Mars

It is again a metaphor created by story tellers. As it is, some following generation of young minds can read it literary, and think of migrating to Mars.

As is the metaphor of the blue chrysanthemum of one-way ticket, or the little prince, or any other tale examples. The race needs heroes to set examples, and every graduation scale of statistics. That makes the telling of tales infinite, while history depends on circumstances and has natural boundaries.

Teachers need to repeat stories adjusting them to the current circumstances. Adventurers do not need to repeat them, neither do the Dreamweavers.

Both of them need the urge of curiosity, however. There is no more need of words. Dreamweaving is the ability of repetitive play of a world, turning sometimes the angle of viewing it. The very action is spell-bound. Whenever a metaphor becomes true, dreamweaving changes its direction. We are our best enemies, because we are at the same time fnite and infinite.

We carry both ends of the absolute in our brains, who are the grand creators of circumstances.

I need the whole place for a Shelter

That is, sometimes I apply th homo mensura principle to the universe and treat it like a living body. I want no interefense of annihilation throughout my own lifetime. I want it for a shelter, the whole imaginable universe. My singular existence is carried out here, and I do not any part of it to be blown, i.e. to become unimaginable. I do not want it to lose the tiniest particle of its substance: there is no waste in the universe, because every part of it is used again to create new parts of it.

Someday we shall disintegrate and add to the formation of parts in the vast space, spreading out and recombining. We may get out in all our hostility and differences, yet, the process is not finished. We enjoy life as it is.

Influence

The generation of disobedient trouble-makers, the strong-heads and the obstinate of every humankind historic project, those who couldn't be influenced, manipulated, bribed and survived threats, torture and death... Those people have proved that humanity can survive the fear of death. Patience is resistance's other side, for it is sufferance of our soul.

Horizons

The arrivals hall of Frankfurt airport seemed half empty and had nothing stressful to my mind but the big ad up near the ceiling saying 'RENT a KA'. I had only the nylon bag with my slippers and my handbag with my documents and the big file containing the dissertation I was to present at the conference in Saskatoon.

The German passport control officer, a shiny blond with too many white teeth in her smile, had kept nodding to the passengers in the queue up to the moment her glance had fallen on my brand new international passport with the Canadian visa inside. 'Stop! Stop!' she had gasped but I had nothing that horrible about myself. She started asking questions making me feel disgusted at the fanatic robocracy of that intercourse. Upon inspecting my ticket and visa, she had asked, probably a routine question that had made me furious: 'What is the cause for your stay in Frankfurt until 3 p.m. tomorrow?'

The rage made me answer looking down on that servant to airport machines: 'I would not stay a second but for the lack of suitable flight and the evident desire of your country to use some of my currency for your hotels.' That had produced her strange reaction for me, for never before that had I seen such a servile transformation. 'Yes, Madam. Thank you, Madam. Have a good stay, Madam'.

Pfu. So it was like that.

I repeated the exercise at the hotel reception. Wow! It worked! I blinked at the vanishing illusion of the freedom of personnel in Europe. They were trained to answer accordingly to speech patterns.

The departures hall was empty when I arrived there around noon, unable to hold my disgust with the local pride of the hotel, taxi, and airport staffs and desiring to get away from that provincial place that looked to me as canned beef in its own sauce, and have a breath of air up above the low horizon of grey sky over grey houses and roaring highways.

Then the hall began to fill with talkative people: a group of teenaged students who were going home, families who were… who were emigrating from Europe, it dawned on me, Germans mainly, travelling to Canada for a longer period. I felt as carefree as the teenagers who were just tourists.

I changed my shoes for the slippers and was ready to watch how the great transatlantic airbus shot into the thick layer of clouds and kept flying above them at nearly 12 000 kilometers height right into the blue of the late June day. The clouds formed their own country, following, perhaps, the relief of the ground below in their own order. Had there been anything below? I was too happy with the limitless light blue day to think of grey old Europe. At some point there was only dark blue, nearly black plain below with white pieces floating: the Atlantic, I guessed, with the icebergs.

The air hostess informed us we were on Canadian territory and then repeated this in French.

And the day was 31 hours long.

I remembered an old French tale where the hero carried a white hen under his arm while singing a song:

> *The day before me; the night behind me.*
> *Let me become visible to the world.*

The sufferance of our souls, the time's abuse

Julius Caesar, Act 2 Scene 1

There is a city I visit in my dreams. It is spread under the soft rays of an all-time season that can be summer or a snowy hint of winter, a windy day of flowing rising water, a hint of fall in the Upper Street and blossoming spring a few yards down a connecting alley to the boulevard that has come out of the past of childhood. This city has a changing name, too. While you are walking, the meanings change – of both time and places: so many meanings that could be found in dream only. When you are awake, your mind cannot see any track of logic: what's been perfect in your dream is now lost.

Hunger

Hunger can be of different type. It's so, because food is of different nature. Food is information. There is the food for our bodies, and the food for our minds.

There is the food for our senses, and there is the food for our wishes, and for our will.

There is also the fine food for our soul, which we start to think of in the face of death or when we know that we are standing in a one-way doorway. And it is the high speed blue mist of the zoom we experience.

We remember that as a gap in memory. Each time we zoom. It is in the nanos of the noos. It is inexplainable, so we refer to it as a special heritage.

When a gap stops bothering us, we are ready: flesh has had it all. This is the hunger of the soul.

And in this sleep of death what dreams may come

Then we start dreaming. Not always we dreamweaving – not all of us can do it. Most people release their nightmares. Only those who have no debts can create the state of the blue zoom. You cannot carry heavy

objects that do not belong there.

Epilogue

Independence?

Some Piece of Philosophy, Some piece of witchery.

No one owes any other person anything;
No one is due to serve any human body;
Every living thing is due to Old Terra only;
Every living thing owes service to old Terra only;
You can't stop muddy waters with fences;
Nor can death of institutions be stopped with planning
armed defenses;
What shall instant billionaires do?
When the old continents suffer their revision in the
2020s
How can specter provision be cleared out of guilty
minds?
Our Future is not paid by Past Services in the run of the
spiral
Our Future is measured only by Future bits of creations;
Otherwise we enter realities of Fake Value
And the stars cease to shine and turn into black tunnels.
Just forget and continue anew;
And let memory turn into myth
Remembered in the Earth mud only.

Part 4. The Peacock's Flight

Prologue

The Music of Life,
Magnetic Attraction,
Glorious dancers
Generate a view that resembles
A Peacock's Flight
The Peacock is courting his lady
Lowering graciously his bright magic blue neck
Laying his crown to her feet
And spreading the fan of his tail
While dancing.
Thus the sky is courting the Earth
With glorious feathers of Aurora Borealis
Crowning her as the mother of life
And opening a glimpse to the stars
Inspiring in small folk a hope and a fantasy
Of getting out onto the Milky Way
For the lifetime of the race.
Thus the heart sends light at each of his beat
For life, creating a fire-bird that sends nightmares
Back to the cold realms of chaos.
Or gives birth to new stars
Attracting the eyes of the dreamers
Closed in the womb of the Earth,
And eager to be born in fire
Even if they pay for the glamour
With the single thing they own
Their life.

Explanation

This is a Tale of Nostalgy, comprising a dozen of single cases. Nostalgy is often the reason that keeps the world moving on. Birds are not to blame of people's wishes. Nor are they responsible of urges for destruction.

And it is about the Earth, seen as a living creature. Of a more complex nature. It contains the female and the male beginnings which are tightly woven into the magnetic field of its crystal lattice. Each period, when the season of love comes, the Earth dances a fiery dance of Aurora Borealis, courting the Sun and the stars, who send her their kisses of light and their seeds of life as tiny particles carried away by the solar wind.

Nostalgy is connected with the earth's magnetism, which is woven in the genes of the ancient human races and often inherited by their further generations, who are referred to here, as the Natties. The year of 1959 is the year of great changes in the worlds of the Earth. Then the peacock danced in the night, attracting particles of cosmic intellect to help reduce the destruction mania of the human population, whatever the reasons.

Nostalgy is connected with the migration of vast masses of population to places which affect the crystal grid of the Earth – it is the call of the natural elements in the organism of people, that causes them return to their roots or die. But people have discovered how to disobey it: by bringing up a generation of cosmopolitan survivors.

Nostalgy is a rare disease that affects people who keep the memory of their genes.

Intro

Misha was on duty. He minded the apparata in the orbital station. Stardom was not expected tonight, nor any extraordinary phenomena on the night side of the Earth, above which they hung. August was a quiet month, seen from above.

That was why Misha was bored and fixedly surveyed his coffe cup, thinking of his his unfulfilled love for Alexandra. There were no figures on the cup walls, for the coffe was instant, and he saw nothing to distract him from the wasted first half of his life.

Therefore he failed to notice the beginning of the light's dance. First in the left corner of his periphery sight something colourful trembled, and next the melody of the machine signaling something exclusive, made him raise his head and look at the screen.

Over the volcano of Yellowstone a light was rising in a magic dance. The Telescopic vision was followed by a voice message: *"Registered broadcasting of unusual radiance in the area of the volcano Yellowstone-1 "*.

An incredible figure of a bird in flight was rising above the dark conical heap of the volcano. A swish of giant wings, a second swish and opening a glorious tail of peacock blue-and-emerald green, and fiery yellow, white, red and purple. But the volcano was not active and only the light show continued.

Michail was standing like a salt statue with his arm on the alarm button. He had pushed it instinctively, ahd had no idea he had done it until the siren screamed sharply like a peacock challenging his rival. Michail had never before seen the Aurora Borealis which made the Earth look like a dancing peacock in the sky.

Ivo

– There is no more beautiful thing in the world – Ivo said, – than a pecock's flight. When the peacock opens his wings and flies up into the sky, and his tail follows lightly behind and colours the world with a brilliance of rays, this is… this is a melody of lights in the endless blue sky.

Ally was staring at him in astonishment, while he raised with his forefinger his soft cap in the lolours of the rainbow, that was a gift from a friend, and scratched his forehead where it was too tight on his head. Then he sniffed, wiped his hand in his picturesque coat, and nodded:

– You know that I breed some special birds: Guinea fowls, mini-hens, doves, and pheasants. I look after a couple of peacocks, too.

– Since when? – Ally inquired, trying to mask her shame of her thinking low of Ivo as a failed local journalist, who had been given a job as a night guard of the Jewish Market and his duties included clearing of the toilets. He had mentioned he bred hens in his country-house yard.

– I have always kept two cocks. – Ivo said conversationally. – I breed them just for their beauty, they do not rank as the common white doves or the Guinea fowls, or the tinyChina hens.

Ally had asked him about those: she had once asked him why he bred such strange fowl and he had answered then: „*Because they are beautiful! For pleasure*".

She heard some acquaintances of hers passing behind her back and calling her by name. She turned round to say "hello".

– What tales is Ivo telling this time? – Asked the elder of the two sisters. Her voice was full of irony.

– He was telling me about his peacocks – Allie said honestly. – How they fly.

– Aaach! I have seen one of them fly… – Tanya's voice softened. – One had flown from our neighbour's yard in our village, and had perched on a tree in the lawn of our godfather. We all went out to lure him down, but there was no need of that because he suddenly flew above our heads and landed near the hens, to dance. It's an incredibly beautiful show.

Ivo was smiling absent-mindedly while he was counting the coins left by the two women for using the toilet, and then turned again to Ally:

– You must have passed along the yard with the peacocks at the farm openmarket. It belongs to the boss of that place. He loves to watch their dance, too. Just pay attention one day to the front yard of the Major's Hall, they are walking among the green vines and scream, and dance, you can't miss them. They are white, - Ivo added.

Ally nodded, charmed and raised her hand in a final salute. Ivo raised his hat gallantly and beamed a pure white smile at her.

That man had slipped out between the teeth of time. But he took it as if the Creators had forgotten to inform him about it.

Preiously he had been one of the journalists in the single local newspaper, responsible for the cultural events columns. He took autographs from all the celebrities he interviewed, both, popular or unknown, who used to create any piece of art, whether good or not. He was nice and polite and he talked with people. Some friends jokingly assused Ally of flirting with him. She was tolerant and somehow he was interesting to her, for she had not often met persons who had fallen in the gaps of time. There were, however a category of young women who orbited round him: a former partner, and a current partner. They brought two or three young girls with them, and all looked alike – as people who hardly met both ends, but never really cared about working.

They took out of him everything he earned. He did not mind. Otherwise he spent his money on alchohol and was often drunk and unable to do his duties, but he was still polite and no one of his bosses really minded. He was never mad, and never said a bad word against anybody. Sometimes his brown eyes had an absent look and his face became carried away and sad. He had no hatred for the surrounding world, only let sadness show up on the surface of his existence, not despair, only sorrow.

Ally couldn't tell what happened in his head. She had told him once about the effect of „ the differentiated Accelerator", when a few dozens of nano particles of different polarization met with *standard* air. It looked like a live rainbow spreading in a rose-form in the light blue air – for a very short time that sufficed for the human eye to catch a glimpse of it, and then leaving to the mind to wonder whether there had been such a phenomenon or its was only a vision of one's imagination. Ivo had listened carefully as if the machinery in his head classified the information.

That day he had met her with the announcement that the peacock had perched in the early morrow on the roof of the old two-floor country house and then flew on the emerald green lawn to court the lady on the other side of the fence, and have enough space for his dance-show. It was October, but it was still a mild autumn – like a spring. And it was evidently a suitable season of love-dance in the sunlit open space.

Ally or Alexandra, who hated to be called "Sashka", had promised to help him find some temporary job abroad. He had to care for three daughters. She wondered whether he could find someone to care for his Guinea fowls and peacocks .

The Bridge of Kadina or Cruel Flame

The old bridge over the Struma, the silver river, was hunchbacked and narrow, with one lane for the cars, no good view of the traffic, but it was still sound and its stone walls were thick and had only little broken spaces. I always joked whether it would let me pass, whenever we travelled in my car on business to the most distant places of the district neighbouring the ost southwest district part of our country where the state borders of Greece and Macedonia were. /Today the official name of the state is fixed to Northern Macedonia, but here, on the Balkans we never cared to use it, for we have known each other's history for times immemorial, and knew what we meant/.

So I deliberately teased my colleagues, repeating the same mantra and watched their reactions.

– Hey, do you think I am going to hit the road straight this time?

They responded differently: from total disregard to polite protests, while Vera always screamed – she was really scared.

I was also scared to drive along that bridge, but they all thought I was joking, except for Vera. The blond girl instinctively believed me... or, probably she knew the old tale of that bridge... Now, I come to think of it, she must have known it. I always drove along the broad and straight new bridge. When we reached the centre of the village, I turned left and drove along the narrow old bridge, following the hump first driving up and next lightly descending on the opposite side of the river, and pulled up in front of the Youth Hall. I kept my eyes widely open for other cars, but the traffic ran along the speedway and did not bother much about that ancient scaring tale accompanying the old bridge.

The Struma followed its course playfully, shallow in the young summer, and clear. Down bellow the bridge, in the sand-bottomed pools the small fish waved their tails happily because there were no fishermen to scare them. At that time of the year fishing was probably forbidden, or people minded their own business and did not care for fishing holidays.

Both banks of the river were full of willows, that stood with their feet in the cool water and their silvery leaves shone like fine smiles in the sun. The river was broad and slow seen from the left side of the bridge and the bottom was covered by thick mud. It wasn't scary, though, because the water was transparent and one could see all the fallen branches and thr roots that were washed in the fresh stream.

What was giving me the thrill, though was the bridge, itself. Probably it was due to its form, or probably it was too narrow? It looked rough but it was steady and inspired the idea of a sound construction.

Each time when the car reached the top of the cyrved bridge, it jumped as if it had reached a porch in a doorway, and the bridge suddenly seemed broader, the day beamed as a normal, usual day, and the shadow that held the bridge seemed to let its grip. Our secret unexplainable fear vanished like a sigh and we all felt relief and enjoyed the day.

The next time we happened to go on a business trip together, I followed the same route, curious to check whether the same extraordinary feeling will obsess us. It was the same: a cold fear up the narrow bridge, a jump, a sigh, shadow behind you, a bright day before you. The bridge fascinated us with its spell-bound story we had not heard in its complete version.

———•———

My colleagues had left the car and had entered the new Youth Hall cafeteria. The building was a neat new house in the style of the old Bulgarian architecture. I was still busying myself with the car, but, in fact I thoughtfully studied the bridge. It was a solid construction. I knew from my father that bridges needed to have special linking details that held them. I knew about the old tradition that masters needed to immure the shadow of a young maiden. It had two narrow windows on both sides of the river. *So, it was hollow after all*, I thought. I continued to muse on this idea. It must not have been because of the spring water floods – the bridge was much higher than the river banks. The windows gave it the air of a fortress.

I sensed being an object of close survey myself. I raised my eyes and saw an ancient and very thin man who was smiling. He was sitting on the opposite side of the river at a small table in front of the windows of the cafeteria.

- They are windows – he said immediately after I looked him, answering my unsked question. The young bride was closed inside the hollow bridge – there is just enough space inside for a standing woman. They used to hold her baby for her in front of the windows to feed it.

The granddad seemed to need a company, and since I was unwilling to get inside the café and join my eager to light their cigarettes friends, I sad down on the second chair and prepared to listen to his tale. He was pleased with my sudden attention and his inspiration came to tell me a cruel love story in full detail. He knew the people from the village, and ge gave the details his personal interpretation, that was not mentioned in the records of folk rituals.

He told me that strange tale at length, and where I stared at him in disbelief, he repeated – commenting on the story of the young bride, Kadina.

- *Here the field is broad and flat.* – He started, and I nodded in approval, because I had been driving along the roads between the two mountain ranges that closed the narrow river gorge, and knew that the winding road descended towards the upper river valley and towards the big village, spreading at ease in the middle of the field.
- *The river has no natural barrier. In amcient times there were dense forests and the streams that came from the mountains above filled it with the water from the melting snow in the spring or from the heavy rains in the early summer and in the mild Autumn.*
- *The river flooded the fields. It was not the present shallow and mild stream, but thundered between the rocks, muddy and fearsome.*
- *Every summer the people used to build bridges to connect the fields on both sides, and each autumn and spring the river carried them away.*
- *They continued living on with this trouble until one day a stranger walked along the white road from the town and stopped to rest at the hot springs in the upper end of the village to wash his tired feet and talk with the local people. They shared their main trouble with the river, and he said:*
- *Find me eight apprentices from the village to help me, and I am going to build for you a sound bridge that the river shall not cary away.*

The news spread like a country fire, and till dinner time, the stranger was surrounded by eight strong young men, and the elder invited him to stay and gave him a word of approval, for the word meant more than a signed agreement in those times.

There was a small farm building in the yard of the rural school where the master could live, and the young women were eager to bring food to him.

Manol was the name of the master and he had come from far away, building fountains and bridges, and arcades, everything that had domes and archways that could connect people on their routes to the sky.

On the following morning they started searching the two banks of the river for a suitable place of the bridge, they took measures, made calculations and planned what they needed. The Master said they needed some of the graniterocks and some old oak trees for support.

There were hills on the opposite side of the river with ancient sacred places and big rocks on the steep lawns. The forest was old and tall.

All the oxen carts from the village lined in a caravan and fetched the materials needed for the bridge. All the men took part in this. In the meanwhile others dug for sand and made canals for the still water, that took it down the fields.

The Master and four of the apprentices prepared the places where the bridhe had to step on the ground and where the main supports should be constructed.

They made the banks higher and put stone blocks along them, and the heaped earth used to slip back into the riverbed and open hot water springs rushed between the slabs. Once the river carried away the stones prepared for the construction of the bridge, but they were huge and didn't go that away, only paved the muddy bottom and made it sound. In the beginning of the summer heats the banks of the river dried up and the work went faster.

The masters spent all day around the bridge, while their wives took turns fetching lunch and dinner.

When they finished their long daily work, Manol sat down to rest with his back propped against the stone wall and watched the clouds, drifting in the sky and the sun setting behind the mountains in a pool of gold.

Then he got up and continued the work on the water fountain with two tubes – one for hot water, and the other for cold. He did it all alone, not asking anyone to help him and no one learned the secret of how he had managed to capture two springs in the same fouuntain.

Then he sat beside it and watched the stars.

Some other hungry eyes watched him.

He was still young, healthy and strong, and somehow different from the local rough men, and he attracted the eyes of the women — the local beauties: round-faced, fair and rosy in the cheeks, with high brow and artistic eyebrows and lashes, and big dark-brown or green eyes. He never looked athem, for he had work to do and that made them even more insistent in their rivalry to draw his attention. There were, too, some other kind of eyes that followed him: sharp, calculating and jealous, with accounts to settle, using his lack of interest.

The construction of the bridge grew, there was only a little left to reach the end of work. The workers were exhausted. The Master melted like a candle and closed in himself. He stopped chatting with the people.

One of the apprentices told his wife to bake a big pie and roast a rooster. Another one ordered a whole lamb cooked — their strength was running away as if the soil on which the bridge stood drained it.

The young bride of the youngest of them, and the most cheerful one, Kadina, with a breast-infant on hands, started coming twice to fetch them atray of freshly baked bread, roast meat, butter and honey, summer apples and wild-rose-wine.

Another woman's eyes jealously followed her with a gaze that carefully sliced her time, scheming to get rid of her. Words of mouth spread easily in rural communities: words of happy solution to a problem, rumours, horrible rules born in evil minds...

There was a summer storm one evening with thunder and lightning and heavy cloud that came down as rain. The raging river flew towards the bridge, but only took away a few smaller stones.

The masters of the bridge remained on guard till midnight. They sat in the shade he built over the strongest of the hot springs and watched the bridge. When the rain was over, Manol told them to go home for a full rest and come in the morning for the final stage of the bridge construction.

So they went back to their homes, and came on the morning calm and happy. Only two of them were missing.

The first of them came late and said:

- *They've been discussing our work down in the village: they say the river gods want a gift, otherwise it can take away the new bridge.*

- *That's all stuff and nonsense* – Manol interrupted.

– *Lads get back to work and let's make it hollow inside with two narrow openings on each side. Whenever the river is high enough to flood the bridge this is the way to let incoming air dry it. Come on, get up and start work.* Are you all ready?

- *Stoyan is not here* – *one of the apprentices said.* – *while we were on our way here, Pavlina called him to mend for her the door of the sheep pen.*

> – *Do you remember when he wanted to marry her and sent his people to make the offer to her father, Angel, one of the elders. He refused to bless their marriage, although his daughter wanted him. He sent his gifts for a second time; while the bargain continued, Kadina crossed his way at the Easter holiday dance in all her young grace, and he noticed her and hastened to mary her. She took him right before the old man consented…*

The others nudged him to shut up, because Stoyan had come at last, dark as a storm-bringing cloud. Without saying a word, he started work. At some time, he gave a kick to the bucket of the stucco and shouted at the aid to add more lime from the pit to the sand.

Pavlina had managed to mutter some words that his pretty bride was constantly hovering about the construction, ready to serve the Master. Her pity was burning inside him like a snake's bite.

He continued his work, but his eyes saw no longer the bridge, but the eyes of Kadina smiling while she was handing a towel to the Master, and caring whenever she handed a plate of food over to him.

Pavlina had shoved a snake-rumour into his heart and now it was winding and whispering.

The bridge was growing and spanning the river held by triple domes and four stone columns, and two openings like narrow windows at the two sides.

The artisans talked often about giving a gift to the gods – a young and pretty woman – to beg for their mercy and keep it steady. The gift had to be beautiful.

Manol did not pay attention to their talk but the others warned their wives not to hurry to serve them the daily meals.

Kadina only continued to come twice a day, caring about them, and served the best dishes to Manol, but he never raised his eyes to her.

Stoyan followed her and the colours of the summer day grey grey and frosty under his heavy blu-and-black gaze.

They had almost reached the end of the construction, and he said:

- Now it is time for me to leave you, my lads, while it's still hot. You know how to complete the job. Be blessed and farewell.

He washed at the fountain with the hot and cold water, waved and soon vanished down the road that followed the river valley.

The men began the final stage of the work.

They closed the first dome and sat down to rest before they closed the other one.

- Ech, only if some young bride would bring us a cool drink… – someone began and another one added under his breath:

- The one that comes first should be the one whose shadow we must build in to keep the bridge sound.

And then all stood silent because a slime shade had fallen across the bridge: Kadina had come with a silver pot of cool milk and was searching for Manol to serve him first.

The searing heat hit Stoyan on the head. He jumped up, took her by her elbow and dragged her into the opening of the unfinished dome and started to build. She cried and begged him to let her feed the baby, but he wouldn't listen and closed her inside the bridge leaving only a narrow opening to raise the baby to her breasts.

The old man was telling his tale in an even, singing voice, while I listened to him stunned.

- Such were the people then: their life was cruel, and their actions were openly hostile. – He concluded.

My colleagues had drnuk their cups of coffee and smoked a couple of cigarettes. Now they were coming out.

Julka was walking in the shade of Valio, and Nelly, wo was a close friend of Valio's wife was waching her with steel-like piercing eyes.

The granddad nodded a couple of times:

— *There is some saga hidden here, too. People are cruel. The bridges springing over the gaps of the world stand upon underpinnings of defeated rivals.*

I recalled the picture of Julka being sad with the refusal of Valio to paint her portray, and Valio justifying that with his wife's jealousy.

Julka was the big love of Valio, but he had married Venetta, instead, and had children.

I spent the next twenty years overseas and then returned home, but of all my friends Julka was not there and no one would tell me where she had gone. I walked towards the city centre, and there, on the first wall there was freshly stuck an obituary.

At the same time they were opening an exhibition in the city Gallery of Art. I waited for two days to pass, and on the third evening I went to see it. In the main place there was a picture as if drawn by the Master who was the patron of the gallery.

A young, dark-haired woman was standing in front of an old-style house, while in the back there stood the misty domes of the Bridge of Kadina.

The eyes of Julka were sending beams of soft light. The note under the picture mentioned a five-digit price in dollars. There was a piece of cardboard which said: "Sold".

I ran into Valio at the exit. He was humpbacked and greying.

His wife, Venetta was proudly walking beside him, her eyes shining yellow with the greedy selfish fame.

There was no chance of avoiding them.

- Did you see the picture "The bridge of Kadina"? – Venetta asked me. – It is Valio's masterpiece. Now they shall take it for an exhibition in Manhattan.

All the visitors of the exhibition were to pass over the humpbacked Bridge of Kadina, The Young bride over the Atlantic. And the bridge was not going to fall, because the shadow of Julka was holding it.

Nostalgy

The Trans-Atlantic airliner landed and stood still under the ovations

202

of the grumpy passengers and suddenly they all moved and formed two lines at the luggage belt.

Suit cases of various size and colour, traveler-bags and rucksacks were jumping heavily out of the opening and landing on the belt with a final sigh, and the belt screeched as it moved in a circle, dragging them out of their formal lives.

They stood round it. No one spoke. At certain intervals someone rushed and caught a bulging shapeless suitcase.

There was a rhythm in the sound of the screeching belt – pieces of memories,like the ringing voice of a gutar were falling in the big silence, and from those broken pieces pictures flew up in the air and danced there as if in a trance, spell-bound and spell-generating.

They went far away from them, and at the same time they returned and were looking for the place they wished to go back to and stay – somewnere, sometime undefined in the future, probably, creating a parallel world without pain.

One more suitcase fell fron the opening, a second one right after it and a huge soft bag. The screech of the belt was like pieces of brocken laughter, that gathered in a melody. It knitted a silver-thred bridge that connected the future and the present by a belt of starry sky, binding the blue Earth . They were returning home on it, spent a blink of a moment at their roots, taking new strength from the soil, and continued on their routs. They left one by one and two by two, pushing their overloaded luggage carts with objects of bustle and hue. They didn't look back.

They moved forward followed by a trail of misty pictures of the old homeland, where they were young and happy, beside a stream with blooming orchards around the banks, and the sun rising in a pool of fiery light over the green peaks of the Balkan's young summer... and melted into the mist, seen of by the melody, which was to see them back in.

4. *The Perfume of Roses*

A human cannot always live up to the standads of abstract reason. There are periods when one lives down to the standards of instinct, which are rooted in the nature of the the spaces or stages of life. In such cases an individual discovers the many faces of truth. One's senses depend on the tradition and the emotional belonging of things.

A tiny glass container of rose oil in the bottom of my pocket turned into a generator of identity of my original self there before I crossed the electronic door that scanned the incoming foreigners at Calgary airport. Back still on the Old Continent, international check-up officials let it pass with reverence. Maybe they were doubting they might be under the control of *langoliers*: they simply asked me to put it on the rolling belt of the scanning machines, and then let me take it again. Some smaller souvenirs like a cigarette lighter, they made me leave. It had no scent. It was too tiny to set the place on fire. The rose, however, passed. There was some magic in the scent of the rose, or in the word meaning a scent of a rose. A symbolic power that drew my concrete human image homewards, where it began from the scent of the Rose Valley.

I have always had a weak spot for scents and subconsciously I classify them as beautiful. Some of them are surface-manifested, while others are the expression of the essential feature of an identity.

According to the Ancient Eastern calendars, the flower-symbol of my zodiac-sign is the tulip. This cannot be true. There probably exist tulips with beautiful, velvety scent, but the tulips cultivated in gardens are beautifully coloured, and do not smell. They cannot bring me back home.

The rose is a different case.

Once I bought five special young grape-vines at the farmers' market in Veliko Turnovo – This was our capital city and a centre of Balkan culture and education of the spirit. They were sold to me by two brothers. One of them told me he wanted to ake a present for me as a bonus. I threw a longing look towards the sunny-yellow, but he said: *"not this one"*/in our culture yellow is not a good colour – it is the colour of envy/. Then he handed to me a huddling dark red rose. I did not protest, and thanked at length, although my eyes voted for the yellow one. I took it at home and planted it in my garden and it thrived there, giving me ten long-stemmed velvety scented flowers. Gorgeous and with the perfume of home

Later on I found a yellow rose with the colour of a summer morning sun and the scent of rose wine. An old granny gave it to me: she tore a branch of a climbing rose that I was looking at in awe, and ordered me to plant it under a shade in a jar and water it every morning. *"Roses like heat and water"*, she said. It grew up and akes bunches of flowers.

There are two kinds of roses: one is beautiful; and the other kind are those that can be made into jelly and wine. Both kinds have a specifc odour, which can bring you home.

When you taste them, they become a part of you.

Once back in my teens I perfumed my letters with rose perfume. They were not addressed to anybody, but I was young and in love, and the paper smelled well when perfumed, and the receiver neded no name, because I knew who he really was, although I never sent him a letter. I never looked at him. I knew that we were not a real match: we could not be happy together. But every time I looked in his direction I felt weak. That was like the perfume of the rose.

The rose-bushes in my garden love me. They are always happy to see me and meet me with permanent flowerbuds. A tiny glass bottle of rose essence cost my way back home. This is the valley in the heart of the Balkans for me. And my heart has its own needs and is not interested in logic, but aches and draws me back to my roots.

A tiny bottle of rose perfume is the essence of possession for me – I want this land, because it smells of youth and young love, and of roses. My dreams bear the scent of roses and this does the magic of alltime space. If I am ever to pass into the higher stage of life, which is independent of body-needs, I'll probably keep the memory of the rose perfume. Itcolours the worlds I weave up, gives them a flavor and taste, carries the keys to my possessions, creates the feeling of dejavu. The fragrance of home.

No one can persuade me that life of a human is in constant fight or annihilation of all other lives that stand in one's individual route.

People are unevenly developed. Those who stand in our way we see as our enemies and wage wars with them. Wars are a primitive way to realize our possession of our individuality.

There are probably other ways of declaring the possession of our existence. Yet, in this Universe comprised of stars and emptiness, we continue to stick close, leaving no space for our individual comfort, and wage wars, whose end is decided by those who stand out of them; those, who do not turn the forests to ashes and the ashes to deserts of ex-foreign possessions.

Probably that is why we are settled in the periphery of the night sky, because we still udergo a hard and long apprenticeship befor we become Creators.

Probably those who have completed that stage of training, can cross the shortcuts connecting the lands of the Creators and discover new ways to all the possible worlds, while barbarians still have to study and repeat the class.

Shall we ever learn to love and tolerance. Without rivalry and hostility. Without the humiliating practice of standing on our knees and bow, while leaving ourselves depend on the mercy of those who trump over our heads. And be free of binding circumstances that raise walls to our worlds.

It is so primitive to wage wars and make heaps of gold, which we imagine can buy us life. But life is not sold so cheap. It is reached in the long practice of the kind to mindweave its own route to the status of creators.

It is like the fragrance of a constellation, that dances in spheres of light like the perfume of a rose that brings us home on the wings of the solar wind.

And we shall no longer teach our children to fear the different creatures. The very young infants have no fear: they know the future, they play in it, and overcome aches. Then they grow up to comply with circumstances of society and to them dejavu as a possession of their own space of time means only aggression.

There are no other hostile creatures, than those created by fear. There is just us… and the stars, and the moral law which bars fear and never creates nightmares of the worlds that are in our possession.

A Blue Persian Carpet

- She is leaving this time for England, and then – oberseas. – Angy is complaining as if I am not present.
- You shall accompany her – my brother, the foreigner states.
- No I'm not going anywhere – I've got no business there. – says Angy angrily.

- Don't you tell me it's not your business. Who else do you think shall go with her. – My brother-in-law, Mohammed is raging.
- Will you take me on your trip? – Angy asks uncertainly and I am surprised at last with his consent, and start worrying that it is too late for me to start travel arrangements for Boston.
- Then you travel with her to London – Mohammed orders, still failing to mind my presence. And thus the question is settled finally.

This is a whole month in London, then – Oxford, and a couple of days in Cambridge, then – again in London. Angy is extremely pleased, in fact, he behaves as a local guy.

He is not allowed to get a card for the oxford libraries at such a short notice for it took me whole month to decide he would accompany e, but that does not bother him because he is free to study the town while I am busy reading, he can walk in the parks and visit the museums... besides, he liked Cambridge better.

The book-store had four spacy floors and an underground floor where the books for learning English were sold. He liked the store immensely. There were old books of antiquarian value, with huge brown leather armchairs and small tables, where teas was served to special clients while the book-sellers discussed the value of the books.

And then there was London again with the British library and the useum area. We decided to start with Victoria and Albert Museum. What we first saw was a blue Percia carpet They switched on the lights every twenty minutes so that the colours wouldn't wear off.

It was large and thick. Nothing remarkable. Except for it was genuine. But its value was not told in words. But for shared by word of mouth. The real thing couldn't fly. Later on we saw theexamples of Persian carpets in the internet. They were red. That one was blue, like the sky woven up with ornaments and vines that surely meant something... something lost. Maybe it was rare for its own time of creation. I've got a brown and beige, and white. Thick and colourful. But the genuine one was like a negative and had all kinds of wonderful ornaments typical for the carpets of Persia.

There were also in the same hall some porcelain vases and cups, all in tune with the carpet.

When we got back to the boarding house, it turned that the young people whom we shared a room with, knew nothing of the fact of the existence of such a museum. They had come to London for some concert in Hyde Park and were not interested in anything else.

I was thinking about the numerous tales about the great carpet artisans of the Ancient East: they created outstanding artefacts all their life and got no recognition. Time doesn't help identifying their pieces of art, but just flows on and reaches a time when everything can be reached at hand. And it cannot be recognized better, than by spreading the tales of the magic flying carpet by words of mouth... until... until a green guy believes in tales, and creates a device that can send carpets in the air.

And Empires used to rob the concuered lands off their artefacts, but not of their memory. It it hadn't robbed it, it would probably fade in the course of time and be powdered with the dust of oblivion. Dust to dust and ashes to ashes are the "gifts" that history can only inflict on all hand-made objects of art. Oblivion lies in the foundations of our dejavu.

In the tales, repeated again and again in all storages of human memory, thare is kept the idea of all the carved wooden safes, full of precious stones and fine textile, with flying carpets, and horses, and with boxes of medicines that could cure every suffering.

How much is forgotten, and how much is preserved in tales, which are our metaphoric mysterious signs, that can challenge our curiosity, because we cannot bridge the gaps in the logos only by the poetics and pathos of dreamweaving tales.

The fairy tales are told to children, and researchers. Some day someone tries to create the magic things that are described in the fairy tales. Sometimes they work. Why are we usually filled with sorrow, when some magic stuff is excavated from ancient sites? They always fit somewhere in our day. The name of the artisan is hidden, but the tale mentions the work of art, and that is sufficient.

For example:

Once upon a time there lived in Percia a man who used to weave carpets of singular design...

This is all and it is everything.

Statistics

The E-generation has no talk to speak of:

Hurry up tell me all before the battery's expired.
No way forward, no way back.
I cannot move. I'm caught up in traffic.
We're late.

If you repeat it 18 times and add a rap tune, it can become the hit of the summer. There in no meaning in it. There is nothing else, only words that have ceased to picture a world as catch-up phrases having nothing in common with tomato-sauce. Only those words that blind my mental vision. They are all the words.

Maybe they are a special code? The tasteless image-weaving of *langoliers*?

These finally end and the text starts globally:

Stay with me. I'll never be alone – heart-breaking plead of some young soprano. Repeated many times, Musical pause, second part – the same as the first.

Some more words to the same stile, that can fit a line.

I mentally click an emoticon, red with rage.

Then I tune to business-reasoning. If the teens learn to speak a tongue – their mother-tongue, or the global tongue of chatting with their mates, - in the discothecue, then they need no further education and school-control, and today's teachers have to look for something else to do for a living. For teens have already been using their own deep structures and metaphors, to signify their simple meaning, which elder generations cannot access nor accept, or asses.

Statistics…

How many have emigrated over the last twenty years.

What is the number of the first year shoolers' enrollments?

How many University students get onto the shuttle bus in the morning?

How many teachers of world languages are needed all over the country?

How many of the active teachers of foreign languages imagine they are only instructors, and how many of them accept themselves as educators – does the school children's age matter?

What is the number of those students, who take part in the "Work and Travel" program, and become potential emigrants even before the end of their first semester at University?

What is the nuber of the abandoned houses in rural areas? How many are still inhabited, and cared for? - Those are aesy to count on the fingers of one hand.

How many of country homes are renovated and financially kept functioning, for nostalgia reasons?

– I have collected some data for analysis – I begin to explain timidly. – What I need is some statistics model – could I get some training by your faculty?

– No roblem – the professor of the Maths Department says optimistically. – We'll do that for you. – You just write down what results you need us to achieve.

– What comes up – I carefuly explain. No play with the facts. – I cannot be certain that empirical data fits into preliminary schemes. – By far I've worked according to the public opinion published by social media, and it is based on emotional exaggeration. Besides, you know that opinion is not a criteria to be trusted, it can be easily manipulated.

– Eeeech, don't tell me such a nonsense: what you order, we calculate. Whenever you are ready, just call me.

– Thanks, I'll call back. – I say the polite words because I am brought up to be polite with people who are redy to do a favour to me.

I hope he doesn't really expect me to call back.

Statistics continues to spread wild and raw, out of tables and coefficients, and sow panic and frenzy.

Once again on the question of Statistics. This time from a different angle:

– I don't like potato soup. – Angy told me once when we were discussing what our favourite things to eat were.

– Aggie doesn't like potato soup – Angy's Mum confirms. – When he was very young we enrolled him into the village kindergarten. They used to serve them potato soup for lunch and he used to run out shouting indignantly, and get to his Granddad in the Cowshed.

– It was nasty and bland, with tomato peels floating over the surface. – Angy adds. – And my Granddad used to treat me with an edd, baked on newspaper the plate of the iron stove.

– What's that? – I ask curiously, for I hear about that recipy for the first time in my life. In the meantime I continue stirring my personal idea of potato soup, and the summer air is full of the delicious smell of well-stewed potatoes, red peppers, fresh onions from the garden and fresh mint.

– Well, you tear down a piece of the Worker's Deed newspaper / that was the daily newspaper of the communist party – the thickest, and therefore used for farious purposes cheapest – only a penny – paper/, you put it on the stove and crash the egg over it. It is yummy.

– Sure – I say thoughtfully and switch the electric stove off.

– Mmmm. – It smells tasty. What are we having for lunch?

– Potatoes – I say cautiously and begin to pour the stew in the dishes. It looks good and the steam gives off a delicious odour.

No one objects. Angy and his Mum start working with their spoons and lick them. It is not exacly a potato soup. We use to call it a casserole – vegetarian but nuch thicker than simpy a soup. And there are no tomatoes in it. Tomatoes don't match with potatoes. I hate tomato peels in my meal, too. And there is nothing so bleating than stewed tomatoes in much water.

– I got the impression you won't eat potatoes – I tease them when they have a second helping.

– This here has nothing to do with that potato soup – and Angy points down with his spoon. He's grown fatter and his wedding suit no longer fits him. His Mum is happy because Angy's star sign is Scorpio and his, otherwise sunny, character is awful, especially when he is hungry, and he is happy now and does not raise debatable topics.

An egg on a piece of newspaper – I think. *But how am I to get that kind of paper. Today's papers smell thickly of offsette print, besides they have thick pages and are very small.*

In the beginning of her stay overseas Annie used to come back home every summer. In the fourth summer she called back and said she would go to the French Rivierre . On the following summer she excused her not coming back with a business project and said she had not enough days for a vacation. So she travelled in a jeep to the Niagara Falls and then she had booked tickets for an opera at the Metropolitan. During the next six years she even didn't bother to call me and I have not seen her back. Probably she managed to hide nostalgia with being busy there. Maybe nostalgy is a kind of habit and one can get used to live with it.

The end of the world is coming, and we live down our last fears, make our last money, and even start travelling as if for the last time.

Then we find suddenly out that this trick with the end of the world was just a fake news, and we hide behind a façade of self-imposed nostalgy. We are perfectly aware that it is no sickness for a special place, but for a special time, and it involves going back to the time we have been dreamweaving, and then – to our current affairs and sometimes fail to bridge the gap.

The immaterial memory of our childhood has been filled by the spectre of our sweet dreams, and we leave it to replace our disappointment and aches.

Next we recollect this picture and it replaces the home-sickness we imagine we have for our deserted home-place.

The first question foryour self-identification the world over is *"Where do you come from?"* It makes you feel bound to a certain spot over the surgace of the Globe that is no longer important, because it is simply some cluster of country-houses. The proper question is *"When have you been happy?"* – but the Web does not find the difference. It is such a pity.

Love Apples.

When finally I got back to the Balkans, I drove to the village of my mum's relatives. My mother and my Father were there, too, and my granny and granddad were the same as they had always been to me in my childhood. The tomatoes in my mum's garden were ripe and I went in the garden at small intervals and picked a large overripe tomato, wich peeled easily, and ate it, its juice running down over my hands.

   –   Come to lunch – mummy called me, – there is chicken and rice.

I went but before that I picked some splendid ripe tomatoes.
Mummy was laughing:

— You ate a whole bucket of tomatoes.

It smelled like home. In the sandy soil of the Mid-Balkan, source water easily went through and reached the roots of the plants clear. I, in fact taste the soil at home together with the juice of the tomatoes. And the sulphur of the Canadian soil gradually cleared off my blood and the taste of life as the very action of my existence, returned.

The sky was blue and burnt by the July sun, over the wavy hills the hicory was in full bloom, and along its roots was gathered its bitter juice. You clear that from the small stones and the sand grains and chew it into a gummy stuff that makes huge balloons.

We roamed the mountain hills with my granddad, amd I ate everything I could, restoring the taste of the earth: the white pine needles and the pearls of pine juice, the sour leaves of the grass, that had the funny name of goat-beard, the little sweet yellow pears.

Some place overseas 10, 000 kilometres away, where the sky was the same blew colour and the hikory, and many other grasses and herbs, I could recognize, but couldn't live, because the soil was not the same, there were some people who I had become my friends for ever, although there were still doubts hovering, about my true relations with Bill who was teaching Shakespeare at that time. I miss that happy time sometimes, but I do not feel pity I have left them, for they are not within the scope of my possession. There is not the irresistible call of blood that is the sign of homesickness. My life is within the possessions of a certain place where my times are entangled into a knot of past and future, now, as a presence.

> The tomatoes grew ripe and splendid, and in lavish heavy
> bunches on the plants in the garden of my home.

The French brought them to Europe once and they grew them for their beauty. They thought the red tomatoes were poisonous and called the green ones *"the apples of love"*.

They might have been right. Love is possession. The life juices of the earth that loved me, passed from the tomatoes in my blood restoring the possession over my life, that had called me back. For blood, it is said, is thicker tah water, and is susceptible to poisoning.

My two young sons stood close by me, lest I could go on another trip overseas. Angy pretended he didn't mind, but his eyes were spakling green.

I travelled for shorter periods later. Ten years after the first long trip, I was back home again. Angy kept making salads to me from the tomatoes that grew in my own garden. Who can tell for sure those Renaissant French gardeners what had in mind when they called the tomatoes "the apples of love".

The apples of Love. Love is magnetic. It can bring you back home. That is why it is a part of nostalgy.

The Promised Land

Two teenaged girls leaned on the wall between the two rows of waiting halls. They wore hand-made heavy silk dresses – green and yellow, with golden embroidery.

Their father ordered them to wait for him there, while he went to take some food. The girls leaned elegantly on the thin light-grey wall like a finely lined picturesque relief. One of them took out an old black book with oval corners and shabby from use. She opened it and started chanting the pages, while bending back and forth like a young apple-tree. The other one stood before her, shading her from random curious stares. Their hands were thin and tender with long fingures, but a pair of them held the Koran without any strain, as if it was a dove's feather, and the other pair of girl's hands were clapped together like an unopen lily in a gesture of a prayer.

They looked extremely scared. They had left their home for the first time and here at the Amsterdam airport, they became aware of the stranger's world around.

Their father came and gave them each a bottle of sone drink. I looked away so as not to disturb them, but for a moment had a glimpse of the white hands catching the bottles, while the prayers still hovered round their pale faces. Shortly after that they moved to the line for New York airliner, which quickly flew turning round the wall of the waiting hall and slipped through the electronic door of the scanner.

I had tried so hard to feel what they felt and sense what they sensed, that I failed to notice I had begun to slip down off the seat in a trance, hypnotized by the rhythm of their chanting. I stood up with a jump and started to walk over to the bureau of the Boston flight passenger services, where two chocolate girls in shining white blouses and beautifully ironed blue suits, smiled at me, checked my ticket and asked me if I was OK.

- I feel some strange loss of energy – I beamed at them in answer to their politeness, and some freckles moved on my pale face.
- Oh, I know what you need – the taller girl smiled broadly, came up to me from behind the plastic desk, and pointed across the diagonal of the free space. – Over there is an Irish bar, and Joe can make for you an energy-rising drink of chockolate and cream.

I thanked them admiringly, and next minute I was standing in front of Joe and was telling him my problem.

Joe was red-haired and his face was covered with freckles.

- You feel out of energy, don't you – That was not a question but a firm statement. Half-turning to his left, he caught sight a pleasant girl with plain blond tail, who was standing at the bar. – Meg shall serve you what you need. One euro. Please.

I had only seven coins of one euro each and placed one of them on the barplot. Meg took a long glass and fild it with sweet thick, splendid chocolate from one of the guilded taps behind her back, while she was smiling and talking something soothing to me. I guessed I might've probably looked as scared as the two girls with the Koran.

I tapped the coin on the plot, but she said:

- Now wait – here comes the most important part!

Then she moved the glass under the next tap and topped it with a cream tower, taller than the glass itself.

215

— Glorious! – I exclaimed, mesmerized.
— Really! – Joe said. – I told you Meg is the expert. I felt my inbuilt linguist immediately read it in my mother tongue, and even translated them as my closest friends.

I took my glass, bit into the sweet peak of cream and looked around for a place to sit down. My head was no longer dizzy.

Opposite Joe's place there was a pizza bar. I took a large piece of pizza with white cheese and spinach, left there another of my coins and sat at a round table to fight the energy crisis.

When I finished with the pizza, I had reached down to the melted rich chockolate drink and the clock above my head counted three hours to my flight.

I took the glass in hand and walked slowly along the long alley between the two rows of waiting halls. I reached my section of an open waiting space, but there was a red rope, so I walked to the opposite wall and sat down with my back to the wall.

An aged Rabbi stepped on the path. He looked as taken out of a picture book with his black top-hat, greying forked beard, black stained long coat, a small cardboard suitcase, an ageing plump wife in a long black dress, two big sons in old-fashioned grey suits and small, round caps on their balding heads, one younger son - also in suit and a cap, two daughters in home made brocate dresses and long black plaits, and a baby-daughter about three or four years of age in a high cart.

He placed his family on the empty seats opposite me: the mother first, then the infant girl, then the other girls. Finally he took the last seat opposite my own, and his sons stood up before him. He opened the suitcase, which was full of old books, and showed something to theboys. They nodded and walked away, probably to check in for their family's flight.

The baby had grown restless in the meantime, but she made no noise, only wriggled in her cart, and the father of the family ordered the two elder sisters to mind her and push the cart along the free alley. Then he got up and vanished behind the corner, only to come back in a few minutes withhis sons, and a whole bag of boxes of chockolate custard. He gave each of them one. The baby stretched out her hands and received one, too. The old lady opened the plastic box for her, put it into her hands, and gave her a spoon. Then she calmly ate her own chockolate, leaving the baby.

The two elder sisters were for a while left to themselves, and gazed at the jeans and the jackets of the passing foreign women. Their own dresses had suddenly become hard and heavy, and made them feel uneasy. When everyone had eaten their energy stuff, the Rabby gathered the cups and the spoons in the bag and handed it over to his youngest son to carry it to the rubbish bin. The mother took a handkerchief out and wiped the chockolat off the baby''s face. The curly-headed baby beamed happily, but her sisters played the roles of young ladies who were busy to mind her and turn their backs on the baby. The Rabby uttered no sound of reproach but took the handle of the cart and walked her up and down the alley.

I watched this quiet and soothing pantomime, where each member of the family knew their roles and acted out accordingly, without any loud protest or quarrel, or any other demonstration of disapproval or disrespect. Then I gulped my cold chockolate and looked around.

In the waiting hall opposite me there was movement. Three slender strong officers in uniforms stretched a red silk rope to trace the line of the passengers coming for passport control, and hung a board marked "VIP"-passengers. No separate queue, all of us were treated as VIPs. In my homecountry there was a separate exit for VIPs who were mainly some footballers and pop-singers. I was too busy to watch that show, to make comparisons. I did that later.

„Ths is the check for my flight", I said to myself, got up from my seat, nodded a farewell at the Rabbi, who had been also watching me, and stood in the quickly moving queue. They remained calmly to wait for the next flight overseas. The two-meters tall giants – one golden blond and two dark chocolate were checking our passports and handbags, asking each whether we were carrying liquid stuff or metal objects.

- I've got a tiny glass of rose perfume to remind me of home – I said and took out the bottle of essence of my coat pocket, and held it up between my fingers for them to see it.
- How fine – One of the dark chocolate giants flashed a white smile, and made a sign, – Please, go.

Holding the rose oil in my pocket, I suddenly became aware that I had only that small thing to remind me of home. It also began to dawn on me that it might turn too small to take me back home again.

She'll come back

"Twelfth Night" or How Far it is to the other End of the World

    — You're ment'lly sick, Lad, – Plamen continued to wind up.

He and Angy had been sitting for two hours at the "Fish" and drinking beer steadily. Plamen had returned to their hometown to arrange the things of his heritage and sell the house that stood closed after his parents' death. Then he was to return to Chicago, where they lived with his brother and his family. They had developed some smaller business there.

Angy had met him accidentally on his way back from the school, where he worked, and had complained to his old friend that Mary, his wife, had departed to the US for an unknown period.

That was in his esteem a chance one in a million, that should not be lost.

    — Does she call home?
    — Yes. On Saturdays we talk for half an hour. – that is when I call her from the cabins that are next to the flower shop. She hasn't called for two weeks now – it is she vanished completely as if she's gone under the ocean.
    — She's gonna leave you. I can tell you this. – And Plamen waved his swollen forefinger at him, but Angy obstinately shook his head.
    — She's not.
    — Why didn't you leave for the States with her?
    — I've got no work in the States.
    — Hey, Bro. you know, your head is as strong as a dogwood log.

Angy raised his glass of beer in a careles sign of salute, and sipped off the foam. He did not look bad, not at all. Shaved, clean, ironed suit. Somehow he looked to Plamen refreshed as a man who was cared for.

- Have you found some bitch… – he started his inqiry again.
- No – Angy shook his head and waved a hand in a sign of horrified negation.
- So, what have you been doing now?
- Nothing. I've been waiting for her.
- You're mentally sick, Lad.
- We've discussed that alredy. – Angy said. Tell me something new. Tell me what are you going to do in Chicago.
- Why, I have not a constant employer, but I've been working here and there, but mostly I am busy with my son-in-law – training him some practical skills that men are best at.

Then he told again the story of his brother's luck in finding a good employer, and marrying a good wife, and settling down like a normal family head.

Angy gave half of ear to his story, while he kept thinking that Plamen had no relatives here and there was nothing to hamper him from settling for the rest of his life there. And Plamen had let free the snake of doubt that bit at his heart: "what if she doesn't come back?"

But Angy knew what he knew: he shouldn't get distracted from his main care. He had to suppress the snake of doubt. She had always come back. He knew the old rime: *wait for me, and I'll return, just wait for me very strong…* He knew he must give her freedom and not search for her too intensely to make himself boring. She had too much energy to use up. Let her go. He was the one to stay firmly here and she 'd miss him more and more. The ones who had called her through the global web, were unreal, they could not secure a home for her. He saw them as some cobs that were weaving their web-realities round her. But he knew she never let someone tie a knot round her. She would recognize the situation and come back. Her place was here, beside him.

He knew that for sure. And he knew that she knew it deep in her bones and blood. He needn't explain that.

But still there was a dark space down in his stomack, that gaped now as large as a cave.

- What are you thinking of? – Plamen stopped telling him his own story and stared at him.
- I was thinking of how she travelled to Canada and returned after 12 days. – Angy said.

Plamen was familiar with the details of that story. The case was from the end of 1990s, when it was very difficult to get a Canadian visa. Mary had got it at once. For six months. Angy's sister and her husband, and two children had been living there for 7 years and had discussed their emigration many times, whenever they were calling. Both, Angy and Mary, refused to hear about that. And then, Angy's wife left for a world conference to Canada. For 12 days. No joke.

- Now, what is the expiration date of her visa? – Plamen asked.
- She's been issued two visas: the first one is for six months, but the second is for five years.
- Hah, Lad, this time she won't return to you.
- What could she be looking for in Canada, that she's not got here? – Angy began reasoning.
- Your wooden head, brother – Plamen said emphatically. – It's not to be found anywhere in the world.
- Ah! – Angy said happily.

Then they took leave with one another, and Angy went back home, opened a link to his blog, and began writing satires on the migration waves' problem. The third of his closest friends, Rumbo, had advised him to start composing satires in a blog, while he was alone. And Angy did it. Thus his day was busy, he composed satirical verses and published them, then he answered the comments.

This time the doubt that Plamen had thrown into his face, made him feel uneasy. He began to search for the thick volume of Shakespeare's plays, that she had brought home with her the last time she had returned. There was a handscript inside the title cover by someone called Bill and a few words ordered in a playful joke. Nothing, really, to be worried of. Now he wondered if there was anything hidden in the deep text? And how far was it to the opposite end of the world?

Then she had hovered online to check her Skype days on end. Once he sat quietly behind her back while she had been delivering a Skype lecture to the students from her MA coure. She discussed "A Midsummer Night's Dream for a round hour by the clock. She was talking about the four types of love that were to be found in the play.

She was sitting at the PC display with her back on him and speaking, as it looked from his position, to the blue screen. To no audience live.

Quite ridiculous it seemed to him. But she followed the yellow and blue squares on the monitor, which probably were notes and questions, because she paused to comment and answer to silently asked questions and commented on invisible notes. She finished and turned round to look at him.

- Why don't you give your lectures at the University? – Angy wondered.
- Half of them are at home in Maccedonia, and the others are back from work and are free now. It is 9 p.m. Who attends lectures at this time? – She softly explained.
- Why don't they come to classes in the daytime?
- They go to work in the day. It is very expensive to do an MA course – she shrugged her shoulders and Angy stopped bothering her with questions whose answers were evident in the crisis.
- Still… it is funny to talk with the computer all by yourself.
- You speak into the telepnone receiver all by yourself, don't you?
- It's not the same – Angy insisted.
- No, it's not. – Mary agreed.

Now, while he was answering the comments, friendly jokes, or the jealous pricks, concerning the poems in his blog, Angy thought it was true, it was not the same as talking to no body. He addressed the messages of friends or fought with rivals, as if they were real men or women, without asking them who they were behind their nicks and avatars. They answered in the same way, and because he knew who he was, he accepted their messages as words, addressed to his genuine self.

He had refused to get a skype account. „ *Who need me, will find me* ", He obstinately persisted. That was his individual magic sentence. If they did not find him, he would know they hadn't needed him. All was sheer vanity in that case – pointless, empty busy-body of a man. This was a test.

> He then searched the Web. He found it. The beginning of The 12th Night":
> *If music be the food of love, play on… http://shakespeare.*
> *mit.edu/twelfth_night/twelfth_night.1.1.html*
> *O spirit of love! how quick and fresh art thou,*
> *That, notwithstanding thy capacity*
> *Receiveth as the sea, nought enters there,*
> *Of what validity and pitch soe'er,*
> *But falls into abatement and low price,*
> *Even in a minute: so full of shapes is fancy*
> *That it alone is high fantastical.*
> - You are not jealous at all.

– No – Angy lied bravely. – He couldn't help it. It wasn't fitting into his public image.

But why, but why was he thinking of Othello:

Iago

> *O, beware, my lord, of jealousy;*
> *It is the green-eyed monster which doth mock*
> *The meat it feeds on; that cuckold lives in bliss*
> *Who, certain of his fate, loves not his wronger;*
> *But, O, what damned minutes tells he o'er*
> *Who dotes, yet doubts, suspects, yet strongly loves!*

Othello

O misery!
http://shakespeare.mit.edu/othello/othello.3.3.html

———•———

We had reached "The 12th Night" with my MA class of English Philology – the extended course on Shakespeare. I had never before dreamed of being given a permission of Shakesperean studies, and that explained my detailed, even boring detailed lectues. I had secured the text in English, and in Bulgarian, and had it printed on transparent sheets, ready to project it. I had a video of the Play, as well, but even so, the text was quite difficult, and the students failed to understand it, let alone, enjoy the video. The practical class in the reading of Shakespeare was almost near its end, and I dared ask the question: *„Dear Colleagues, woud you like some change – there is a Canadian professor of literature who would like to give you the next lecture on Shakespeare?"*

– Superb – the students reacted, charmed, because I had become too particular with boring details, and the prospect of listening to a professor who had come from the far side of the world, looked very attractive.

Judith was sent to my classes by a world society I was a member of, to show her round the place and take her off the hands of the organisers for a fortnight. She was a certified professor, therefore being a guest lecturer at another university was part of her entertainment. We had become friends online. Back then, in 1997, our university was still young and ambitious, an we were blessed by a special room for internet communication. I spent hours on end there, in the e-classroom, typing long and funny e-mails to numerous friends abroad. They included my professional connections, and all my private students from the high school graduation class, who were potential emigrants. I had been checking their essays online and their personal essays, needed for the successful adaptation the world over.

Nick, my best student, was sitting for the entrance exams of an American university. He composed various documents and papers, and sent me over to consult him, and boast with the favourable answers he was getting.

The teenagers from his group were of that type of humanity, who would not take a 'no' as an answer and were not used to accept failure.

To me it had been exceptional and inspiring to be at a click's distance from the world over the Ocean. That seemed much closer, than my usual routine of stressful classes, for which most of my colleagues were not prepared, and my bosses never failed to note my rare errors. The Web, on the contrary, needed me update to information, but then lavishly sent back letters of praise and gratitude, and invitations for exchange projects.

Judith conscientiously fulfilled her professorial duty, and we took her to unusual routes, even for us: at first I took her to my friend Irenah's birthday party with a fancy home-made tart, red wine and, veal stew, and lfe folk dances, which she enjoyed enormously. Next Diana offered to take us to Rila Monastery, and found an old friend who took us to the lead roof of the tower of Boyar Hrelyo; the stories of that guide were sweet and funny, we enjoyed them and Diana took us for a second go, to Melnik winery caves. There we tested their latest vintage wines, and Judith tried to lure a small grey donkey with a nettle stalk. She also had a collection of stickers on bottles she tested indeed.

We, that is my group of friends of young faculty took her round the town and she finally stopped worrying about her vitamin pills and threw them into the toilet of her hotel, because she did not want to trouble her husband by telling him she had not been drinking them. At the end of the fortnight period, we took her to the capital city of Sofia, and I was dismissed from doing the duties of a tourist guide, manager, PR and advertising atachee. She stayed one day there and next she sent me an SOS-mail: „*Come ASAP. It's so boring here!*" So I took a leave and remained her official guide till the end of the month.

She invited us to a world conference at her university next year, which was financially impossible for us, but she booked our air tickets and some dayly expense funds.

I sent an e-application for a visa to the Consular office in Belgrade, and then I sent my Passport, and they sent it to me back in a short period with all the stamps and permission to visit and stay inCanada for six months.

Before the end of the academic year, I had given a two-hundred-page dissertation to the old professor of linguistics. She returned it to me, shaking her head with disapproval: "*Golleague, she said, you evidently have problems using the definite article in the English language"*. She hissed at me and handed over two pages of hand-written notes, where she had taken out the pages with the "mistakes": she had scrupulously added a definite article to my basic theorethical key word, which was the name of a ragmatic theory, and philosophers normally used it without any article. It was my last week brfore the summer vacation, and I had some free time between the classes. I used that time to go to the open market, where I got some cheap black sunglasses and a white gladinet.

I gave the flower to the professor, thanking her for her labour, went to the library, took out Encyclopedia Britannica, found the page with the article on the theory, and left it open on the professor's desk in the common faculty room, and went out, putting the black glasses on to hide my tears of humiliation. I had never before that suffered the pain of deliberate injustice. So I gave the students a written assignment to discuss a sentence of Shakespeare, who seemed to have sentences, fitting every case of life:

> „ *To be, or not to be, that is the question:*
> *Whether 'tis nobler in the mind to suffer*
> *The slings and arrows of outrageous fortune,*
> *Or to take Arms against a Sea of troubles,*
> *And by opposing end them: to die, to sleep*
> *No more; and by a sleep, to say we end*
> *The heart-ache, and the thousand natural shocks*
> *That Flesh is heir to? "...*

The academic people are gossips. I didn't know then thet the old witch had treated me the way her professor of English Literature had treated in her day. She had really believed that ambition was the engine of progress, and her attitude would prove educational. But it freed me strangely from any ambition of remaining at a philology department: she lost me – my heart, my mind and my soul – I declared her non-existent. The white flower I gave her meant that – disagreement, disobedience and non-existence.

Then I prepared to depart to Canada.

My colleagues from Sofia University took off 10 days earlier. I was engaged with the Entrance exam for the university and no one would hear of me taking a leave earlier. At last I finished work and got home, threw four sets of thin summer clothes in a small case, and my thick paper, hugged my boys, and was on my way to Sofia airport that would my long travel overseas start. I told them to check their e-mail, and promised to write them from Canada.

- Come back soon, mummy! – they asked.
- Sure, I'll be back in 12 days. – I promised.
- But your visa is for six months – my husband looked at me, worried.
- Ah, that's because they don't have visas issued for shorter periods.

I was as carefree as a bird, and missed to notice then how frustrated all my boys were.

Maybe I was the only person who did not care about all the freedom of movement that the visa secured. I did not need a longer visa. I had nothing to do there besides the task I was invited to do.

I wouldn't miss the merciless, stressing voice of the linguistics. At last I was free to think over and present my research to a world audience, who talked the language I talked and played no dirty tricks with theory.

The long voyage started at Frankfurt airport in Germany at 3 o'clock p.m. on the next day. A huge aircraft with 480 passengers on board, each of them loaded with large trunks and cases. I had the impression of all European population trying to move to Canada.

Next to me two German boys were going to visit their friends for the summer holidays. To my left side across the alley a family of two children, plump mother and lean father were trying to make friends with their neighbours on the plane. The girl was about three years old, inquiring and smiling. She came to me for a chat and I drew some Mickey Mouse pictures for her and showed how to do it. The schoolboys were young and hungry, and I kept handing my desserts to them, and the crusty bread. They shared their ideas of sitting up for an entrance university exam and their results on the TOEFL and SAT papers. There were dozens of east Germany emigrants, who had lost their homes twice and were going to a world without so painful a history, with no smell, no taste, no hysteria for Old World, values – They were going to build new homes in a new world to their individual standards and human relations that involved no political hostility, and no wars and misery.

The exquisite team of the air hostesses /I wondered where they got their practical training/ were treating us very carefully as sick people.

I followed the satellite map of our route that covered about 10,000 kilometres around the Globe which was not that big seen from above the clouds. We travelled to the west with the Sun, and my day stretched over 32 hours, while a part of my age experienced a sudden flash-back.

Down below, there was a dark-blue part of the Globe, with white triangular spots: Nort Sea over the surface of whiah herds of icebergs floated. In a while the plane lowered its trajectory towards the coastline of North America and we were able to see how steep the Ocean bottom fell down after leaving the white beaches. The whales left traces in the water with their huge bodies, and threw up white fountains like strange flowers.

And next up again above a plain of clouds of varied relief, until it was time to get down to land at Calgary airport.

The air-hostesses gave us each sheets of declarations to fill in, where 13 times we were expected to, officially confirm, that we brought no plant seeds, Раздадоха ни декларации, в които 13 пъти трябваше да заявим тържествено, че не носим семена, seedlings or grown up plants, nor any fertilizers, genetic samples and similar stuff. I wondered why the Canadians cared about their fields. We were used to abundance of natural fields and never minded them so tenderly. But we were up the globe now to the North, and the great plains of Canada that supplied corn and maize for the human race. I did not think about that then, but, nevertheless, I noticed the gaping difference of the foreign ways of social mind that sounded to me more like warning.

We clasped our seat-belts, and impatiently watched the spreading view of Calgary, which had quite a provincial face turned up to the sky. There were broad, straight streets and square yards with uniform country houses that looked as orderly as an architectural project. Only a few tall buildigs towered in the center. I had already been to Wienn, Venice, Frankfurt, London, Amsterdam, New York, and Boston. None of them looked so sterile and newly built.

We landed at last, and the passengers clapped their hands in an act of salute to the airplane staff, who had secured a safe and pleasant voyage to the new-arriving future-to-be Canadians.

The elastic corridor swallowed us and our ways were separated at the first crossroad, because the freat majority of my fellow-passengers finished their travel here, while I had to transfer to a local airbus to take me 650 kilometers back to Saskatchewan.

The polite young man at the passport-check desk carefully followed the questionnaire I had already filled and signed, and grinned at my naiive declaration that I was going to a University, and had no intention of walking in the fields.

– Oh, you certainly shall roam in the fields – no way to avoid it. – He flashed a white-teeth smile.

I actually did not get his point then and could not tell if he was jokng, but I smiled back politely instead of giving a verbal answer.

At last he asked the uneasy question:

– How long are you intending to stay?
– 12 days.
– But your visa is valid for six months.
– But I have no business to stay longer here.

Now it was the turn of the young red-skinned officer to blink at me, failing to get my meaning, but he only smiled in a way that manifested he knew incoming passengers better.

He directed me towards the exit where there was a dooryay scanner. My shoes had metal clasps, and they made the door scream. The two uniformed wome who were standing with their backs to the scanner interrupted their animated talk, just to throw a glance at me and laughed again at the simple AI of the door. They thought it funny. I had the feeling of being hit on the head with a very big brick. The cultural gap was so broad that I dropped attempting to bridge it.

A lady police officer came up and offered her help to take me to the exits for the inside air-flights.

Until that moment I had lived with the idea that Frankfurt airport was enormous wit its 5 hundred + exits, overcrouded and very clean.

The luxury at the airport in Calgary fascinated me.

- How long are you going stay here? – the officer asked me conversationally.
- 12 days – I did not waste my answer on polite talk, giving her the core of the information needed. - I'll attend a conference, and then shall be back.
- But why... – she couldn't get over it – your visa is for 6 months.
- I have no other business here – I repeated with the light hearted style of a tourist.
- We have so much work here to do – you'll find your place.
- I had no idea that I looked rather a strange bird against the background of all these people from Europe that had fought for a Canadian visa. I had easily been granted admission for a six-month stay and there was enough time to find a job, get married, and settle down as a regular citizen.

Then nobody would have kicked me out.

She told me that in a hurry, as we walked to another part of the airport. There she left me in line for the domestic flights, where I queued in the wrong direction, forgetting we were within the British queen domination, and one had to stick to the left. The officer at the check-in control snapped at me, frowning, but even that could not affect my high spirits.

The domestic airlines did not stick so punctually to timetables. When we were called to board, there were only some twenty minutes left.

Up to that moment I had to listen to the conversation behind my back between some tight chick and some shiny lcal, about the best pubs in Saskatchewan. The young lady was on a business-trip, and already demonstrated how boring the life of a busy-body would have been, hadn't they booked at least two pleasant places a day. For high-brows. At least two a day.

The funny thing was that I already had a list of the local sights, booked by Judith, and we were to visit the covered cowboy town, the panorama, the French immigrants' town, the residence of Prince Charles, The crafts

Barn, and some fort, and some more… All those were on the conference program, that Judith had sent to me, returning for all the interesting places we, i.e. my group of friends, had taken her to and visited with her for the first time in our lives. The difference was here everything was neatly organized.

I kept silent. After a 32-hours long sunny day, one feels as high as drugged. I could not afford to fall asleep, because I might miss something important. So, at least, I thought then. But then I was so green. Now I sleep instead of wondering. And dreamweave.

The small airbus had just the looks of domestic provincial shuttle. And the pilots bravely flew it, gambling left or right, so that we could see well the landscape below: it was a flat May green lawn in squares and endless straight roads and crossroads each next Wednesday. The squares were taken with green fields of corn, rye, peas and yellow canola in full bloom, and emerald young alfalfa. There werw some low bushes between them, and each square had its own pond, where waterbirds were swimming happily. The plane was flying at a height of 600 meters, and in less than half an hour we were at the airport of our destination. The elastic tube spit us at a newly built place, so clean and luxurious, no one of us had expected in the midst of the nowhere. Most of us were coming from the bigger sities along the West coast of America, or, like me – from the old Europe, which was too overcrouded to be happy. My, it was spacy here!

We were free to go, there were no authorities asking us why we were here, or what was our status, or whatever. When I left the corridor from the airbus, I followed it to the luggage belt and the elevator down to the ground level. There were some people waiting at the small loby in the bottom of the stairs. Some bony individual with a bushy beard and greying hair around a balding head, was holding a hand written sign with my name on it.

We had to behave politely. I could not pretend I hadn't noticed him. "Hello!" I said. "That's me".

The bony guy's face lit up at seeing me. „I am Bill. And I teach Shakespeare! "I wondered for a second.

„*Judith asked me to take you from the airport, because we do not have so many taxis hereabout. She told me you taught Shakespeare*", he explained.

It began slowly to dawn upon me, that Judith possibly thought I would have thus a common topic with Bill to share, and so she had sent him to see me at the airport. I didn't mind, in fact, for the freedom I felt made me quite an unusual speaker.

„*Where is your luggage?*", Bill asked me bravely, and he did enjoy it, when I pointed at my small and soft leather suitcase. Judith had arrived to Bulgaria with three very large suitcases, and a heap of vitamins and a detailed list of instructions to take them regularly, by her caring husband. They were really scared we might be suffering famine down the East of Europe.

She never opened her suitcases, forgetting them in the hotel. It was a hot summer and we got a couple of bright-coloured silk T-shirts. As for her vitamins, she kept regularly taking them out before dinner, then she glanced at the fresh salads, and the sweating bottles of red wine, or fruit juice, and hid them again with a sigh. That was in the first decade of her stay. Then, she followed our advice and threw them in the toilet, because she was frustrated with the thought of explaining about her bold act to her husband who, was a philosopher and much older than her. One cannot fight with philosophers, when they had something to debate on.

So we jumped into Bill's jeep and drove off to the conference opening party.

Canadians are not afraid of long distances. It took us nearly an hour to the university campus, where I checked in, and tried to have a fast shower. I could not switch on the warm water, because I was trying to turn the tap round, instead of pulling it up. So I washed my hands and face with the cold water from the bottle I had in my nylon bag, changed my travel clothes, used lavishly my perfume, and in after ten minutes only, I got down, and Bill drove another hour to the covered museum-western town.

For the two hours of driving along the straight roads of Canada, Bill and I became as close as a brother and a sister. I told him I no longer taught Shakespeare, because our department boss managed to find a professor who could teach only that course, and for the next year I had to prepare new courses on Modern British literature, American Literature, Semantics, and theory of translation.

All the same we compared our courses on Shakespeare, and got immense fun aut of the similar reactions of our BA trainees to the same topics on the questionnaire.

Judith had asked him to hand me an envelope with 25 Canadian dollars for daily expenses. They all looked very special to me with the Queen on one side, and a duck on the other. Judith might have supposed I was dying of hunger, but we from the East of the old continent thought air-portions were more than sufficient.

After two hours of animated chatting and self-irony, it became clear that Bill was freshly divorced and still wounded in the heart. His wife had walked on him, and he still suffered his loneliness. „*Aha!*", the red alarm button was started in my head. „All of us start making crazy things within our singular circumstances." Judith was evidently attracted by her colleague, but she had a healthy family. Ah, that Shakespeare: *Whoe'er I woo, myself would be his wife.!* He seemed to hold all the keys...

I told Bill how I had been questioned if I had the intention to go around the fields. He found my declaration that I was going to the University, not around the fields, absolutely funny. „*Oh, we shall be going around the fields, of course. Eberything around is crop fields.*" I felt like I needed a hard slap on the face, to wake up: hasn't it all been about the crops, because Canada fought to become the breadbasket of the world. I excused with being jet-lagged, and we went on joking about our own latest experiences in the same way.

In the covered Western Panorama town, we found some of the friends of Bill, standing in the street of the Sheriff's Office, where there was a prison. They invited us to see the prison, and locked us there, which was a local joke. We paid a coin each, and they released us.

Just then, my colleagues from Bulgaria came over. "In stead of saying „*Good evening*", they greeted me with a question: „*Where did you sleep in Germany?*". „*At the airport hotel, of course, that was included in the airfare. Judith had booked it for us because we had a 15-hour stay in Frankfurt before the long flight overseas.*" „*Why did we spend the whole time on the settees of the waiting room!*" They threw at me glances filled with envy. Bu we were some of the VIP guests of Judith, an she wouldn't have us arrive exhausted in Canada.

When Bill and I were released from the prison, we joined his friends and went to the welcomw party together. We entered the reception hall of the Panorama, and sat around a huge round wooden table for twelve, Bill's colleagues, me, and some American friends of theirs. My colleagues went to search for a Slavic company.

Well, we had speeded up, happy with our sudden freedom of shared avademic experience, and that we could turn every story into a joke. It did not matter we didn't know our names still. The other participants in the conference looked us with envy. An elder lady from Amsterdam asked me while we were queuing for a drink how many times I had visited an academic event in Canada, adding that it was nice to meet old friends overseas. „I arrived two hours ago, and this is my first visit of the New world", I said and she gaped at me in astonishment. Then she looked so pleased, that we asked her to join in the merry company of newly acquainted mates. So she did, and we became really a gang of strangers, who shared the same experience, and had common topics of discussion.

My Bulgarian wrist watch showed 7:38 a.m., but they supplied me with a cocktail of jin and some green fruit inside, for breakfast, they said... And so we continued merrily for 11 days, and on the 12th morning Bill pulled up in his jeep to take me for a leave brunch at Judith's place, before my flight back home.

I had met Bill's ex-wife during the conference proceedings, a blond young-faced woman with a pink face. In fact she came to see me out of curiosity. Probably, she had heard the gossip that Bill had been attracted to some foreigner, possibly aiming at marrying him and become a legal Canadian. I never had imagined what stories people, whose job was connected with literature and communication, could weave up.

I just kept the high level of noisy talk and telling interesting stories about cultural gaps mainly in the lobbies and the corridors of the conference sites. We attended responsibly the different conference sections and the plenary meetings. I was in the Pragmatics section, and Bill was in the literature section. So I met Judith's husband more often, but nobody minded that. In the night everyone went to their places, and did not interfere with other people's life spaces.

My colleagues from Bulgaria came back to sleep in the neighbouring rooms in on campus, but they were the most eager romancers of all. I did not care then. I had my own schedule to follow in 12 days.

But I had promised my boys to return back home in 12 days, and they had promised to see me in at Sofia airport. You don't cheat in such cases.

When the time came to take leave, the long man Billy, who cared for his beard, that, according to him, made him look like Shakespeare, hugged me and admitted: „*You know, I have fallen a bit for you!*". I got really frustrated abd made a funny statement: „*So have me!* /instead of: So have I"/, I said it out of my wish to be polite, not noticing the mistake, until I noticed the green stare of Judith. *"She has blue eyes"*, I thought, *"Why does it seem to me she looks at me wih a green gaze?"*

And my Bulgarian colleagues, who had brown eyes. I then experienced what was it like when blue and brown eyes let the green monster of jealousy stare through them. I didn't pay much attention to them, then. I was eager to get back to my boys.

It is all for the sake of play – a Midsummer Night's Dream" – OK, OK, 12 nights… What nights, though, we had been involved as players in twelve long days on the stage of the green fields of Canada. And I left in the 11th day, with the idea of reaching my home on the 12th night. The green monster got lost in the time of the long flight overseas.

I do not remember why I departed alone. Probably the others had booked another flight overseas, or took advantage to stay for another fortnight in Canada.

At Calgari airport I got a book by sone unknown author to me – Terry Pratchet. On the front cover the title read: "Interesting Times". I got on board of the same airliner, I had arrived by, and the airhostesses recognized me. It is strange to watch those experienced staff-members rejoicing to see the few brave passengers who dared to return home to the Old Continent.

I remembered a Russian rime from the Stormbringer's Song: *We sing songs of greeting to the crazy brave heroes' glory.*

The return flight was very comfortable, because there were very few of us and each had three seats to stretch our tired legs. I read the funny book, I had, watched the map showing our route, watched the play of clouds in the summer sky. I was mighty interested by the show the plane's crew made for us, travelling on the line of the day and night. It was beautiful to watch full day on your left, and full night on your right, noting how small the Globe was, and how dependent on the shadows of the cosmic bodies.

At the vast and overcrowded airport of Frankfurt the speakers loudly announced the flights both in German, and in the language of the place of destination. The flight to Sofia was announced in German and in English. Probably there was no need to hire a Bulgarian speaker.

There were very few travelers to Sofia, and they were, probably, not supposed to be Bulgarians, for Bulgarians almost never booked return tickets then. The exit gate was 5 hundred-something. I reached the short board-pass check queue.

Three plump men with golden suitcases in hand, immediately stood before me in the queue, totally missing to see me. „*Oh!*", I sighed with relief. „Now I am really home!" There was no sleeve out, and the exit gate spat us on top of a back, metal ladder. The airplane of the Balkan airlines was waiting for us to climb up at some 50 yards.

The young airhosts of the Bulgarian plane, three girls in badly sewn uniforms in orange, and a tired young man with a stubbled beard, were very polite, and made desperate attempts to talk in English.

We stayed there in the end of the airport and did not take off, because we waited for some other plane to land and take the brave passengers back to Bulgaria.

In Sofia, sweaty customs officers snapped at us we have our declarations filled in. They looked disdainfully at the negative answers I had given on the topics, whether I carried arms, gold, jewels and whatever they thought was valuable to customs. „*What do you have in that heavy travel-bag?*", One of the two lady officers shot her question at me. „*Books!*", I snapped back. There was the fat volume of Oxford's edition of the complete works of Shakespeare Bill had given me, some books on logic I had bought on my daily expenses, and the volume of Terry Pratchet.

And my big volume of the rejected project for a dissertation, which had wone success at the conference. „*Go*" the customs officer snorted disdainfully, and waved a hand, gratifying me her permission to move.

So I went out of the exit for the arrivals amidst a crowd of silent friends and relatives, who had been wondering what the trouble with the midnight plane of arrivals was. They rushed towards me for some piece of news. „*They are OK. Now they are busy writing their declarations.*", I said and the relaxed people sighed with relief.

A slimmer, and younger Angy, walked towards me, holding our two boys by their hands. „*We thought you won't come!*" Angy said with bright light-green eyes. „Come on, mummy. We've been waiting for you for one hundred years!", the younger one said. Angy grinned in his best Scorpion's style: "*The most reliable Guardians!*"

We needed half a year to stop writing letters on the e-mail with Bill.

At last his wife forgave him and returned to him. We all were happy with this sudden mercy. But there was still hovering behind a trail of some said words, true, yet not lived through.

Then it was February. And the three of my best Guardians were again seeing me off.

And it tok us many long months before we stopped using Angy's blog to talk with each other and meet outside the virtual reality and inside life itself.

Today I am driving back home after the lectures at the University. Westwards. The round low hills of the local ranges of the Balkans melt in the blue mist and the golden-pink sunset. The rose-colored sky in the tender touch of the Solar wind spreads over the whole young summer blooming horizon. My eyes are full of the emerald spring, and I am back, set free outside all the dreamweaving about summer nights and all the types of love existent in the imagination of poets.

Because to my experience Love is only one: all the time and all my life-space in this world. The Earth is round and everything is finally brought together. The beginning and the End.

The web also begins and closes in the corner of my study where I am chatting with the world, all alone, stretching a hand across the keyboard to reach all my friends and all the interesting events now and here.

Angy quietly walks behind my back, and checks when I'll be ready to go for a walk under the buzzing transmission lines, which let me hear the web all the time, along the path to the local dam, slapping in the wet from May rains green and blossoming world.

His mother was one of the local beauties who had inspired the Master to paint their portraits on the background of their natural countrisde landscapes, the blue- eyed and golden-haired grand daughter of Angel, and his father was dark-eyed and shrewd – and Angy is with green eyes. That genetic table which made life difficult in our high-school days, had really worked in his case.

Green-eyed and sunny like the joyous May, and sharp as a steel knife when his strong, persistent nature took the control. Eyes – colourful, the colour-blind officials had filled in his identity documents. Colour-blind, the doctors had ascribed a diagnosis, and he could not apply for that reason at a military pilots' school. He was lucky not to be given that chance, because he is so absent-minded in spite of all his natural wisdom, that he was certain to crash into Mount Kilimanjaro or one of the highest summits of the Balkan.

But *the green-eyed monster* did not peer through his eyes. It ate Angy's heart, and he shrunk back, while the radiance of glorious May was lost in the emptiness of his day and made him shiver with cold. He never let the green-eyed monster look through his eyes.

- Good for you, then.– Rumbo tried to sound ironical. – You are a philosopher, so you are clever. Why don't you find some yaoug lady but waste your life writing stuff in blogs. You are still in your best years.
- I am a monogamous person – Angy said. – I need no young ladies around. I want my wife back beside me and our sons.
- But are you aware how many pretty ladies are suffering for love of you this minute? – Pumbo stated, although he could hardly move his tongue, for the brew had hit him in the head.
- Now, look here, bro, – Angy began, – do you remember our ancient Eastern philosophy exam questionnaire? You never say to a woman that she was pretty, before she'd married you and spent all her life beside you, giving you all her support in good or in bad times, bred your children, cared about your home, walked with you until her last day with you, whatever you were, and given you courage to live on.
- Blimey! – Rumbo said, – in the dark all cats are black, you say.
- Don't't count your birds until Autumn comes. – Angy made his contribution to that talk of general nonsense.
- You bet she'll come back…
- She'll come back. Her Guardians are here, beside me. Blood is thick – it will bring her back home.
- Hail to thee, Philosopher – Rumbo said in his slow accent, accentuating his admiration.

Angy was flattered and felt high, then he ordered some more beer.

9. *The Scent of Will*

„*I shall not return here*", Julka had said before her departure, and did not let us see her off at the airport.

It was the end of August, the heat was unbearable, and the fields were abandoned and yellow in the burning sun.

Septrmber caught up with her arrival at Montreal, sunny and warm. It didn't make her head noisy with high blood pressure, and nowhere was there a trace of burnt yellowing grasses. The streets were straight and neat. The parks were clean, and the flowers had a curing effect on her aching soul.

On Sunday they went on a trip to the Falls. Incredible surreal blue colour of the Niagara and the shining water powder on the blue raincoat, they had given to her to keep her dry when the tiny boat sailed close to the falling masses of water, joined in an impressive glorious thunderous show that suppressed the painful noise in her ears of voices that had remained far of. She even did not wish to ever imagine herself on her route back.

Then everything began anew. The new impressions from the various sights she was seeing, which gradually turned into a routine, the new noises, which gradually she began to comprehend as speech or other signals.

She couldn't say she was not satisfied with her life. She had friends, she knew all the people living in the neighbourhood by face and by name, she had her favourite places where she met people she already knew. She had not yet decided to have serious personal engagements. She enjoyed her freedom and depended only on herself, and that was not bad, not at all.

„*I'll marry there*", she had said before she left, „*and I'll settle doun to live there*".

The pain that had made her start on that jurney, had subsided long ago. However, she did not risk to remarry. She even avoided a second dating with possible candidates. She kept going to work. She kept going for walks, excursions, parties, and shopping tours. She took part in her office-mates daily gossips. She watched the world news on the TV. Until she got bored to death of routine activities, and gradually closed herself, ceasing to take part in the life of the neighbourhood, and the activities of the city.

Until she had walked out early one Monday morning in September, and reached the underground station to catch the train to her office. She raised her eyes to the clear pale blue sky, looked at the sunlit colourful flowerbed, the clean streets... and shivered with the sudden strong sensation of defilement. She was sick of that all. A row of square houses, ordered for a picture, stable and looking the same every morning. Never different, not a touche of individual character. She was bored to death.

The underground station was crowded. There were various passengers. This morning, however, they were extraordinarily ugly, noisy, spitting on the platform, there was one in dirty clothes, evidently returning from a night raid.

She reached her office building and entered the lobby in defilement, looking for a place to sit down for a minute while her sickness was over.

- Hey, Jull, – Marie, the secretary saluted her – you are coming this weekend to Concord, aren't you... Oh, are you OK?
- Yes, – Julie said hypocritically, thinking she wasn't telling a lie. „*I just can't stand you all any more, all this artificial culture of robos,*". At that second she became aware what Marie had been telling her.
- Am I coming where?
- Oh, don't mind me. – Marie laughed. – You haven't checked your mail yet! There is an invitation from the Femminist Society. For a trip to Concord followed by a tour of Harvard.
- Really! – Julie said. – 'Sounds good to me. – And visibly she felt better.

They were slowly inspecting the souvenir stores of Concord.

The rain had begun again, streaming down heavy, persistent, autumn, lavish. Julia was sick with its monotonous clatter of the salt water drops on the brown- and red beech leaves. Concord was amidst an old forest. There were uniform countru houses, all made of wood and with tin roofs.

They hid from the rain in one of the local museums. Wooden house, painted grey-green. Large. Spacy inside. Dark and full of large photographs.

There were some other accidental visitors, who were guests of local familes: solid elderly, imposing probably very rich, and important to thr nation, to have their family homes in the musum area of the emblematic town of Concord where the Declaration of American Independence from the British crown was announced.

Aged couples. One of the women moved with the help of a metal frame. She was smiling, but she couldn't fully mask the lines of the pain her every step gave.

Julia looked at her with compassion. The old woman suddenly felt she was a friend and her brown eyes looked at her in a hope.

- Arthritis – she said confidentially, and Julia nodded. – When it's damp like now, I can hardly breathe with pain.Tthese wooden houses become awfully damp in the Fall and in the winter it becomes cold.
- Can't you move someplace drier? – Julia sked, and the woman smiled back bitterly and… proudly.
- My sons are in New York. – She said. – One of my daughters is in New Mexico, and the other one is in Europe. My husband spends most of his time in Washington. – Julia noted for herself that her new acquaintance never used "live".
- My boys invite me to stay with them in New York, but then no one will stay here. I must stay on and keep their home for them.

Julia blinked. She failed to get the message.

- I am the Mother of the family. – The woman explained simply. – And here is the home where my children belong. I must stay here, so that thet have a place to return to, someday they need to return to their roots. I keep that place for them. Where are you from? – She asked without a pause.
- Montreal – Julia swallowed. „*The Balkans*", she thought. „*Where my children are.*" The salty rain was filling her nose, and she searched for a handkerchieve to wipe her tears before she burst into sneezes.
- Oh, it's colder at your place, – the woman said, meaning Montreal. Then she added she was going to be operated on, soon and she hoped her pains to stop during the next winter.

It was a cold winter. As early as November the snow fell and everything became icy, ashy and grey.

There must have been sunny days. Julia did not remain. She got pneumonia after the trip and it took some time befpre she was able to return to work. At first she joined timidly, and as time passed, more and more energetically she joined into the functioning of the Machine that they pretended to control.

In January she raised her head and noticed the ice on the streets, and the nasty heaps of snow on the pavement that the municipality services had failed to clear

She went to her office and switched the PC. The first thing she did was to send an application for a leave. She motivated that with her need to improve her health. Then she booked a transatlantic flight.

She finally reachd get home on a grey and frosty winter day. There was no snow. Everything looked pathetic: small, abandoned, black, dirty, empty.

She entered her home, which had no central heating installation, and was very dark and cold. They saw her in, they had lit the stove burning some beech logs, and it radiated heat, but Julia had frozen inside, and could not get warmed. She ate her dunner, got up from the table and washed her plates and her kit.

There was not much conversation.

She did not remember the following few days, either. She had the strange feeling of standing on the bottom of a huge precipice. She felt she had made a mistake, but she needed some time to recover from the shock of her own action, before retuning to Montreal. She could only patiently wait for the due spell of her recovery, and endure the grey emptiness of her miserable roots.

„*I must keep the home of my children*", she heard the voice of the old American lmother, ringing clearly in her ears. The lady that could harly walk in the pouring rain.

Something turned up inside her. Gradually, she managed to clean her house to an acceptable state. The rest of her time she browsed the internet. Her friends were not online: they mostly stood at home, or their pictures could be seen on the obituaries, stuck on the electricity poles around the neighbourhood.

There was nothing left to move her from the inside: she felt no love, neither sorrow. The world was still. On the outside she was polite and accurate, easily entered in polite talk with all her family and relatives, but there was no one inside her – not a breath of her former self.

Until one morning the sunrise woke up amidst the green leaves of the apricot in front of her window. It was May and her garden was in full bloom. She had personally put it in order, for the sake of just ordering it. It was so easy. The people around her annoyed her with their neglect of everything they did, as if they had ceased to live here and expected someone else to care for their homes. She needed to set an example, to show them it was not so difficult to do.

She got out in the young green blossoming, sunny, scented morning. She could sense the earth breathing. Opening her flowerbeds and stretching her body like a child, who had just woken.

Something rose in her.

Fear. Lest she ciuld lose that fresh breathing.

Nostalgy, that made her hands raise on their own, and caress the flowers and the young trees.

On the opposite low mountain range, the freen May forest fell in rich bright folds, full of white blossoming trees. Birds were singing.

She had been missing them. The lack fell down on her like an iceberg, which immediately started melting down in streaming rivers of nostalgy.

That feeling did not leave during the next three years.

The incredible pink-and-golden sunsets made her fear she might miss it if she departed again. She stopped her car and looked at the starry sky for hours. She feared she might lose the stars again. She was learning to recognize the colours of the day and night of her homeplace, where they were not the same as in the wide world overseas.

Then the gaping precipice had closed, and the ground was flat again with no traces of wounds, whatsoever.

She felt at home in May. And her home was everywhere around her. But she had to find the route to her roots.

So that her own children had a place to return to.

10. It is so Easy

The airplane was flying low over the summer green folds of the Balkans. Alexandra felt faint.

She remembered the case of the museum cleaner at Baltimor port. She had heard them chatting in her mother tongue with thebus driver, while the group of visitors entered the Looking Glass House. The elder woman said under her breath: *"Ah, you are from the Black Mountains"*. Alexandra had been puzzled furst, and then had tried to say "hello", but the woman had bent her head, pretending she was busy, dusting some invisible particle from the top shelf. When she had tried to go near her, the woman had pertinently looked away, and lifted her feather sweeper in a protective gesture.

The house had belonged to one of the early American writers and had a mirror-architectural design. It began with a spacy sitting-room, continued with a series of smaller rooms of different use, and ended with an analog of the sitting-room. Each room was decorated in a singular way and contained different valuable artefacts from the history of America. She started taking pictures, but the software, for reasons unknown, made the pictures in the form of a kidney.

She wanted to say "dood-bye" to the strange woman, who was cleaning the dust, but she had started an endless conversation with the museum manager. The manager was holding her by the hand and was trying to soother down. She threw a hostile glance at Alexandra, that probably accused her of having disturbed her subordinate personnel.

So, Alex now repeated under her breath the words "Black Balkans" that had an enchanting rhythm, and went further, translating it into "the wild Balkans", "the Genuine Balkans", "my Balkan", and "the jealous Balkan" that could ruin one with their incredible, magnetic radiance – the sense of nostalgic pain.

Her mind continued to switch off for paticles miliseconds that were sufficient for it to replace the actual pictures with the picture of a young girl in a red dress, all in white dots, roaming a Balkan meadow. The knee-high grasses brought the scent of wild mint and clear, snowy water of a full stream. The feeling was that a group of colourful neutrino particles were speeding in the cyclotrone of her mind, with the velocity and weight of nostalgia, that had caught her savagely by the throat and did not let her take in a breath of air.

Down there the map of the Balkans spread on the video-display of the plane, still unrecognizable, but bringing up uexpected details of scenery, colour, smells, and movement, saved in the nenory of Alexandra. She took a few deep breaths, and stared at the monitor, hungry for more details.

In a while she would be down there. She wouldn't let her mind become victim to the paranoya, created by nostalgy. If there was an urgent need, she had the slill of calming down or speeding up the pictures that her memory handed. But now it wasn't the proper time for that. Now she had to be rational.

It was the time of fastening their seat-belts, when her mind switched off again, and she fell into a black deep hole of bottomless hate. Back on the surface of her mind, she became aware of a failure in the Global Web. There was some high quality intelligence, trying to get emphatically in touch with her own self. That idiot, Senko, had been talking once of the "peacock's tail", and letting the peacock fly. He was drilling about Ivo. In his drilling chant, there was some evil shadow. He hadn't got back home for 33 years, and had developed deep hatred to replace all the things that he had once loved, and that he had felt nostalgy towards.

There is nothing so cruel as homesickness. It occupies one's brain little by little, and settles there for years, inert, but ready to be activized by a word, colour, scent, melody, or by a dream. Each case is singular. The common thing of all is that it acts like sudden freezing dead some part of the brain, its two most aggressive faces being hate and the fear of losing a single grain of your memory.

Alexandra shivered at the thought of losing a single stalk of grass. Assen had become paranoid about his duty to release the peacock from his cage

Fear rose in her, and quickened her mind. It started turning the pictures of nostalgy that lay between her and Assen.

There was no sense of her struugling to search the signals between the plane and the area of departing aircraft. She was to search all data by direct linking to the web, if the Web did not refuse admission of her telepathic touch.

She had instinctively clasped the bracelet tightly. The voice of Chelentano rang from that mobile device of the Global Web: *"Registered nostalgic attac. What's going on?"* She could not speak. Her throat was tight, and wouldn't let out a sound. She could only grasp the cracelet of connection and send a telepathic message: *"Fear"*, that the Global Web duly registered. *"A wave of peacock colours. Flight. Smooth movement. Fan. Speeding up"*.

The Web read her, but was denied access to any possible way of connecting with her mind. The idea of nostalgy floated through her minds like an iceberg, suggesting a key to a human exit of the Web, because fear would paralyze the ability of a human individual to act.

"Through our weakness to resist influences, we are gradually turning into accessoires of the Global Web ", Alexandra thought.

She found the address of Senko, and activated the link. There was a screensaver like those that the teenagers used to cover their personal links: a moving picture of the end of the world.

The Perfume of Longing

It is raining. The rain brings gusts of a perfume, which makes me long for something that is full of warmth and love. Overwhelming love. The perfume comes from the blossoms of hundreds white flowers of *Lilly of the valley*, or as it is called in my mother tongue *Maiden Tears*. They have spread all over the front garden and are thick and full of flowers.

Gusts of longing. Someone somewhere is in love. Secretly. Not shared. Yet.

Green dreams. Easter colourful meadows. Dreamweaving – dreamreading: a sacred wish coming true.

Rumy lived above the bookstore in the closest neighbourhood. It was a brick building of tewo stores and a garden on the back where her grandmother kept the usual flowers for that area: Ladie's heart, some tulips and primroses, some wild hiacinths, blue and dark-red clrmatis, blue acacia, and garden peonies. There was a park with old chestnut trees and linden trees, thet kept thick shades, and behind them were the lines of the railway all overgrown in wild poppies, camomile and blue flowers. The entrance was on the back. One had to enter the small yard first through the green garden gate opposite the park. Then one entered the yellow-and-brown front door of the house with rhomboid ornaments, thet made it look different from everything else, and stimulated one's imagination.

The yard was long and narrow, but there was enough space for the climbing roses, and the bed of Lilies of the valley, which Rumy's grandma kept for their scent.

There was a shed of gardening instruments in the end of the yard, and there was some space between the yard and the railway, which smelled of heated in the sun iron, and some black stuff that was used to oil the engines and the wheels of the treains. And red, white and pink white poppies, and the emerald grass of May, that made everything as fascinating as the wizzard's kingdom of Oz.

There were two bunkers in the park – city's bomb shelter from the end of the World War II, now favourite hiding places of the children from the neighbourhood in the young summer heat. Everything was covered with magic emerald rye-grass, neatly cut.

I was a frequent visitor at her place, because I often went to the book store for some notebook, drawing sheets, coloured sheets we needed at school, rarely for a real book, because books were of limited production then, I cannot remember if our textbooks were sold there, but all the additional books, papers, and devices, we could get there.

Her family approved of me as one of Rumy's close friends, and often invited me inside. I never asked them to pick up a flower for me, but Rumy's grandmother felt that I admired her flowers, and often left me wait for Rumy among them.

I, then, was not aware of the simple fact that it was the perfume of the white lilies of the valley that fascinated me. While I was watching the red, yellow, and rose climbing rose-bushes, the garden was dominated by a fine, dark-green perfume of longing, which made my fantasy drift away in an eager search of something one could not speak about, something sweet and painful something…

Rumy was in love. She did not tell about it, though.

And it was not only her, that was awakened for love. The other girls from the gang often discussed boys and giggled, made their skirts shorter, talked something with whispers, and pausing each time an outsider came up near them, discussed some aspects of their growing bodies, of which I already knew the Latin words, but the latter challenged only further giggles, strange looks, or unwillingness to share.

They came to ask me of advice, concerning matters of flesh that I stil had not experienced, and about affairs of the heart, I stll had not lived through. I only knew the words. It was strange they followed my advice, and none of them complained. There must have been practical wisdom woven in the words, I guessed.

Dark green and white gusts of scent. It reminded me of something that was not there and then with me. Therw was someone connected with it somewhere.

I still cannot recover that image completely. I cannot tell my reasons for writing this either.

It was the rain, and the grey air through which we all moved. And this pressing feeling of waste.

I went out into the front yard. There were thousands of scented Lillies of the valley. I picked a huge bunch of them and it is now in the porcelain vase, its smell taking the whole space of the dining room. It is warm in the room. There are gusts of green-and-white waves of a scent, hinting some impossible desire. They remind me of a perfume in a spherical glass bottle, "Sweet Poison".

Once a teenaged school-leaver gave it to me, because I frankly told her she was not ready for the university entrance exam. She had failed, but no one else had dared tell her what she needed to do. She thanked me for the special care she said.

I opened the bottle out of sheer curiosity. I could not leave it until it was empty.

When I arrived in Calgary, all my things in the soft brown leather suitcase smelled of that exciting perfume.

But I had ceased to sense it, because I had already fell under the control of the scent, and it no longer registered in my mind. Until I managed to get outside it and back to the source. But that's another story.

—•—

– Hello! – Greeted me the bony bearded man, who was holding a plate with my name on it in professorial handwriting. He was standing at the beginning of the staircase wiich lead away from the Transatlantic arrivals' gate, and had the stressed look of someone troubling he would miss me, and fail to fulfill Judith's assignment to take me straight to the reception party hall. – I am Bill and teach Shakespeare. – he hurriedly ifentified himself.

– And you look like him – I kindly noted as expected of me. That was the one-man the Welcoming Committee amidst the mid-country of Canada, where to people would kill to get a visa, and I made it an imerative to be positive, because the conference that began on the following day was one of a row of opportunities to stay longer.

– I was sent to meet you – Bill emphasized he had fulfilled his task.

– I don't teach Shakespeare any more. – I informed him. – A new colleague applied at our department, who could teach only Shakespeare, and the boss gave me the course of the beginning of the English Novel plus a course of theoretical semantics, in case I felt bored.

On our way from the airport to the University campus, where I checked in, and failed to wash my hands because I had no idea how to turn on the tap that was to be pulled up, instead, we drove on to the site of the reception party, we continued to share personal information. We listed all the courses we were reading so far, and bravely made fun of stupid bosses, fearing not being overheard and given nasty warnings.

We had two hours of spare time to walk round the covered museum-town. We met some other colleagues, who had managed to come earlier for the conference, and made friends with them, for I was jet-lagged and still high up in the air, and Bill was proud of himself and relaxed after he had managed to take me to the conference site. So we formed a noisy and merry croud before entering the reception hall and get some drinks and food. There were large round wooden tables. I felt at home and that helped me become the center of a laughing company of newly-introduced old friends.

I am somewhat of an outist, usually. I don't mix up with people at parties. I cannot make jokes or tell them so they are funny.

The other participants in the meeting party watched us enviously, probably imagining thet we have been friends for dozens of years.

We made friends as fast as possible, and as many as possible then and there. There was a mixed aroma of roast salmon, lime, bouquay of wines and perfumes. Through it I could trace a thin weaf of fresh dark-green and white perfume of longing. I, then, could not tell why.

-   Do you know what? – Bill said, – she arrived only two hours ago, flying overseas from a distance of 10,000 kilometers.
-   Ah, so you're jet-lagged, someone of the local people tried a guess.
-   My day has been longer than 32 hours, but I don't feel as if my time has lagged behind – I said, – I feel home with you here. – They laughed at my rough compliment.

I did not admit it was not the whole case. I felt there was only half of my true self that had managed to get in through the entrance. The second was still standing at the scanner gate, grumpy and impatient, waiting for me to get back for a reunion. It was standing there as an invisible print of thin, tender longing, hard to sense, perfume. The scrupulous AI service had stopped her at the border.

While I was passing through the e-gate, the officers stood with their backs to it, engaged in a merry chat, and their hands crossed. The door was scanning in case some crazy immigrant tried to bring in dangerous piece of iron. The door started. Turned on the red lights and let the siren of alarm at my passing. The lady-officers turned up immediately, looked me all up and down, and started giggling, pointing at the metal clasps of my summer shoes. They found it so funny, and in a few incredibly long seconds turned the alarm out.

The scanner-gate shut up finally, and eyed me with green rage.

I got out, stepping in a freshly woven dream and walked forward.

I knew something was left behind, that shadowy part of me, which was stubborn, strong-headed, resistant and uninteresting.

The other side of my Self was in the center of a glorious show.

Bill told me he was jut divorced. And he was not his complete self, either.

It was merry, noisy, funny, brave and... decent. The days passed: one, two, three, four... six...ten.

Our peeling selves were filling with life, and the wounds were healing in a novel reality, which was not the same as true. There were glances exchanged without comments. There were approving glances on the side of Bill's colleagues. There were glances of disapproval and dirty little smiles on the side of my colleagues.

Towards the tenth day of my stay in Canada, I knew with certainty that I would use my return-ticket back. I would travel alone, without my colleagues, who had checked up for a later flight overseas.

At the Calgary airport, I lined in the wrong place, because I was the only one passenger in the departures queue. I lined three times, to reach the ticket control officer. She snapped angrily at me, but did not mind, and beamed at her merrily. The moment I stepped across the e-gate between their world and my own, a swift breeze of longing moved along me and went back to Canada. I was free from a charm…

And I happily walked towards the gate for the overseas line.

My boys met me at the airport. My younger son spoke up for the three of them:

– Hello, Mummy. You've been away for a whole month.

I was away much longer. I became invisible.

Much mor time took me to recover from the lack of a self and be able to travel *There* and *Back*, without any hesitation. Bilbo, the keeper of the gold ring knows all about it. He had stood up against the dark country of *Mordor*. And resisted it. And survived.

———•———

There costs so much time of the existence of your self, when your ticket is one way. The scent of home got fully lost.

I was a part of an experiment. My original self peeled down like a sheet of transparent folio. Then a B-Self came off and only the frame remained. I knew it must ache, but there was nothing left to feel the ache with.

Next the frame vanished, and in the mirror there remained a former, younger and familiar face. And a faint perfume of longing.

A persistent feeling of longing for a spell of something-to-be. Naughty and carefully that face looked at me from the mirror. Where had this self-willed face been hiding all that time, and what this rascal had been doing *There*, and how had she managed to reach me back? „*Do you know?*" A question flashed down my mind. „*I have always known*", I thought in answer. *„We kept sending e-mails for a few months, and then Bill returned to his wife, and this time they were happy together."*

Green leaves and two rows of white curly bells. A thick strong scent. It doesn't bring oblivion but awakens the desire. For a free flight.

There and Back. The Ring of the worlds is intact.

I take out the volume of Shakespeare's plays Oxford edition, and open it. There is some note written down in the hand of Bill. I did not read it then. I am not going to read it now, too.

But I know how its play of colours looks played on the violin.

———•———

... not even déjà vu. Then the ground shook and dreams sprang up and formed miriads of stories. Images came up – familiar, close, and at the same time they seemed alienated, because they had their own power to influence people's minds, and their own voices to whisper rhymes and chant spells out.

The doors between the worlds opened and the grandmas and granddads departed. But they did not left completely, because they returned now and again in their grandchildren's dreams, and when one stretched a hand to touch them, one felt hard flesh, and their voices were more powerful than ever.

... and she could get into them and be them. And have an unusual power of control.

It was a time of confused minds, and confused directions of departure.

People rushed to leave – where to, they could not tell. They just knew they had to leave. Because the Earth was changing its knots of magnetic power, and the crystal grid that held them, took a position in the direction of theStar. The load of all those people had to fit in harmony. I knew not for what reason until there came up the story of court dance of beauty and love.

But then I was not in any position to know that, because it was not yet dreamwoven up to fit the changing winds of the stars. There were similar cycles recorded in previous spiral circles. In their current metaphors of poetic vision. The doors were opening, and talk was going about of the wholes of fire... but none of them were actually experienced by humanity.

There was some awareness coming as echoes of dragonways: separate pieces of knowledge, tiny particles of intuitive awareness, that could not get us to a whole picture.

The City of Souls departed after 30 full orbits. Then more doors opened and echoes of other worlds came faster and clearer, but people could not understand the messages, for they were not trained to trust their psi-senses. They had lost patience for the others' personal spaces. They were thinking only of their single bodies and small stories. The global Network was already energized and was developing spaces to store all the words for a time when people could be able to read them in universal contexts.

The City of Souls had nearly reached the borders of the Solar System, and the larger Planet kept sending at irregular intervals its holo-image, but the people didn't notice, carried away their daily disputes. They could see the images in their own heads, which were now illusions, drifting into the Solar Wind.

That was the reason of the first disorders of the Mental Routes connecting the worlds throughout mullty-dimensions of the Vast Cosmos.

And then the Sun erupted and seared the cooling land, which had already lost a big deal of its energy with the departure of the City of Souls.

The Global chrystal lattice got refilled during the next eight complete orbits.

And then it shook all over and closed the doors.

Mankind was happy at last.

Knowledge remained, but only as a memory.

It started to reset itself, but it was like an echo in the tunnels of the world. The Program had been self-improving, and the basic command to follow was *replay*. The algorhythm was to replay all the memory files and clear repetitive stories away. There were so many strange stories of strange individuals.

There were no real or natural earth humans behind them.

They appeared, multiplied and spread globally, debated, told old-fashion jokes about the human race, repeated again and again old debates about presidents, leaders, and policies.

The very few Natties who volunteered travelling in time received the current holo-emissions in their shelters, until their feeling of a dejavu became too strong and they went to sleep.

By Earth humanity standards it was the next 3 millenia.

But what else is time, besides an empty space in the vast Universe? Time is not a dimension.

It is a possession of the skill to create a dejavu.

On the basic experts' professional labels in the infosphere

The Creators - they remain anonymous for safety reasons.

The Translators - anonymous, because they are familiar with the initial codes of information, and the information as a purpose of encoding.

The Artists – commonly muted, because of their numerous trials to take the shortcuts between the worlds.

The Erasers – almost no one knows about them, because they are to erase all the open shortcuts between the worlds.

The Guardians or the Mothers - those who save the memory heritage for their next generations, at all costs: they have no moral barriers, mercy, remorse.

The Programmers – those, who define the algorhytms.

The Story Tellers – those, who tell about the events in the mixed codes of fractalia and save the memes as Metaphors or Riddles.

Sometimes The story-tellers are used as Erasers of memory.

Time is not important.

The moving forces are the passion for new toys, the tales and the fear of death. Tne latter is only an abstraction, though.

There is also the race of the Popular ones – but they do only one function: they take the popular name. Temporarily. But time is just a circumstance. Ache is the regulator of succession of priorities.

The Recognisers or Plagiators. They recognize the pieces of universal mosaic, and sometimes are helpful in arranging them.

The Dreamers – those who connect the random worlds.

The Poets, who can sing out a world of a sudden emotion.

I am a dreamweaver. In this part of the vast cosmos – The Dreamweaver.

And everything was going to be OK, if I was not entrusted the mission to find, connect and erase certain objects of the absolute memory.

Within the plain dimension of history, the humankind like to leave memes on stone walls, so tat history keeps them. Isn't that funny?

There was a documentary film on our TV, about a discovery of an inscription on a stone wall somewhere in the nort-eastern corner of Bulgaria, dating as far as the furst Bulgarians on the BalkansThat was fake news, because it turned to be no elder than 20 years: a popular Artist and musician had carved it by order of some political figure, and now he had to prove that he was the author.

All my tales are published under a nick – they are parallel realities, which secure a longevity to my pieces of mindwork, but shall be difficult to read the name of the author.

All tales woven in word of mouth or in mind-pictures, shared in empathy, live longer, and they do not treat the name of the author as the single sign of identification, but the singularity of the product. So, names are also multy-dimensional, because they meet the wish and the actual in a hode of a singular reality.

The names of the tales for children are quite funny, where the characters are presented as avatars, wearing a nick of a hero, which symbolizes their essence. When the hero is insignificant, we normally do not hear about them, nick or not.

This case is similar: soe insignificant man bears the first name of Shakespeare and has a beard, but lacks the original multy-dimensional space of Shakespeare's thinking, neither can he create a possession in an imaginary reality of dejavu. Because that individual is not a Creator. The status of a Creator is not a question of a bargain. The Creator weaves up worlds or alters worlds to fit the signs and the minds of the time, and still leaves them keys to fit the future times of the kind.

And next the realities we construct, gather around a name and challenge
the name to explode and shine. They are like solourful projections of
the Self, a constant Self, that remains one and the same. The value of its
possession are transparent like a starry sky.

An unusually warm January. The show has melted into sticky black pools, because the asphalt cover of the country road is uneven and broken.

Showdrops are showing bravely their heads like the raised bayonets of an ancient army. They are there since December but now they are seen, white and green flags of victory over the winter. The earth has open itsbreast, giving off odours of young lilac bushes and vines of white and yellow jasmine . I go out to breathe in their freshness and trim the early woken garden. The salvia bushes and the white lilac are the most difficult to trim.

Then I sit on the garden bench that was once a shuttle-bus double seat, fastened with iron nails and three wooden planks, painted cobalt blue, that Angy made for me. I sit there and plan what and where to plant in the beginning of the spring. There is not much space and there is much to do. Ant it is then, that I become fully aware what possession means. The Earth possesses us, and we possess it. It feeds us, and we feed her. We return home, where the starry sky is open and bears the smells of home. The scent of the stars above matches the energy of the earth and gives birth to our individual routes and homes – the liltations of our nostalgy.

We are all F(x), which is a limited but open set of features, to other worlds in a multy-dimensional space. And that is all. A question of a singular choice.

Where does the peacock fly to?

Ivo was not to be seen outside. She wondered if he'd come back home. Alexandra was looking around eagerly to see some old acquaintance who could tell her. The girls from the café were still there. They had grown a bit older and heavier than they were some 12 years ago. Their familiar faces popped up on the surface of her memory. She smiled at the two of them: she remembered she had never learned their names.

– Has Ivo returned?
One of them laughed:
– He is always here. He's never been away.
Alek held her breath.
– Is he here today?

The woman pointed somewhere behind her back.

The cage with the white doves was fastened up at the corner of the building, which was no longer pale ping but bright orange. Ivo was just getting out of the thorny bushes in the small flowerbed. He brightened, when he saw her.

– Wow, see who's come to visit us: an American embassador!

Aleck hated him to call her that way, but the man was full-heartedly stretching his hands out to her while explaining:

– I was arranging the alpineum stones.

She threw an absent glance at the white stones heaped in the middle of the flowerbed-to-be, but she had not really time to discuss that.

– Ivo, do you still keep the peacocks?

He beamed a white teeth smile at her, and that lit up his reddish face and masked the dirty coat he was wearing.

– I want to ask you a question – Aleck continued, without waiting for his reply. – Were does the peacock fly to – what is the direction of his flight?

Then she insisted:

– It is important.

Ivo reacted immediately:

– From west to east.

He managed to pronounce it in capital letters.

Then he beamed in a broad smile and explained:

– He flies towards the rising sun, so that his lady can see him in all his splendor. If he flies together with the sunrise, it shall blind her.

– You are making fun of me. – Aleck protested, while Ivo's eyes sparkled with laughter.

– No, I'm not. The peacock perches on a high place early in the morning, and when the sun rises, he flies towards his lsdy, and his tail makes a new sun in the blue, iridescent with all the colours of the rainbow. The peacock flies towards his lady and desires she to see him together with the whole world.

– But before that he had flown over the fence and perched on the tall tree, hasn't he?

There were sparkles in the soft brown eyes.

– Then no one saw him: his flight was in the hidden spell of time. No one minds yoy when you fly westwards, because you are invisible, while you move in the wrong direction. You aew outside the normal flow of the Earth's time.

Alexandra took her head in her hands.

– Are you here for that reason?

– I am like the peacock; who else would take care of my ladies.

– That idiot Assen, stole something from the Labs – she was surprised by herself, with the sudden impulse to share that piece of information with Ivo. Ivo was nobody and she could tell him the secret worry of her life. – I got a message from him that he is going to let the peacock fly tonight.

Ivo was smiling and nodding. He didn't seem to be listening.

– He wants to blow up the world.

– He cannot blow up the world. The world is bigger than an open peacock's tail.

He had evidently listened to her.

– Peacocks want only to get likes from their ladies.

Aleck made a vain attempt to insert a big paranoic BUT. Ivo raised his hand:

– Don't stop him, don't break the flight of the peacock. She knows that he is courting her.

"Who is *she*?" Aleck asked silently.

– People are like peacocks: they never care who else is watching their love-dance.

The shabby man nodded at her, and then he graciously turned to meet the next clients of the toilet.

Aleck had no idea how she had reached the open space in the colourful walkers' alley.

"I am like the hen of the peacock. How can I be so blind?"

– So from the West to the East they move in their dance – she muttered loudly.

"To the female bird", the script on the display of the communication bracelet, said.

11. The World below

Misha had never before seen anything so beautiful. The Earth was

257

dancing in the gusts of solar winds and was crowned by particles of life that could be woken for life in its womb only with the help of starlight. But they needed her motherly embrace, and the stuffs of life that the Earth contained, Some might mutate, but others would live on to the cosmic harmony when light turns into music.

Misha thought about the powers of the dance of love: they were not connected with violence: violence gives birth to monstrosity and annihilation. The dance of the lights was a glorious courting.

He knew the theory about solar winds, but now he felt spell-bound by instinctively reading the might of love and youth. He blocked the buttons of the emergency alarm: love is not a catastrophe and the urge of blood should not be let to lead to violence.

He also had another insight: nostalgy is flying back home to a space of time:

This is no country for old men.

It was like a sudden flight of a dancing bird.

He made a full record of the show and sent it down a present that ran in tune with his psi-waves and spread with the global infosphere.

That suited the next generations of youth: the impertinent, obstinate, disobedient, difficult to influence, the strong-headed and the long-lived, the Milleniums, the Natties, the Dreamers, and the Gamers.

They were to skip present troubles and vain efforts of blowing the Eart. They would appreciate the court dance of the Globe and keep it for the sake of its sheer beauty.

12. The Peacock spreads his tail out

There is, probably, somewhere someone quiet and good of heart, with whom we can silently walk throughout our cutual world. And reach anyplace, anytime. A glance, a smile, a hand stretched to help, an agreement to choose a path to follow, down the street you like to walk, in the town where it is pleasant to live, where you won't feel uneasy of the passers-by who are good acquaintances of yours.

You walk taking unlimited pleasure of the whole this peace and harmony, hand in hand, minding the route and not letting the other a sudden fall in the coming dusk and the exhaustion of keeping on living.

There must be such a combination: you both seem to like the same things and you remain unchanged for each other in joy and in sorrow, in trouble and in relief. There must be... But it isn't the common case.

Nor is it always possible.

What is possible is the attraction of different natures and making deep traces along the route, change and loud crying silence, impertinent and constant walking hand in hand, debating presence... each time... It is possible in real life.

One lives in negation. One lives with losses and longings, dreams and promises, failed hopes and wasted opportunities, routes not taken, jobs not completed, present, not planned, and growing boredom with the same routine, and then sudden awareness of your own insignificance and depression of the final balance of a life, spent in place you don't like, at a job you hate, among hostile people, who never understood you, never cared for you, never given a copper for you.

In moments of clear awareness, you turn round and see you, in fact, have everything.

In moments of pain old failures heap and make yout self-assessment misty.

And there is a strong sense of the end coming, but you cannot judge how close it might be. You only know that the real life is heavy, and that there is nothing new under the sun, for billions of singular lifestories had bee running parallel, repeating most of your own steps, feeling the same warm sunlight and hapy in their own way to have it at their only one present moment of life.

The ancient philosopher said as a correction of fear of life, and of death:

The sun is every day new... and into the same river we enter or not...

Absurdity

I am in, and out of my time of reasoning.
That can be gathered in a tiny shell of sparkling
stardust.
I don't think of Notime. I can sense it.
It is the inevitable algorithm that holds our Back
memory and our future plans –
I pass through doors opening in nightmares or in
dreams woven in the lights of life, leading out of the
emptiness of chaos, that is not a world yet.
Such is the algorithm that is natural for us –
Given as a key that is no more but stardust.
Whatever we could do, whatever we could say,
That is the end of glory –
Particles of stardust woven up in
An unending Cosmos:
Possessing us as aeons.

Epilogue

Brain is the Master

The brain, ah, the brain!

What the brain likes to keep:
Not emotions, neither senses
Nor your deeds that you boast of
Just some wishes and some dreams
Sometimes rimes of childish blubber
And strange skills of questioned price;
What remains are just so stories,
Your fears and your gains,
How to weave up magic tales,
How to fly and get inside
Each single meme and cell
Singing out mind to life.
Probably.

Lightning Source UK Ltd.
Milton Keynes UK
UKHW041706301119
354496UK00004B/98/P

9 781728 395937